THE SOULMATE

IAIN MAITLAND

INKUBATOR
BOOKS

Published by Inkubator Books
www.inkubatorbooks.com

ISBN (eBook) 978-1-83756-238-1
ISBN (Paperback) 978-1-83756-239-8
ISBN (Hardback) 978-1-83756-240-4

Iain Maitland has asserted his right to be identified as the author of this work.

THE SOULMATE is a work of fiction. People, places, events, and situations are the product of the author's imagination. Any resemblance to actual persons, living or dead is entirely coincidental.

For Michael, Adam and Glyn.

PROLOGUE

My name is Sharon. I was born with the surname Meier, but I prefer Meyer. I am sixty-two years old. Lately, I have been writing poetry of sorts. Love poems from my heart.

I have spent all my life longing for a soulmate. And now, at last, here she is.

You are my soulmate, my one true love.
I have searched for you all my days.
Knowing you were out there somewhere.
All I had to do was to find you.
And now I have, my darling.
We will be together forever.
Holding hands. Laughing. Loving.
Our hearts and minds as one.
Our souls entwined.

This poem does not scan nor follow grammatical rules. I

do not care. It is from my heart. For the great love of my life. That is all that matters.

I love fully and completely and for always. I expect my soulmate to do the same. To love me back as much as I love her.

I have had what I thought were soulmates before. They were not. They are dead now. In my heart, I know this is the one for me.

PART I

MY ONE TRUE LOVE

1

THURSDAY, 29 SEPTEMBER, THE EVENING

I have a new friend. Her name is Philippa Kelly.
She has asked me to call her 'Pippa.'
I believe we will be best friends forever.

We met at this evening's book club, where literary sorts get together to talk about 'the book of the month' chosen by one of the group. The idiot — Alan — picked this month's read, *Of Mice and Men*. The events are held after opening hours, 7.30pm to about 9.30pm, at a café in the seaside town of Felixstowe in Suffolk. Every last Thursday in the month.

Felixstowe is a shabby seaside resort on the east coast of England. There is a port here too, the biggest for containers or some such in the United Kingdom. The town is full of crude and foul-mouthed dockers and their wives, mainly mutton dressed as lamb.

When conversation falters, I sometimes call our book club 'a jewel in the literary wasteland of Felixstowe,' and it always generates a chuckle from everyone other than Alan, a retired librarian, now a Citizens Advice Bureau know-all, who shakes his head and mutters to himself, 'Stupid old woman,' I suspect. Alan is writing a novel and thinks he is better than us. He is a fool.

I was the last to arrive, as I had to walk back home to collect the gloomy book that I'd left, half-read, on my bedside cabinet. I studied *Of Mice and Men* by John Steinbeck at school forty-five years ago or so. I remember the story well enough.

The café owner and book club organiser, May, an earnest and dreary middle-aged woman, pushes four tables and sixteen chairs together into the middle of the café. We have never had more than a dozen people attending — just seven or eight of us are regulars. It gets me out of my cramped flat. My GP says I must not shut myself away and dwell on matters.

I noticed Pippa immediately, sitting quietly on the other side of the table, a new face amongst the eight there (excluding me). She was, I thought, mid to late thirties. Slim and elegant, with a bob of brown hair streaked with blonde highlights, she wore a simple black top and skirt and shoes with a blush pink cardigan and a close-to-matching handbag. She was simply mesmerising. I sat opposite and smiled warmly at her. She smiled straight back as though she were thrilled to meet me.

May opened the conversation, introducing 'Philippa' and, after various hellos, offering her view of tonight's book. As well as making mugs of tea and beans on toast, May writes excruciating poetry where every line has to rhyme with the one before or after. She also plays the guitar with her gormless husband, Ray — 'May and Ray,' I imagine — and they harmonise traditional folk songs. At the Christmas book club event, the room full of tinsel and false jollity, they sang in the second half. She was red-faced and whispery, and he overcompensated by bellowing out the words in the flattest voice I have ever heard.

May led the first half of the get-together well enough. She goes round the table, asking for everyone's comments in turn, being encouraging to the shy and quiet ones, the mousy sisters, Joanna and Moira, who work in shipping admin at the docks. She is brisk with those who want to dominate the proceedings: Paul and Stephen, the two gay men with their flights of fancy, and Elaine, the fifty-something widowed housewife and utter nobody who never stops gabbling nonsense. Dreadful Alan, of course, is always desperate for attention.

Having gone round the table, May finally came to me — the 'elder stateswoman' as it were — and asked for my thoughts. I made two or three salient points, partly from memory and also from my Google research earlier that evening. I was pleased to note Philippa, as I thought of her then, smiled and nodded at everything I said. Alan sat there seething, as he had just garbled what he had wanted to say, and one of the gay men — Paul, I think — had pulled a face, which everyone had seen. Alan was livid, I could tell, but sat there quietly stewing. Poor old Elaine seemed confused and just kept smiling inanely at Pippa.

At the interval, everyone — led by Elaine — made a beeline for Philippa and flapped and fussed around her.

I held back, knowing, from her glances, that she really wanted to talk to me most of all. There was an instant connection between us.

And then Alan barged his way through, asking if she was a writer. I saw her shaking her head. Before he could drone on about himself and his stupid book, May was calling us back to the table.

The second half of the evening is often a mixed bag, as we talk about the book a little more, debate the next book we are going to read, and then one or two people will share what they have been up to. Last month, Elaine revealed all, with breathless excitement, about her visit to and the (endless) history of the lighthouse at Southwold. And, previously, Paul and Stephen have told us, sniggering and giggling, about a trip to Amsterdam, their glances and smirks at each other indicating there may have been more to their visit than they spoke about.

Tonight, after we'd agreed the latest Richard Osman would be the next read, dreary May allowed Alan to take over. He said he has written "a modern version of *Of Mice and Men* ... an update for the twenty-first century." There were looks between the sisters, the gay men and me as we tried not to laugh at his pomposity. Stupid Elaine just stared slack-jawed at Philippa. Alan opened his pad and read the first page or so. He thinks he is teasing us, exciting us, expecting us to encourage him to go on. He really is the most terrible bore. Cue pained expressions from the sisters and stifled smirks from the gay men. Elaine looked her usual dumbstruck self.

I simply stared into space, as I have been taught to do when I wish to stay calm. I did not, as I sometimes do, chant, either in my head or out loud, om-mm-mm. That would be rude. I may, I think, have hummed. I do this to distract myself at tricky moments. I must have done this louder than I had intended. Alan got very angry and upset, and everyone, covering their laughter, had to calm him down. Other than Elaine, who just seemed her usual, baffled self. May brought the evening to a close soon after.

As we were leaving, I could sense Philippa wanted to

strike up a conversation with me. So as everyone said their goodbyes, Elaine taking an age, I took some time putting on my coat, fiddling with my book and the contents of my handbag. We both contrived to 'bump' into each other at the door.

"I'm Sharon Myer ... Sharon!" I said, reaching out my hand.

She took it in her soft, limp hand and held it longer than necessary. "Philippa Kelly," she replied. "Pippa to my friends."

So I added, "Hello, Pippa."

I gestured, as if to say, 'Are you going this way, Pippa?' She nodded, and we walked towards the town. She said she'd just moved to Felixstowe. I replied I had lived here for ten years. She told me her husband, Peter, had got a job lecturing at the university in Ipswich, and her teenage son, Dom, had started A Levels at the local school, and she needed to find "something to do." I answered that I was on my own and "kept myself busy with this and that."

"I'm forty," she added unexpectedly. "Last week."

I replied, "I'm sixty-two."

She answered, "You don't look it!" Although I do, we both laughed.

With careful questioning, I learned her parents had died earlier in the year and that this move was a 'fresh start,' having lived in South London, 'a horrid place.' I sensed undercurrents of grief, loneliness and something more, a sadness, a vulnerability, she did not want to share with me, at least not yet.

Then she stopped suddenly, and I thought she was going to hug me. But she didn't. She pointed to her car, a new black Audi 3, and asked if I would like a lift home. "I live in Picketts

Road, Old Felixstowe," she said, adding the number. I am round the corner in Bath Road, but did not want her to see where I live. I said, "No, I'm not that far." And so, after some hesitation about shaking hands or hugging or kissing cheeks — we kind of just waved merrily in the end — we went our separate ways.

I have not had a close friend — an intimate friend, shall we say — since I came to Felixstowe ten years ago.

I just know Pippa is that special person. My best friend forever. And maybe more. My soulmate.

I do hope nobody dies this time and spoils everything for me.

I AM SOMETHING OF A WALKER. Not one of those pretentious, 'look at me' types I see striding out in a bobble hat, hiking boots and trekking poles. On pavements in Felixstowe! I have no time for such affectations.

I wear what I'd normally wear, other than a colourful rucksack over my shoulder instead of my handbag and, of course, a pair of sensible shoes with thick rubber soles. I have a flask of tea, a bar of chocolate and a bottle of water in my rucksack for sustenance (as well as my trusty Pac A Mac plastic raincoat, just in case).

There are plenty of nice walks from where I live in Bath Road — down and along the promenade towards the leisure centre and the pier one way, Cobbolds Point, the Martello tower and Felixstowe Ferry, with its little jetty and pleasure boats, the other.

This morning, after last night's book club event, I am walking back along Bath Road into Brook Lane, heading towards The Dip, where there is a kiosk, beach huts and a lovely view of the sea. It is about halfway to the Martello tower on the way to Felixstowe Ferry. I will sit, as I do some mornings, on a bench, sipping my tea and watching the container ships from China and elsewhere coming in and out of the port. I have a small pair of powerful binoculars.

I walk, as it is almost on my way, up and down by Pippa's grand home, a detached house set well back from the pavement in Picketts Road. It is big and wide with a living room window to the left and a dining room window to the right. The front garden goes all the way round from the left to the back. There is a driveway sloping up to a garage to the far right. There are no cars there. Pippa and her husband must both be out; I think he must be at the university in Ipswich. I imagine she is out shopping, somewhere smart and sophisticated like Bury St Edmunds.

I stop outside the house, on the pavement on the opposite side of the road, taking off my left shoe and shaking it into the gutter. My feet, my toes in particular, are always rather sensitive. I do not want to have any stones in my shoes.

There is a boy — Pippa's son, Dominic, I assume — at an upstairs bedroom window, gazing out. He has a look of Pippa about him, slim and slight with shoulder-length brown hair. He is bare-chested.

As I stand there, he sees me looking up, and he stares back for a moment or two.

I watch as he reaches down and pulls a black T-shirt over his head and torso. I walk on as he turns away.

At The Dip, I sit on the bench and pour myself a cupful of tea from my flask. I walk somewhere most mornings, if it is dry and warm, to get out of my flat, to take some exercise, to avoid dwelling on things. In the afternoons, I sometimes paddle in the sea by the pier, or go to the library, or pick up milk and bread from the Tesco Express in town. In the evenings, in a notebook, I write the key points of my life story, looking back over the events that have brought me to where I am today. It is something to do. I take half a zopiclone tablet to see me through the nights when I am wide awake. In truth, I use them rarely, as they send me into a deep and troubled sleep, and I do not come round easily.

"It's a short-term solution for your insomnia," the efficient young female GP said, writing the prescription in front of me. She then added, "Take one, or half of one, as and when you need it. Come back and see me in a month."

She asked a few generic questions about my mental health. I do not think she knows anything about me, nor mental health, really. I knew how to answer them well enough. She did not ask what she should have asked — the 'why' of my insomnia, the depths of my despair — but just scribbled the prescription and sent me packing. You get no more than seven minutes with a GP at my practice, if you get to see anyone at all. It would be easier to see the King of England.

This bench is not the best place to sit and blank your mind and soak up the autumn sunshine. It is exposed to the always-sharp wind on this coast. Also, there is a stream of passers-by, half of them walking dogs. I like dogs. I used to walk them for people for a few pounds, but someone reported me to the benefits people, who cut my money, so I don't do it anymore — even though I need every pound I can get. I prefer dogs to people — men, really — who will sometimes stop to pass the time of day. I wish they wouldn't. I am polite but brisk with them, sending them on their way by putting my binoculars to my eyes or getting up and going if they do not take the hint.

I walk back to my flat the way I came, along the clifftop and Foxgrove Lane, and then I stop and turn again into Picketts Road. Pippa's Road, as I now think of it.

The boy is in the garden to the side of the house, throwing a tennis ball for a dog, a small but overweight, sandy-coloured cross-breed by the look of it. Running here and there it goes, mindlessly fetching and returning the ball.

I stop and watch for a moment. And then the boy notices me. He goes to turn away, old women like me being invisible to teenagers, but I call out cheerfully, asking him what type of dog it is.

"A Labrahuahua," he replies, not as dismissive as I'd expected. "Half Labrador. Half Chihuahua." He looks at me, my face, judging me, and then adds, "Mother was a Labrador. Father was a Chihuahua." I think he is going to make a ribald remark, like he'd make to his mates, but he does not. Instead, he laughs to himself, picks up the ball the dog has dropped at his feet, and hurls it away. The dog gives chase. "Dotty," he says. "She's called Dotty."

I don't know why. It has no dots at all. Someone, the father no doubt, trying to be clever-funny.

I stand there, trying to think of something to say to him to keep the conversation going. I cannot mention I met his mother, Pippa, last night, as I do not want him to think this is anything but a chance encounter. But I would like to know more, to get a sense of what he is like. Teenage boys are mostly dirty monsters; 'beasts in the field,' Mother called them. I doubt this one is any different.

"Shouldn't you be in school, young man?" I say, trying for a humorous manner. I regret it instantly because of the look on his face. I wanted to strike an amusing tone, leading into a conversation of the subjects he did at school. Woodwork or English literature, for example. To get a sense of him. Not that it matters; most of these little brutes follow their ignorant fathers down to the docks for a life of pilfering and petty crime.

I was rash to ask the question and hold my breath on his reply; it will, whatever he says, reveal something of his personality.

He could have said, 'I've got the morning off ... for the dentist.' Something like that. Instead he sneers at me, this nasty brute of a boy. "Who the fuck are you?"

He picks up the ball at his feet, whistles to the dog and walks off. He turns as he reaches the house and stares back. Such a look of contempt that it unsettles me.

THERE IS something about Pippa that is simply entrancing. I cannot explain exactly what it is. I feel sixteen again. But it is more than a schoolgirl crush, a 'pash,' as we used to call it.

She is a natural beauty. There is a radiance, too. And a calmness. As if she understands everything in the whole wide world. I do not have the words to describe her perfection.

There is a bond between us already. An instant friendship. But I long for more. Not just companionship. I want love. I want her to be my soulmate.

I cannot wait for the next book club evening — three weeks away — to see her again. So, each morning this past week since I saw the boy, I've been walking up one side of Picketts Road, a long, ambling stroll, and back down the other. I am aware of Pippa's house, of course, and I glance at it now and then as a passer-by might naturally do. I do not stand and stare; although I stop, more often than not, to take a peppermint from a packet in my pocket or to tie up a shoelace.

I have been doing the same in the afternoons instead of going into town and pottering about. There is a Spar supermarket at the top of Picketts Road and along the High Road going out towards Felixstowe Ferry. I now get my daily milk and bread there, and a chocolate bar as a treat. I have it later with a cup of tea whilst watching afternoon programmes. I like a nice quiz on the television. It passes the time and allows me to keep my brain active.

Mornings and afternoons, I've not seen the husband's car parked there. Nor Pippa's. She seems to be out every day, and I wonder whether she has got a part-time job. I can imagine her working in a gallery, effortlessly charming clients into buying peculiar works of art. You don't get many galleries in Felixstowe, though. Charity shops, mainly. And the ever-busy Poundland, of course. Pippa would not shop there. I have not seen the boy Dominic again, thank goodness. He rather frightens me — not physically, as he is whippet-thin, but because of his aggressive manner. I think he must be going to school regularly.

This afternoon, taking a mint from a packet in my pocket, I watch as a teenage girl, pushing magazines and leaflets through letterboxes, drops some leaflets by accident on Pippa's doorstep. A telltale sign for burglars that nobody is at home.

I know my civic duty. When the teenager has gone, I walk across and go towards the front door, picking up the leaflets. I pause, looking around at the houses opposite to see if anyone is in a garden or watching from a window. They are not.

I look up at Pippa's house, for signs of anyone at home. The windows are all shut. I peer through the frosted glass of the front door between the two big windows of the living room and the dining room to either side. I then press my ear to it. Nothing.

Holding the leaflets in my hand as though ready to deliver them, I look through the front window into the living room. Such a long and spacious room, front to back, tastefully decorated and expensively furnished, with paintings — what look like proper originals, not prints — on the walls. Exquisite, that's the word. I stand transfixed at this rich and comfortable lifestyle, and then, checking again to make sure I am not being watched, I walk to the back of the house.

The garden is well cut, trimmed — manicured, that's the word I'm looking for — with a simple, what looks like, hand-carved wooden table and matching chairs. Expensive. I move to the windows — a patio door into that big living room, a kitchen window, such wonderful cupboards with a central breakfast bar, and what must be a gorgeous dining room beyond. There is also a building that must be a converted garage or an extension to the back of it; I gaze through a window, and it looks like an artist's studio.

I stop and listen again. There is no one in the house, and I feel encouraged to investigate further. I imagine Pippa here, stretching out in her lingerie, reading a magazine in the living room, preparing a cocktail in the kitchen and painting abstract art in the studio. I pull at the patio door, but it is locked. I then tug at the door handle of the studio, and to my surprise, the door opens. I stand there in the doorway, breathing in the atmosphere, the perfume, the scent of

Pippa. I shut my eyes and imagine myself watching Pippa painting or sculpting something divine.

Then, from somewhere inside, upstairs, I hear the barking of a dog. The mongrel dog, Dotty. It spooks me. I think she must have been up there all the time, perhaps lying on the bed next to the little brute. I expect he is teasing, taunting the dog with a ball or a treat. He is that type.

I imagine him hurtling down the stairs as teenage boys do, running into the kitchen, taking a bottle of squash from a cupboard, grabbing a handful of biscuits from a tin, going to the sink by the kitchen window, splashing squash and water into a tumbler. Then looking out and seeing me standing here. I have experienced similar moments in my life and know what can happen. Within seconds, he'd be out, pushing me against a wall. "What the fuck are you doing here, you old bitch?" His breath and spittle on my face. This incoherent yob from South London.

I panic at the thought, shutting the studio door as quickly and as quietly as I can. I walk by the patio door, frightened now, although he is not there, and then I am hurrying down the drive and away. I hear more barking. I imagine he is now at the living room window, holding the dog, watching me go. Thinking dark thoughts. I dare not look back. I must be more careful in future. Then I am on and along Picketts Road, moving quickly out of sight.

IT HAS TAKEN me two days to recover from my fear of being discovered at the back of Pippa's house. I dread what the boy would have done if he had found me there. And I worry that he saw me leaving, and what he will say and do if he sees me again.

I've been about my daily business, seafront walks, visits to the town, writing notes on the key moments, the turning points, of my life story, without going anywhere near Picketts Road. It has been hard, unbearably so. I could not stop thinking about Pippa. Each minute of every day.

Tonight, this Sunday evening, under cover of darkness just gone 10pm, I am walking up Picketts Road once again. I cannot stop myself. I am obsessed. I hold an old dog's lead in my hand, clutched to my face, as if I am in distress. If anyone stops me, asks me, I will say I am looking for my lost dog, a Jack Russell. I will play on their sympathy.

I am outside Pippa's house, looking up at it in the moonlight. There is a light on at the upstairs bedroom to the side at the back, the horrid boy's room. Sitting on his bed, crouched over looking at his mobile phone screen, doing what teenage boys do in their bedrooms at night. The bedrooms to the front are in darkness. I do not know if Pippa and her husband sleep there together. Perhaps they sleep separately. I do hope so.

There is a light on downstairs, at the living room window. The hallway and the dining room to the right are both in darkness. Two cars, his and hers, are on the driveway side by side, his black BMW, two years old, and her new Audi. So, Pippa and her husband are inside the house. I have an overwhelming urge to peer through the living room window to see if they are there, sprawled together on the sofa or sitting on separate armchairs.

I check around, and then, holding the dog lead high, I walk a way up the drive. I stop, out of curiosity, at her car and look inside it. I do not know what I expect to see — something quintessentially her. An expensive beret or a silk scarf, maybe. But the interior is empty. I look inside his BMW, and papers and files and books and magazines are scattered across the back seat. There are bottles in the cup holders between the front seats and crisp packets and chocolate bar wrappers shoved in all the spaces. Without thinking, I pull at a handle of a door at the back of the car. To my surprise, the door opens.

I stand there, deciding what to do. I have a sudden urge to take handfuls of papers from the back seat to see what they are. Then, later, shoving them down into the big bin at the back of my flat, never to be seen again.

As I hesitate, I hear a noise at the gate, to the far right, on the other side of the garage. A wheeling, squealing noise — it sounds as though the grey refuse bin is being brought out for its morning collection. I notice others are already dotted up and down the road for tomorrow's round.

Before I can react, let alone move, he is there pushing the bin out. This tall, skinny man with his dark greying hair brushed back and his salt-and-pepper beard. He is wearing a striped dressing gown over his navy pyjamas. The trousers are too short, and he looks stupid with his bare, hairy ankles showing. He sees me straightaway, my hand still on the handle and the door open.

He leaves the bin where it is and walks round the back of the car towards me. I think for one awful moment that he is going to hit me. But he does not. I am, when all said and done, a sixty-two-year-old woman, small and solid at five feet four inches. I am not a threat to anyone, certainly not a six-foot, physically active man in his late forties.

"What are you doing?" he says, looking at my hand, the door handle and the open door. It is a neutral voice, carefully balanced, but it could turn to anger quite quickly. Like many men, he likes to be in charge and does not want to feel he is not in control of any situation.

I hold up the dog lead and swallow and stumble over my words. "I ... I'm looking for my missing doggie." I know well enough to make my speech sound as though I am close to tears.

"Well, you won't find your ... doggie ... in the back of my car, will you?" It is more of a sarcastic statement than a genuine question. He puts his hand on the car door and looks at me as if to say, 'Take your hand away.' And so I do. He closes the door, tells me he's going to wheel the bin out and then go back inside to get his keys to lock the car. And then he says, like I am a nobody, "Go on, off with you." He jerks his head dismissively.

It is as though he has seen right through me, this pretence of a lost dog, and he knows I am up to no good. I turn abruptly and walk down the driveway, heading to my flat.

As I get to the pavement, I glance back, just to see what he is doing. He stands there, by the gate, watching, and waves the back of his hand towards me this time, dismissing me as if I am nothing.

It is that second dismissive gesture that makes me angry. That I am no more than a fly — something of no importance to be batted away. He is an arrogant and unpleasant man. He is the spider. Now. But he will be the fly. One day soon.

2

WEDNESDAY, 5 OCTOBER, NIGHT-TIME

I live in a flat, tiny and horrid, in Bath Road near the sea in grubby old Felixstowe. It's part of an Edwardian, three-storey, detached house — grand in its day, but well beyond faded these days. Cars pack both sides of the road, and there are braking, hooting and reversing noises at all hours. Even now, so late at night, as I lie restless in my bed.

The landlord, a widowed, retired music teacher from a posh school in Ipswich, lives on the ground floor, where he plays his out-of-tune piano loudly and often. He is old and hard of hearing; I think his mind is going. Whenever our paths cross these days, he seems confused and uncertain, no matter what the conversation. I live on the middle floor, at the front of the house, minding my own business. A young and vigorous couple, male and female, Mr Grunt and Mrs Groan I call them, live at the back. I call them this to amuse myself, but they are anything but funny.

An oddball of a fellow, a prematurely bald, unemployed man of about forty, lives upstairs under the eaves of the roof.

I often hear him creeping about and rocking on the floor-boards. That is what he is doing tonight, keeping me awake.

It is at night-time, now, when I feel most anxious and depressed and unable to sleep, that I have decided to start writing up the notes of my life story. To transfer them from my notebook to a proper A4 book. My usual GP — the older man, not the brisk young woman — said a while ago that it was a good way to 'put things in perspective' and to 'move forward.' The words 'at last' unspoken, but hanging in the air.

Psychobabble nonsense, really, I know. But I have been writing bits and pieces on scraps of paper and in my note-book. Not so much an autobiography as a memoir of sorts. Just those parts of my life that might be termed 'turning points,' moments that ultimately led me to my sorry state today.

Alone and poor and with nothing to look forward to in my life. That's the perspective the GP talked about. And Pippa, the wonderful Pippa, is my way forward out of this hellish life. My only way. My last chance of love.

The man upstairs — the oddball keeping me awake — has lived there for almost three months now. When he moved in, I was polite, friendly even. In one conversation, as we passed at the front door, I shared my opinion of the thoughtless previous tenant — a shiny-suited insurance man — and how he kept me awake most nights with his kung fu exercises.

Of course, I had assumed, as I have done to my cost before, that the new man upstairs was a nice, balanced fellow. But a month or so ago, I refused to sign for a Royal Mail parcel delivery for him — you cannot be too careful — and he somehow found out. I think the landlord must have seen me open the front door and refuse to take it from the postwoman. And that somehow got relayed back. Anyhow, no matter; the man upstairs has since turned against me. Such a spiteful sort.

It is 12.17am, and I will struggle to sleep tonight, at least until exhaustion overwhelms me. The man upstairs is moving about. Stomp. Stomp. Stomp. Loud enough to keep me awake. Not so loud that I can complain to the landlord (not that he'd do anything). Stomp. Stomp. Stomp. He walks heavily, the floorboards creaking, out of the bedroom above me. He fetches a glass of water. I hear the pipes screeching. Then a hop, skip and a jump as he returns.

His bed is directly above mine. All is silent. I wonder if he will now go to sleep and end my torment. But, as it does most nights, it creaks, on and on, and I feel increasingly ill at ease. Then it stops suddenly. There is another long silence, and then he is up again to his bathroom, where I can hear the pipes groaning back into life and the flush of the toilet. My unpleasant imaginings make me feel sick.

The man upstairs is still moving about. There is a floorboard directly above my head, and he stands on it, leaning this way and that. It creaks. Then stops. Then creaks again. He does it slowly at first and then gets faster as he rocks to and fro. I imagine him laughing. He thinks he has the better of me.

He does not know I have a key to his flat. When the last tenant left, he knocked on my door, handing me his set of keys to return to the landlord. I had spares made. A useful thing to do. If I wanted to, I could go upstairs when the oddball is asleep and stab a knife into his stupid fat face.

GONE TWO AM, and all is quiet at long last. I look over the notes I have made about my life so that I can start writing them up more formally in an old desk diary for last year. I bought it for fifty pence, negotiated down from one pound, in a charity shop the other morning.

I try to tidy up the original notes in my mind before writing anything in the desk diary. I want to avoid crossing-outs and corrections later. I want my story to be neat and tidy, 'just so.'

I am writing as close as I can to my natural voice. I think, with any piece, you should be able to 'hear' the person writing it. This is what I write.

My mother, Walli Meier, came to England — of all places for a German Jew — in 1939 when she was eleven years old. She was smuggled here, along with other children, by family friends. Her parents, my grandparents, promised they would join her after the war. She never heard from them again.

There were, when I was young, fanciful stories of her escape from the Nazis — of forests and hot-air balloons and being covered by tarpaulin at the bottom of a small boat as it crossed the channel. I was never sure what to believe. My mother's relationship with the truth was never a close one.

In her teenage years, she lived in various places in and around Belsize Park in London — a housemaid in a GP's house early on, a kitchen help in a restaurant later. A servant in all but name. She rarely spoke of being a young German woman living in England in the 1940s. Of men approaching her, and more, in parks. She was told by the GP to say she was Austrian if challenged, as she often was. I imagine her life must have been hell. These experiences must have shaped her in some way, made her what she became.

In the late 1940s and through the 1950s, my mother cut something of a glamorous figure in the clubs in the West End of London, a 'hostess' was the word used in polite society. There were, I think, many men. They were rich and powerful, and mixing in such circles made her believe she was more established and accomplished than she was.

Eventually, she moved into an apartment off Tottenham Court Road, a woman kept by an older, married man. She made it sound smart and sophisticated whenever she spoke of it, and it may have seemed that way. I think this was when she was at her happiest. Anyway, she fell pregnant with me at the start of the 1960s. Not by the married man, but by someone else, a younger, more dashing version — and a single man.

'Van,' as she called my father, was a Matt Munro type of singer in one of the clubs. She left her apartment and her work and everything to be with him, to start her own family. But then he was killed in a road accident in Soho when she was six months pregnant. She often talked of this and said it was murder. But she was too frightened to go to the police. That tragedy was the start of a downwards spiral. Basement flats to rented rooms to benefits-only bedsits.

My mother and I, thrown together in small and dirty spaces and with little or no money, fought for as long as I can remember. My earliest memory was screaming endlessly in the night, and my terror as a door was broken down and a man — I don't know who — came running towards me. I believe my mother had gone out and had tied me to the cot in the bedsit.

We moved regularly from place to place, each worse than the last. My mother would leave me at home at nights, giving me something to eat and drink and telling me not to make a sound. Often I did, through anger or fear, and there would be more shouting and broken-down doors and suitcases packed, and we'd be on our way again, zigzagging through the run-down back streets of London.

When I was in school, it might have been easier for my mother to get a job to support us, as other single mothers did. But by then, the drink had her in its grip. I do not think she was capable of holding down any job and making money other than the way she did. As I got older, into my early teens, there was the night that one 'gentleman caller,' as she called them, was leaving when he saw me hiding beside a chest of drawers. He looked me over and smiled to himself. She turned a blind eye to what followed that night, and others, all through to my later teenage years.

I read back over what I have written, and it seems a good summary to me. I will write up more notes soon. But that, I think, will do for tonight. It is quieter now, other than the odd car driving by, parking and reversing in the road outside, and I can sleep through that. I must try to get some rest. The early mornings always make me feel anxious and ill at ease.

I hate men. I always have done since those teenage days. I loathed the weight of them on top of me, the smell of their cheap aftershave and the stink of their bodies. Their thrusts and grunts and sudden cries. Then up and away, some throwing a handful of coins back at me. Searching for them on the floor always felt like the final humiliation. I wished they'd just gone.

Women, some women anyway, are gentle creatures. I love the smell of their perfumes, the sweet aroma of their bodies. And those times they touch and stroke and arch their backs in beautiful agony. I let thoughts of Pippa enter my mind, relaxing me and, eventually, sending me to sleep.

I SHARE the middle floor of this house with what I call Mr Grunt and Mrs Groan, a young married couple in their mid-twenties. He is big and muscular. She is blonde and dainty. They both work at the docks; in administration, I suspect. They always look smart as they come and go. He nods, or at least he used to. But he never spoke, let alone started a conversation. She gives me pitying looks sometimes, as though I am dishevelled. The looks make me feel angry, not that I say anything.

My rooms are at the front; theirs are at the back. Our bedrooms adjoin. We share a bathroom and a toilet, more's the pity. The previous tenant, Sian, a local primary school teacher, was clean and tidy. I had a set of rules — tongue-in-cheek guidelines — posted on the door, who could use what and when, and we got along splendidly. She left to get married earlier this year. I was not invited to the wedding or the celebrations after. I have not seen nor heard from her since.

These new people have been here for four months, and are a law unto themselves when it comes to the bathroom and the toilet. Him in particular. He does what he wants when he wants. I bought and put a bolt on the door recently after he'd walked in on me sitting on the toilet. He just laughed, thinking it was the funniest thing. I have hated him ever since.

I'm lying here this morning, after a restless night as per usual because of the oddball's activities. Writing up my memoirs did not help; digging up horrible memories that simply won't be laid to rest. One way or the other, I am always troubled at night.

And I am woken by the young couple doing what they always do at 6.15am or so every morning. He grunts. She groans. On they go. I find it disturbing. Intrusive. They know I can hear. Early on, I used to knock on the wall with my shoe, but they'd shout back, cursing me. They do not care. It is so disrespectful.

After a crescendo of animal noises, they stop. All is silent for a few minutes. But I lie here still, knowing this is not the end of it. Gradually, it will build up again, on and on, until her groans reach a peak and the whole thing is rounded off with his sudden guttural cry and it is all over. At long last.

I hate it here, in this flat, where I feel degraded and dirty; there is no privacy and no sense of decency from those around me. I would leave right now if there were anywhere else to go.

But this flat — rooms and shared facilities, really — is pretty much at the bottom of the heap. Truth is, there is nowhere else for me to live. And I would not give these people the satisfaction of taking my own life here.

Yet there are times when all of this, this hell, is just too much to bear. The grimy oddball upstairs, the dirty couple with their bed banging repeatedly against the wall, and the fading landlord and his off-key piano playing. I feel such utter desperation.

I hear them now, the young couple, outside by the bathroom and the toilet — laughing, playful, running up and down the landing. I doubt, post-coitus, they are dressed as they should be. Half-naked, I expect. I imagine him bare-chested in his boxer shorts, strutting about as though he owns the place. He'll then be there in the bath, sweating and dripping bodily fluids. The thought of getting into the bath after him, even after a thorough rinsing, repulses me.

She will be in the toilet, mopping at herself with sheets of toilet paper, removing what he's left behind in her and down her legs. Then, after a wee and whatever, she will join him in the bathroom, maybe the bath itself, and I will have to listen to the ribaldry, his deep, booming voice and her nails-on-the-blackboard laugh. This can last for thirty minutes or more.

I cannot stand it any longer, being forced to listen to all of this. I get up out of my bed, flipping on the light, folding the duvet back and taking off my nightclothes and laying them out by my pillow, ready for this evening. I look down at myself, and everything sags and hangs. I wonder how anyone, especially Pippa, could find me attractive — or, indeed, how anyone ever did. I pull day clothes from my wardrobe and drawers, dress, and wait for the couple to go to work.

I sit here for as long as I can, as they finish in the bathroom and go back to their rooms. There is much noise, over and over, getting dressed, music going on, then the television, and I can hear them clattering about as they make their breakfast. I bow my head as it — this endless noise and chatter, this thoughtless torture — goes on, from waking up at 6.15am to until they leave for work at just gone 8.30am.

"Fuck off!" she shouts at the top of her voice. "Fuck off!" she repeats, laughing now. I hold my breath, sensing this foul bantering may lead on to another round of sex, this time somewhere in their kitchen area, probably on the table or the draining board. But he shouts back jovially, "Fuck yourself. Fuck you!" And that seems to be that, as doors are opened and shut, the music and the TV go off, and, at long last, they are heading for work.

I pick up my washbag and towel and my bottle of anti-dandruff shampoo, as today's the day I wash my hair with the hand shower attachment at the end of the bath. I head out onto the landing, to the toilet first, then the bathroom. As I put my hand on the toilet door handle, she appears from their rooms. She must have forgotten something and come back for it. She looks me up and down and says, as she goes to the stairs, "Had a good listen, did you ...?" I do not know what to say. Then she adds, "You dirty old bitch."

I feel crushed and humiliated. As she walks away, I could just curl up and die.

3

MONDAY, 10 OCTOBER, THE AFTERNOON

I am leaving Boots in the town, tucking my paper bag of medications into my shoulder bag, and thinking about Pippa. And then I see her. Just like that! She is walking in the same direction, but on the other side of this pedestrianised shopping street.

I swallow, momentarily unable to call out. She looks beautiful with her hair freshly cut into a bob and streaked with brighter blonde highlights. I would recognise her instantly, anywhere. She is wearing a full-length camel-coloured coat, dark brown boots and a matching handbag. She looks perfect. A model!

I feel a sudden flush of excitement. As though I am a giddy teenager again, with a crush on the games mistress, Willy Wilson, at school. I go to call out 'Pippa!' but the words do not come. A twenty-something man walking towards me gives me a funny look, as I am in his way. It is all I can do not to hiss at him to mind his own business and go away.

And now I am walking along this side of the pavement, watching Pippa on the other, slightly ahead of me, going by

Superdrug and the Wimpy, heading for goodness knows where. It is hard to imagine she is going to Greggs for a sausage and baked beans slice.

I am trying to catch my breath and calm my nerves as I walk briskly to keep close, hoping she will suddenly turn to cross the street, looking automatically to the left and seeing me. I will suppress my delight and simply feign pleasant surprise.

She does turn, as she comes almost level with the book-shop on this side of the street, and she spots me. There is a smile of recognition, pleasure even, and she hurries over as though we are the best of friends. I smile at her as if this is nice, but no more. I must not seem too eager.

"Sharon!" she says. "What a coincidence. I was just going to buy the new Richard Osman from that lovely little bookshop."

She sounds genuinely pleased — excited even — to meet me again. I swallow and push a strand of hair back from my forehead. I feel sweaty and hope I do not look it. She glances at me as if she has noticed I am out of sorts, but is too polite to say.

"Snap!" I answer (although, in truth, I ordered a copy from Amazon the other day — it is so much cheaper for those of us on a strict budget). I then wish I hadn't said snap. It means I will have to go into the bookshop, buy the book at a higher price, and then return home to cancel the Amazon order so I don't pay twice.

Anyhow, we go into the bookshop, and there is only one copy of the book left — more are on order and coming in the next day. Pippa and I um and ah, you have it, no, you, with me actually wanting her to have it, as I don't really want to buy the book.

Eventually, to the bemusement of the polite young man behind the counter, Pippa says, "I've got it!" and takes the book and pays for it. And then, oh days of joy and wonder, she turns to me as we leave and says we must share it, that she'll read it over the next week or so, and then ... 'we must meet up' ... and she will give it to me to read before the book club meeting!

If that's not enough, she gives me her mobile phone number so we can arrange the meeting, waits whilst I put it in the contacts list in my phone and then suggests a coffee, right now, in the town. I am beside myself with joy, but do not show it, merely smiling and saying, "Yes, let's." This is where it all begins, our lifelong friendship.

———

"LATTES AND SLICES OF CAKE, then. My treat!" Pippa says as we enter the coffee shop, looking at what there is to eat and drink, and agreeing what we will have. Pippa, a slice of carrot cake. Me, a slab of coffee and walnut cake. "You find us a table," she adds.

The place is almost full, a mix of tattooed young people and what I call 'Felixstowe's Finest,' doddery old couples stumbling about and getting in everyone's way. I end up at the only free table for two, at the back near the toilet. I have to get up to close the door after a silly old man comes out with his flies undone, leaving the door wide open. It's not a nice view: a toilet with the seat up and tissue paper strewn everywhere.

A young couple, him carrying a tray of drinks and eats, her pushing a baby in a buggy, come towards me and stop. They expect me to give up the table for them. Like many young parents with babies, they have a sense of entitlement. I don't move. Instead, I put my handbag on the other chair. They tsk and tut-tut and move away to sit on the edge of a table for four with an older couple. And then, at last, Pippa is here with our goodies.

We move the lattes and the sweeteners and the long spoons and the plates and cakes and the twiddly forks about. Pippa puts the tray to the side, on the floor, leaning it against the table.

We ask each other how we are, and say we're fine. We look around, and Pippa smiles at the baby, and the affronted parents turn away. Then we drop in our sweeteners and stir and sip our lattes.

We talk about the weather, the book club, and the latest Richard Osman, which is passed to me to look at as though it is the Holy Bible. We then talk about the other book club members — the Felixstowe illiterati — until we start eating our slices of cake. Between mouthfuls, our talk gradually becomes more personal.

"I've a job interview later this afternoon. At four. Keeping myself busy," Pippa says brightly, her tongue licking a gooey lump of carrot cake off the back of her fork.

I nod at her to go on.

"At, ah, a boutique in Ipswich." She tells me its name and where it is, near the Sainsbury supermarket on the corner, and then reels off the various brand names it sells.

I smile at her as though I am familiar with them. I buy mostly from charity shops and, occasionally, the sales at Primark in Ipswich.

"I've not worked full-time since Dom was born," she adds, sounding anxious.

"You'll be fine," I answer, eating a piece of my delicious cake.

"It's so different here ... from London." There is a strange, almost wistful, note in her voice. "Dulwich, West Norwood, Streatham ... South London suburbs ... busy, busy places."

I nod, not sure if she thinks that's better or worse than here, so I ask, "Were you born there?" encouraging her to tell me more about herself.

She licks the back of her fork again, which I find most distracting, and says, "I was born in Dulwich. Only child. Daddy worked in the city. Mummy was an artist." She glances at me conspiratorially and whispers, "She wasn't terribly good."

"Peter was from round the corner in West Norwood, Chestnut Road. His father was an engineer. His mother a housewife. Three boys, Peter, Chris and James. They're all still living down there. Well, Croydon and Sutton. Chris and James work together as builders." I note a sense of vague disapproval in her tone, that this working-class family was beneath her.

"Peter was a lecturer in central London; he taught fine art. I was one of his students." She hesitates for a moment before going on, "We, ah, fell in love, and he left his wife and ... anyway." She tails off, as if embarrassed, ashamed even. This mesmerising stealer of husbands.

"And you then had Dominic," I add, in a jolly voice.

"Yes," she replies more positively. "He's been such a joy. Our pride and joy, really. I stayed at home all through when he was younger; painted and sculpted and sold some of it on eBay and later Etsy. But it's not easy making an income from that, let alone a living. I've never had, you know, a show in a gallery or anything. I've drifted away from it lately ... I need to get back to it. Peter's been the main breadwinner, but ..."

There is the longest pause, as though she is going to say something private, intimate even. I finish my cake and turn to my latte, not looking at Pippa, knowing that if I play this right, sweetness and light, all sorts of home truths will come tumbling out. About Peter — there's something not quite right there. I'm sure of it.

She hesitates and looks around, as though she is going to say more, but does not want to be overheard. She said, after the book club evening, that her parents had died and that their move here was a 'fresh start.' And it could just be that they fancied a change of lifestyle and pace and sold up in the big city, bought a bigger but cheaper home here by the sea and have Pippa's inheritance from her parents — £500,000, £1,000,000 or more — in the bank. And will live happily ever after. But there is more to it than that, I am certain.

I think this move is a last chance. The marriage between darling Pippa and the horrid husband is a sham. They stay together for the boy's sake only. I have a kind of sixth sense in such matters. I almost swoon with delight at the opportunity here for me. Perhaps even a new life! For the briefest moment, I see the possible future, myself and Pippa together, living in the lap of luxury in a gorgeous flat overlooking the sea, the nasty husband banished far away. There's still the boy, of course. I will need to think about that some more. I don't want him there. He will be harder to get rid of. I suppose he might go to university. They all do these days, even stupid ones.

"The thing is, Sharon ..." Pippa pulls a face — she is suffering and is about to reveal a confidence and reach out to me for comfort. And I will provide it. I will be her confidante. Her best friend. Her sister. Her mother. Perhaps in time, more than that. Her lover. I go to reach out my hand, putting it on hers.

But there is a sudden flapping and squawking commotion by the door. It is Elaine from the book club. She has come in, spotted Pippa and is squealing with excitement. Pippa turns away from me, no meaningful, long-suffering look, nothing. She smiles and waves back at Elaine and gestures her over. The great fat lump waddles across as fast as she can. It's all I can do to stop myself jabbing my fork in her face as she sits down.

Instead, I smile and pretend I am pleased to see her. Pippa and she do that 'mwaw, mwaw' kissing thing, close but not quite touching each cheek in turn. I busy myself moving chairs to make room for the wretched woman and to avoid the nonsense show of faux affection. And the sweaty great thing sits there all breathless, barely looking at me, her eyes on Pippa, and then says she'll get herself a coffee, and do we want anything else?

Pippa smiles politely and declines, indicating she still has half a latte left. "Cake?" Elaine says and repeats, "Cake?" Pippa declines graciously. Elaine then looks at me with a quizzical look on her face. She does not like me, I know that. And I loathe her and her great big bovine face. "I'll have a glass of tap water, please ... cold with ice cubes ... and a slice of lemon, thank you." Off she goes, put out by my presence and specific request. It's all I can do not to laugh.

As we sit there, Pippa and I, waiting for the return of the ghastly woman, I notice Pippa glances at me and smiles ever-so-slightly nervously. She then looks over at Fatty Bum Bum, and they smile more warmly at each other.

I realise — a sudden flash of light — that they have

somehow or other met each other between the book club evening and now. I have no idea how. Perhaps their paths crossed when out shopping. They have become friendly. And I then wonder if they had arranged to meet here at this time and if, bumping into Pippa in town, I am now actually the interloper, so to speak.

As Stupid Elaine turns and comes back towards our table, she smiles at Pippa and me, looking all excited. I've never liked Elaine. We have had several 'agree to disagree' (as May puts it) conversations at book club events. I can't stand her at all. As people say, 'two's company, three's a crowd.' One way or another, she has to go.

I KEEP things as pleasant as I can during our round-the-table-conversation. I say conversation, but it really involves Elaine gabbling away about whatever comes into her head and straight down and out of her mouth. She suffers from verbal diarrhoea, really quite badly.

A new shop that is opening in town (and 'don't we have enough of those already?'). The book club book (and 'isn't it wonderful?'). A visit she made to Bury St Edmunds, most likely alone (and 'the Abbey Gardens are just lovely even at this time of year?'). On she goes without ever pausing.

Pippa smiles and nods and tries to say something beyond oohs and aahs. She glances at me now and then, somehow embarrassed by Elaine's non-stop stream of drivel. I sit and look at Elaine, who now seems to have a chipped front tooth since I last saw her. I nod whenever she looks across at me, waiting for my moment.

"What happened to your tooth?" I ask innocently as Elaine draws breath. I point my finger towards her mouth.

She shakes her head, flaps a hand in front of her face and seems flustered by my mild question. Then she covers her mouth with her hand as she replies.

"I bit into something last night … it was quite soft." (Probably the last of half-a-dozen doughnuts she was wolfing down as a late-night snack.) "The bottom half of my tooth just came away." She looks ill at ease.

Pippa talks about a friend she had in London who had a similar issue and a 'simply marvellous dentist' — private, of course, not NHS — did something or other with a 'bonded filling … not too expensive.' She smiles reassuringly.

"It's unsightly," Elaine says, sounding as though she might cry at any moment. She still has her hand in front of her mouth. She glances around the coffee shop, which remains busy although no one takes any notice of us.

There is a silence, and I think Elaine will sip her latte and then carry on chattering away. A missed opportunity for me, really. But then — glory be — she actually opens her mouth, pushes her top lip up with a finger and reveals the broken front tooth to us.

There are so many things to dislike about Elaine. The great big lumpy look of her. The brightness of her ill-matching clothes. The hats at a jaunty angle. This childless widow wanting to be everyone's best friend. The assumption that we all like her and are fascinated by her mindless chatter about anything and nothing.

I recoil ever so slightly as she opens her mouth. Enough for her to think I am revolted but do not want her to see that I am. And, as Pippa thinks of the right thing to say, I comment sympathetically, "Never mind. I'm sure a dentist can do something to make it look a bit better." Pippa nods in agreement. Elaine just looks crestfallen. Boohoo.

And so the conversation — the brainless chat — starts over. I enter into the spirit of things, nodding and smiling a little more, not just at Pippa but poor old Elaine as well. It is the stuff-and-nonsense type of talk that passes the time of day. Elaine is subdued to begin with, but I give her encouraging looks. I have an idea for some fun. She then opens up and comes close to returning to her usual, insufferable self.

I offer Elaine a ginger biscuit from a packet of two that has been gathering dust at the bottom of my handbag. She pulls a face, kind of embarrassed, and gestures towards her mouth as if to say, 'I can't eat that!' I've upset her again. I feign surprise, as though I had forgotten her snapped-in-half tooth. I dip my head down and smile to myself.

It is as we are getting up to go that Elaine accidentally confirms that Pippa and she have some sort of budding friendship going on in the background, as I had suspected. Elaine asks Pippa if she got 'the job.' As we are walking to the door, Pippa says, "It's later ... I'll let you know." As I open the door, Elaine adds, "Let's meet and have lunch soon."

I move to go out through the door first. Elaine does too. Pippa is coming up behind her. Elaine stops. Pippa bumps into Elaine, who moves forward just as I step back. Elaine goes tumbling over my foot and lands head first on the pavement.

There is a lot of fussing around by elderly passers-by. (Felixstowe's living dead.) Elaine eventually sits up with a cut forehead and her broken-toothed mouth hanging open. She seems bewildered, as though she does not know what has happened. She looks blankly at me first, then to Pippa, who stands to my side, her hands to her open mouth.

I keep my face neutral as Pippa pulls a little white hand-kerchief from her sleeve and offers it to Elaine. She takes it and dabs at her forehead before looking at the blood on the handkerchief. I think Elaine is about to cry. I wait, Pippa and the old fogies flapping about, to see if she does. She doesn't. Instead, she gets to her feet, crouched over, dabbing her forehead.

I've had enough by now. As I walk home, I realise who the woeful creature reminds me of. Quasimodo. What a sight she is! I clap my hands in delight.

4

MONDAY, 17 OCTOBER, LATE AFTERNOON

A week on from my coffee with Pippa (and the dreadful Elaine), I have been much happier in myself. My days are filled with the same routines, but I seem to enjoy rather than endure everything I do. For example, I have been leaving bits of broken biscuits by benches where I sit, for the dogs. And I have been writing little notes in the margins of the psychological thrillers I borrow from the library — to explain things to those readers who would be better off with an Agatha Christie. In pencil, of course!

My friendship with Pippa has come on in leaps and bounds, each and every day. I texted her that first evening to thank her for my coffee and cake, and she replied almost straightaway: 'You're welcome. See you soon!' Since then, we have been texting regularly, six or so times a day. All sorts of silly, lovely chit-chat! She always replies, often immediately, and apologises when she does not. We are becoming such good friends. I try not to think about Elaine; it is as if she does not exist.

I am due to meet Pippa for coffee tomorrow so she can hand over the Richard Osman book; she is 'a slow reader.' I haven't minded waiting. I have kept busy. This morning, I went into Ipswich on the trusty 75 red bus, to change some books at the bigger library there and, more importantly, to sell a couple of trinkets I happened across in the oddball's flat. He has been particularly loathsome of late, and when he went out yesterday, I had a little look around his grimy place.

As I return from Ipswich late afternoon, I receive a terrible shock. I see the landlord's friend, Francis — a fellow retired teacher, I believe — standing on the front doorstep with a folded-over chessboard and a box of pieces under his left arm. He is a shabby little man with white wispy hair and a stained grey overcoat, a dusty ghost from another time and place. I can imagine him, much younger and oilier, at the private school, hanging around the changing rooms as the little boys got ready for rugby.

"Roger has just passed away," he says to me in a practised voice. I tip my head to the side, put on my sympathetic face, and ask what happened. I do not shake hands or anything like that, as we've only ever met in passing and smiled politely and said hello. And, anyway, he smells musty, as many old men do. I think the two of them used to play games together regularly most afternoons: cards, backgammon, chess, whatever.

He says he'd let himself in as usual just after lunch and saw Roger dead on the living room carpet. A heart attack, he thought. He talks about having called an ambulance and the police and an undertaker, and hanging around for hours. As though he really wanted to get home to watch something on the telly. I'm not sure who came and went, and when, but anyway, the body has now gone. The old man says he called the landlord's son, who is on the way up from London. He gives me his key to pass to the son and says that he's taken back his chess set. It is all rather matter-of-fact as he finally says goodbye and walks away.

I am now standing inside the landlord's ground-floor flat, looking around the living room. It all seems old, a relic from another age, full of bamboo and wicker furniture from the 1980s or earlier. A *Radio Times* magazine lies open on a side table by a chair in front of a bulky old television. Various programmes are circled in red ink.

I go from room to room, idly opening this, looking at that, putting most things back where I found them. There are bunches of keys on hooks on a board in the kitchen. I take the spare key for Mr Grunt and Mrs Groan's flat; it may come in useful. What a horrid place this is. The kitchen smells of boiled cabbage. The toilet, seat up, has a soiled bowl. The bath has a ring of grime around it. The bedroom smells of damp and urine. I come close to gagging as I go through drawers and cupboards and the wardrobe full of his old clothes. Oh, these dirty, sad men in their seventies and eighties.

I am used to old people's living arrangements and their gradual letting go of dusting and cleaning and hoovering. Then, men especially, changing clothes less often, washing and attending to personal hygiene infrequently, until they come to this disgusting state. I pocket what money there is, and a knick-knack or two that catch my eye and may raise a little cash, but there is little here for me.

As I am doing my final checks, I recall a conversation the landlord and I had several years ago, a hot day one summer, at the front of the house. He was using an ordinary dining table fork to dig out weeds from around the edges of the concrete and gravel driveway. The early days of his mental decline, I suppose. I was coming back from the Tesco Express with a carrier bag full of shopping.

For some reason, he started rambling on about his son, young and rich and successful and oh-so important in the city. I think the landlord had just had a birthday, and the son had not even sent a card. And the landlord said — I remember this word for word — "He'll come up as soon as I'm dead ... before I'm even cold."

I looked at the tall, stooped old man in his stained shirt and trousers and sensed his sadness and despair. I did not know what to say to him, so I made a few sympathetic noises, as you do, and added a few soft phrases, 'oh dear' and the like, at appropriate moments. I then made my excuses and left.

I stand here now, back in the front room of the dead landlord's flat, looking out of the smeared window into the road, buoyed for a moment or two by my little finds. Close to £40 in cash. Maybe another £20 in cash for the knick-knacks from that shop in Ipswich. A useful sum, enough for some nice treats, and no one will ever know anything has been taken.

I wonder what this — the landlord's death — means for me, though. I have a lease, just renewed, that runs for another five months. This bottom-of-the-ladder flat is paid for from my benefits and is about as cheap a place could be. I don't really like it here, the noise, the endless tension I feel — just being on edge all the time — but there is nowhere further to fall. At best, I may end my days in a hostel full of battered young women and their screaming brats.

I do not know my rights and am worrying whether, given notice, I could be turned out in a month or two. I doubt I would find much else hereabouts. Everything is being 'done up' by landlords for higher rents. This place is the last of its kind. Where will I go? The thought of possibly being homeless makes me feel physically ill.

And then, standing here in my terrible state, I see the landlord's son arrive, his silver Mercedes, brand new, top of the range, pulling up onto the driveway. I watch as he gets out, this tall, slim man in his thirties with his slicked-back hair and dark grey suit, dripping in self-confidence and certainty.

I know his kind; I can tell just by looking at him. Appearance, conveying success, is so important. He expects to be spoken to as though he is lord and master. Money is the bottom line to him. He will show no mercy. If it suits him for me to stay, I'll be allowed to. If not, he will do whatever he needs to do to force me out.

He locks the car door, then looks up at the house. He is almost rubbing his hands with satisfaction. He takes a bunch of keys from his pocket. I move quickly, before he sees me, to the door of the flat, opening and closing it behind me. I lock it and put the key from Francis under the doormat as though left there for him. I hurry up the staircase to my own flat. I do not want to see this man face-to-face. Not yet. I need to build my courage first.

I LIE ON MY BED, going through the texts between Pippa and me over the past week. The early exchanges were started by me. Pippa was so quick to reply when she could, and so sorry when she could not, that I knew she was delighted to hear from me.

I kept my texting to no more than six or so a day and what might be called 'girly talk' (although I am not a girly-girl sort of person). As an example, I found a marvellous full-length rust-coloured cord skirt on a bargains rail in a charity shop in town — just right for a cold winter — and sent a photo to Pippa. 'Wow!' she replied. She loved it, too.

I like reading Pippa's first texts to me again and seeing how she begins to open up, putting a x at the end and then hearts and emoji faces. I had to Google to discover what most of these meant. They were all sweet and kind. Having scrolled through Google, I sent back messages with suitable emojis. I was careful to be friendly, but not flirty.

As I'm rereading and reliving my thoughts, I can hear the landlord's son moving about downstairs. This mercenary man who drove here just as soon as Francis contacted him. He has not gone to the hospital, nor the undertaker's, to spend a few minutes of contemplation with his late father's body. He has no respect. This disgusting, subhuman being.

Instead, he has come indoors straightaway to check out what is now his. He is opening, rummaging, closing, going to the next cupboard and drawer. Repeating the process time and again. Seeing what he can find, any little treasures, a hidden gem or two.

There's nothing there except smelly old-man belongings that, even if washed and ironed, would be turned away by any charity shop. The socks have holes in them. The pants are stiff. But he has the house, and that must be worth a substantial sum. A ready-made pension for a man who has not yet reached forty.

I go back to the texts. After a few days, Pippa began texting me, starting a new topic of conversation, which we'd discuss, as best you can via texts, to see what the other thought. I am pleased to state that we agreed on just about everything.

We kept to 'safe' subjects mostly, such as the best places to walk in Felixstowe (not that Pippa does!). Naturally, we stayed off certain subjects, just in case we differ. Brexit. Harry and Meghan. The government. Covid. I don't think we would have opposite views. Even if we did, I think we are grown-up enough to 'agree to disagree.'

I did, one evening, when we were having a jolly old exchange, mention Elaine. 'Heard from Elaine?' Pippa did not reply to this. And so I sent the same text the next morning. She replied at lunchtime. 'Not really.' This angered me. I mean, she either had or she hadn't! But I let the matter go.

I stop reading for a moment. I think the landlord's son has exhausted his search. I hear him slam a door, perhaps a wardrobe's, and then another, maybe the bedroom's. I chuckle to myself. Such anger and frustration! I am not sure what he expects to find. Solid gold and priceless jewellery? Tubes of half-used Anasol and crusty, soiled underwear, that's all.

I hear the front door bell ringing. I move to my living area so I can look down out of my window. There is a man in a suit, early thirties but balding already, standing there looking up. I step back. I recognise him from one of the estate agents in town that also deals with lettings.

The landlord's son must have made the call on his way around the M25 of London and up the long A12 to Suffolk. He is a man in a hurry, wanting a valuation immediately. This is my home — I have that lease — but, even so, I suddenly feel sick with dread.

I go back to my bed, trying to lift my spirits by rereading the later texts between Pippa and me. These are the ones where our friendship grew and blossomed. I started drawing her out of herself by paying her little compliments in passing. I sent her a photo of a scarf I had found in another charity shop. 'This colour would suit you,' I wrote.

'Yes! My favourite,' she answered. I have bought and put it aside for her for Christmas. A lovely surprise.

Pippa was most responsive when I asked her about herself and her feelings, 'How are you today?' I did not ask her about the horrible husband or the ghastly son. She shared some intimate thoughts about herself. How she struggled to speak well at her job interview. Yet she got the job! I was surprised she was not as confident as she appeared, and that she worried endlessly about her appearance and talking in public. I reassured her every time.

And now I think it is the moment that I draw her even closer to me — to cement our friendship — by telling her a little about my horrid flat, the landlord dying and his son who wants to sell this place, the roof over my head. 'Help!' I tap into my phone, and then press send.

As I wait for Pippa's reply, lying here on my bed, I am also listening for the landlord's son and what he is doing. I hear him opening the front door, greeting the estate agent, inviting him in, making small talk.

Nothing really shocks me — I've seen too much of life's dark side — but a son doing this within hours of his father dying, even before he has been to see the body, is beyond callous. I fear this man and what he might do. He has no scruples.

They are moving about downstairs, the estate agent

making notes, taking measurements, keen to put the house up for sale and get his commission. I hear one of them laughing — proper, laugh-out-loud — and I wonder how anyone could do that at a time like this.

'What's wrong?' comes the reply from Pippa.

I think what to put. I have, at the back of my mind, an idea that is forming. I need to phrase my response carefully.

'Landlord died. Son here already wanting to sell. I'm going to be homeless.'

I wait for her next response, hoping she will offer me practical help, something more than just kind words, maybe even a place to stay. That studio in her back garden could be made into a warm and cosy home easily enough. I don't think she uses it. As I lie here fretting, I hear footsteps, the creaking on the stairs, as the landlord's son and the estate agent make their way up and onto the landing.

I move to my front door, listening. I am here in this house alone. The young couple are at work. The oddball in the loft is out as well. Not that I would turn to any of them for help. But I feel somehow more vulnerable on my own. My only hope is that the landlord's son will behave properly in front of the estate agent.

They come along the landing to my door first. The landlord's son bangs loudly on it. Bang! Bang! Bang!

I delay, not sure whether to open the door or not. I may pretend to be out. But I am not sure if I have locked this door. Thinking I may be out, he may barge straight in. I hesitate for ever such a while.

Finally, I open the door. The impatient-looking landlord's son is raising his hand to knock again. The estate agent stands there, smiling vaguely, looking nervous.

"Nick. Roger's son," he says abruptly. "We've come to

have a look." He steps forward, expecting me to move aside. I don't.

"Sorry, you'll have to make an appointment through the agent." I smile sweetly. The estate agent offers a practised smile. I glance at the landlord's son as I close the door in his face. He is red-faced livid. I have made an enemy there. I wait, expecting him to bang again, louder still, but instead I hear them moving away, the son apologising to the agent in a voice crackling with anger.

I go back to my bed and lie down to look at my text messages. Pippa has sent three. The first: 'Don't worry. He can't force you out. You have rights.' He can, of course, make my life a misery though.

The second: 'You okay?' Clearly, she expected me to reply immediately. And then, the third, a minute ago: 'Honestly, don't worry. He'd have to give you notice. And you can find somewhere else!'

And that's that. No 'You must come to me' or 'I'll look after you.' She might as well have not bothered to reply. I feel my emotions rising. I switch my phone off and lie here doing breathing exercises to calm myself.

All I can hear is the landlord's son and the estate agent moving about the house. First knocking and, as no one is in, entering the flat behind me on this middle floor. Then the stairs up to the loft, a knock, a moment's pause, and in again to look around.

This isn't fair. The landlord's son should not be doing this. Despite his position as a guest in the house, the estate agent should know better, too. As they go by my door, I hear a bump and a rattle, as though the landlord's son has knocked against it to make me jump, then put a key in my lock and jiggled it to unnerve me.

It does. I feel trapped here, the oddball above and the couple behind making my life a misery with their noise night after night, morning after morning. And now, the landlord's son is my enemy. I have no doubt that he will try to force me out one way or the other. And Pippa, my beloved one, has betrayed me. I wish I were dead.

5

TUESDAY, 18 OCTOBER, THE MORNING

My mood was desperately low all evening, even after I watched the landlord's son reversing his car and roaring away up the road. My anxiety carried on through another noisy and restless night to now, the next morning. Since the young couple left for work, I have been spending ages debating whether to meet Pippa at the coffee shop for the handover of the Richard Osman book. I am so angry with her for letting me down over my 'Help!' message. Eventually, I decide to go. After all, I have little else to do.

Pippa strolls into the coffee shop a few minutes after our agreed meeting time of eleven o'clock. She is wearing the same fawn-coloured, full-length coat with everyday brown boots. But she appears unusually flustered, looking this way and that, as though she expects to see me by the door. She seems on the brink of tears.

I am sitting at 'our' table at the back with, courtesy of the landlord's loose change, two lattes, sweeteners, and two packets of biscuits: one oatmeal, one shortbread; I am not

sure which she prefers. I like both. I keep one foot on a
table leg to stop it wobbling this way and that. I wave to
Pippa, then stand up to greet her as she hurries
towards me.

She hugs me, quite unexpectedly, and I am taken by
surprise but hug her back. I have dreamed of this moment
since we met. All my anger towards her — irritation, really
— for not replying to my texts is gone with this simple,
loving gesture.

I have not been hugged by anyone for years, not since my
friend Monica died. She was my soulmate, for a while. As I
hope Pippa will be — but for ever, this time.

I hug Pippa until, after what seems like several minutes,
she lets go and sits down opposite me. She is all twitches and
glances behind. I wait for her to speak.

She pulls the latte towards her, fiddles with the sweetener packet and drops the little white tablet in, stirring the
latte round and round. More times than she needs to, in an
almost obsessive way. It is annoying, but I smile anyway.
Then she taps the spoon on the side of the glass, chink,
chink, chink, chink, chink, to knock the froth off back into
the latte. I think she is going to start the whole stirring thing
again. And I will have to bite my lip. But instead, she drops
the spoon on a napkin on the table and sips the latte. "That's
better," she says, looking at me at last.

She has a thin moustache of froth on her top lip.
Without thinking, I reach across with my napkin, dabbing
her lip. I think for a terrible instant that I have gone too far,
been too familiar, too soon. That she will pull back, if not
recoil. But she does not. To my surprise, she lets me wipe it,
then laughs as I say instinctively, "That's better, too." I
usually have to prepare 'ad-libs,' as it were, in advance of

saying them. I am rather pleased with myself and my instinctive bon mot.

It seems to have gone down well; Pippa relaxes in her chair and tips her head back, looking at the ceiling. It is a gesture that reminds me of Monica, leaning against the bedhead and smoking after we had made love, blowing smoke rings up towards the ceiling. I imagine Pippa naked for a moment and feel myself flushing. Pippa does not seem to notice as we look at each other and smile, then glance away. I have a feeling that Pippa is about to share a confidence with me.

I am correct. She leans forward conspiratorially. I lean in, too.

"It's Peter," she says succinctly. Then pauses. "I think he's having another affair."

Another affair! As I thought. There is something rotten at the heart of their marriage.

In fits and starts, with well-phrased questions from me and long pauses from Pippa, everything comes tumbling out. It is as I expected, and more. When they were living in West Norwood in London, and Peter was working at the university and she was caring for her dying mother, he had an affair with a student on his course. He denied it, as men will. Got angry, as men do. Admitted it finally, when a mutual friend told Pippa. A young female overseas student.

"Peter went from her bed to mine." She pulls a face of revulsion.

Pippa goes over everything, and, although she does not say it as such, it is clear that they were on the brink of splitting up. But the student went back to Asia at the end of the course. And Pippa's mother died. And Peter was 'very supportive.' And then, of course, there is the boy, the less-than-lovely Dominic, who was doing his GCSEs at the time. And so they 'patched things up' and 'stuck it out' for Dominic's sake.

Here they are now. A fresh start in Suffolk, Peter with a new job at the university in Ipswich; Dominic at the local school doing his A Levels; and Pippa grieving and bereft, about to start work at this boutique to fill her lonely hours. Peter leaves earlier and returns later than he used to do and is different with her, more reserved and distant.

"I'm going to keep going ... until I know for sure," she says bravely about the husband. "I ..." And her voice tails off. Then she rallies with one more comment: "I don't know what else to do ... thank you for being my friend."

"I'm so sorry," I say. I get up and walk to her side of the table and put my arms around her. I don't normally do this sort of thing, but it somehow feels right. My face is close to her neck and hair. I breathe in her perfume. It is all I can do to stop myself putting my face into her hair and taking in the clean, fresh smell.

I wait as long as I can — a moment or two before she might feel uncomfortable — and then step away, patting her on the back for encouragement. She seems pleased.

We move on to other, happier subjects. She talks a little about the horrid boy, who she seems to think is some sort of precious angel, and a genius too. I um and ah and do not contradict her. And how much she likes Felixstowe. And isn't Bury St Edmunds a lovely place? And Hadleigh is terribly sweet. I ask when she visited, and she is rather vague and airy, saying something about beautiful independent clothing stores and gift shops. I sense she's been to these places with the ghastly Elaine, but I do not press, as it might spoil the moment. And she does not elaborate. It angers me somehow.

I am still annoyed — yes, that is the correct word — that she makes no reference to my 'Help!' text, nor asks anything about me: how I am, how things are at my flat, whom I should talk to. Not even that! I had really hoped that she would raise the subject, allowing me to make one or two prepared comments that might encourage her to invite me to come and stay with her.

As Pippa hands me the book, just before leaving, and asks me to keep her 'secrets,' it occurs to me there is a way I can take a significant step towards my goal — my dream of living with Pippa. I can uncover the truth about her cheating husband. Maybe dig up some dirt on the son as well. That will make us so much closer, and who knows where we might go from there? We embrace once more on the pavement, and Pippa kisses me first on one cheek and then the other. As we part, I say, "Leave it with me." She smiles, although I am not sure she heard what I said. Or if she did, what I mean.

———

JUST GONE noon the next day, and I am sitting on a bench by the River Orwell in Ipswich at what is known as 'The Waterfront.' It has been described on Google as a 'cultural and historically significant area.' It is a busy, hustle-bustle kind of place, full of carefully presented arty types, foreign students and older women who dress as though they are thirty years younger.

It is a sunny day, and I am reading a copy of yesterday's *Daily Mail* I found at the top of a bin. I am having a nice packed lunch: a simple cheese sandwich, an apple and a flask of tea. The tea is slightly stewed, but it is quite refreshing. There is a faint smell of vomit and some evidence of it nearby. I do not move, though.

I am close to a number of university buildings along the dockside and can see the doors — the entrances and the exits — of all of them. I glance across now and then, as though I am just passing the time of day and enjoying the sunshine. The reality is that I am keeping watch, although no one would ever know.

On my arrival, I checked, with various receptionists, the locations of the different departments. The entry and exit points. And I have been sat here, the right place to see Pippa's husband, watching everything oh-so-carefully ever since.

His car is in the car park behind me. It was there when I arrived. I was lucky and saw it almost straightaway. I will sit here and wait, however long it takes, until he goes to the car and leaves.

If he comes out with someone, his lover, I will use my phone to film what I see. A hug. A kiss. An intimate touch. Ready to show Pippa when the time is right.

Time passes oh-so slowly. It is now well gone two o'clock; I have been sitting here for ever such a while. I will stay until I see him, even if it is four o'clock or later. No one takes any notice of an old woman like me. I am invisible to anyone and everyone. Not just teenagers. I don't matter. I am of no use to society.

I have my mobile phone resting on my left thigh. When I see him come out of the building with his latest fancy, I will lift it up as though checking my hair — it is something all women do regularly — and I will record them. Of course, they will not be holding hands or even be arm-in-arm in so public a place, but they will give themselves away somehow, fussing around each other as lovers do. I will, if I am careful, get a video with one of them touching the other lightly on the arm or back. It will look damning enough when I turn it into a photograph to be printed off.

I do not know what they will do. I may film them driving away in his car, taking his young lover to a Travel Lodge or some such place for an hour or two's flagrante. They may instead walk along the dockside — there are, I suspect, nooks and crannies further along where they might hide themselves away for something furtive and fast but falling short of coitus. I will follow them from a distance and see what I can record. Their embrace might be enough for that damning photograph; a kiss would be conclusive.

It is now close to four o'clock — it has been ever such a long wait. I have stretched my legs repeatedly. And there have been so many comings and goings that there were times when I thought I might have missed him in amongst the crowds. But the car is still there. Without that, I would have given up long ago.

The doors of the nearby building swing open. I see the last batch of students, the usual mix of deadbeats and ne'er do wells, coming out. I ready myself again, as casually as I can, putting my newspaper beside me on the bench.

I take my phone and hold it up and fiddle with my hair. The mobile phone is pointed towards the doors. I am waiting. Any moment now. I watch, my heart thumping, as it seems everyone is leaving at the same time. On it goes until, finally, the flood of student-types slows to a trickle and eventually stops. I give up. I will come back tomorrow.

Then, suddenly, he appears, pushing the doors open and

striding out alone without a backward glance. I drop my head slightly, just in case he looks this way and recognises me and comes across to challenge me. But he walks on to the car park, to his car. I sigh to myself, ready to turn off my phone, pack everything away, and head for the bus station, tired and demoralised.

As I fiddle with my phone, the doors to the university swing open one last time, and a young and blonde female student, all beehive hair, arms and elbows, knees and legs, comes striding out. I glance at her, then away, and back again. Something, some instinct within me, makes me do this and lift up my phone again, ready to take photographs.

He is standing by the passenger side of his car. She walks to him. He glances around, not seeming to notice me. They do not kiss — the photograph I truly wanted — but he opens the door for her. He puts his hand on her shoulder and then her back and finally, the lightest touch, her bottom, as he guides her into the passenger seat. I watch as they drive away, and then check my phone — I now have all I need to destroy him.

———

TODAY, having spent so many hours looking at the photographs of the horrid husband with the young female student, my thoughts have been turning to the dirty boy.

I am not sure, at this moment, whether I want him on my side or not. It will be hard, given his aggressive nature to me. I'd prefer him on my side, I think, after I have shown the photographs to Pippa. After that, I can plot and plan his downfall.

I walked from my flat up towards his high school early

this morning to see if I might spot and possibly have a conversation with him. I did not see him, though. I did the same at lunchtime, in case he was out and about with his mates, but without success.

Now, in the afternoon, I have been up the town to buy some fruit and vegetables from the greengrocer's by the cinema. As I return to the High Road roundabout, I notice a long procession of the little heathens coming back from school into town. It strikes me that the boy will be amongst them.

I wander up towards the high school with a carrier bag in each hand, by the petrol station and the primary school, keeping watch for him coming towards me, perhaps with his mates, on this side of the road or the other.

I always feel threatened by loud and boisterous school-children, all shouting and pushing and yelling obscenities at each other. I try to avoid making eye contact, and hope that none of them decide to pick on me simply because I am old and vulnerable.

And then I spot him, the boy, approaching on the other side of the road. He is alone and hurrying along, head down. There is a group of bigger boys, four of them, walking behind him, and I get the sense of a pack of dogs about to attack a fox.

I call across before he draws level with me, "Hello!" All the beasts turn and look at me, the mad old bag lady.

I'm not sure if he hears or chooses to ignore me as he presses on. Perhaps he does not recognise me. The pack of boys keeps pace with him.

And so I cross the road, not fast enough for one car driver, who beeps at me, to the derision of the monsters, and I walk alongside the dirty boy.

I move my two carrier bags to my right hand, leaving my left hand free to rummage in one and pull out a brown paper bag of plums. I offer the open bag to him in a friendly fashion. He half-shakes his head as though he does not wish to speak to me.

I go to say something to him, a greeting, a kind word, but he hisses at me to fuck off. I look at his flustered, hot face as he tries to out-stride me. There are catcalls from the animals behind us. "Got your granny to walk you home, have you, dick?" one shouts. There is much derisive laughter.

At that, the boy breaks into a run, without looking, across the road towards the petrol station. The gang of bigger boys gives chase, darting in front of hooting and screeching-to-a-halt cars. He is too fast for them, disappearing into the relative safety of the supermarket.

I carry on my way, soon being forgotten by all the foul children who are walking behind me on the pavement. As some of them push by me, I wonder what it is I have just witnessed. Nothing? Or something?

I will come this way again in a few days and try to bump into the boy, perhaps getting to know him in some way. I will buy some sweets and some gum, and, when I see him, I will cross the road, saying, "Hello! Remember me? I saw your dog. Dotty? How's Dotty?"

I will strike up a friendship of sorts if I can. Then, at some stage, when Pippa turns on her husband and I suddenly appear as Pippa's best friend, the boy will be on my side. And the easier it will be, knowing more about him, to cause a permanent rift between mother and son in due course.

6

THURSDAY, 20 OCTOBER, EARLY EVENING

I 'm walking down the stairs, on my way to get some end-of-the-day bargains at the Tesco Express, perhaps some sweets for the boy, when I stop suddenly. I hear the door of the landlord's flat opening.

He is standing in front of me. He looks me up and down, this arrogant man who thinks I am nothing, someone of no consequence.

I smile politely and step to one side to go to open the front door. He moves to block me. I stop and look him in the eyes, barely controlling my anger. The nerve of the man.

"I'm putting the house up for sale tomorrow," he says in his yobbish, South London accent. It's similar to Pippa's, but much harsher. "Just wanted you to know." He smiles, more of a smirk really, and looks back at me, hoping to see distress in my eyes. I won't let him see how I feel.

I just reply cordially, "I've a lease." I do not add 'tough luck' or pull a face or shrug my shoulders or try to brush by him. I don't want him to see any weakness in me, especially

my fear that I may soon be homeless. Nor do I want to antag-
onise. I hate this man already. He did not even say 'Good
evening,' let alone 'How are you?' as most people would do.
Just came straight out with his threatening news.

"I'm selling without tenants. You'll get your letter of
notice from my solicitor in the next day or two. I'm giving
you plenty of warning, all legal and above board."

I look at him now, this hard-faced man who expects to
get whatever he wants. It's his expression, the contempt at
having to speak to the likes of me, that shakes me most.

"I'm happy here," I say as calmly as I can. "I'm not
moving. I have rights. You cannot just do what you want."

I stop before I say too much. I watch as his expression
changes, this man who is clearly quick to anger. He is about
to say something back, a harder retort, but I am already
turning and going back up the stairs.

He shouts at me as I go. "You're leaving. You're fucking
leaving, alright? Even if I have to drag you out myself."

I keep going up the stairs, steadily, as nonchalantly as I
can. I feel myself wobbling, my legs especially, and I need to
get out of his sight as quickly as I can.

"This is my house. Not yours. You can fuck off out of it."
His voice is full of barely controlled fury. This man with so
many issues. I fear he may come up the stairs after me,
assaulting me in his wrath.

I get to the landing, ready to turn towards my flat. I resist
the urge to look back down, defying him. He would be up
the stairs in a second, losing control of his emotions.

"Do you hear me? Listen. Fucking well listen."

I've riled him. More than that. This man with a short fuse
on his temper. I go into my flat, locking the door and bolting

it at the top, and then lean my head against it, shaking and taking deep, jagged breaths. He frightens me.

I listen as he stomps back into his flat, slamming the door so hard that it reverberates through the house.

I now feel as though I am a prisoner. In the evenings and into the early hours, when I am in the flat, he will make my life a misery, knocking and banging and goodness knows what, night after night, trying to intimidate me into leaving, He will go on until I break down and give in.

During the day, he will sit and wait for me downstairs, coming to the door to threaten and bully me as I go out of the house. I will turn and flee back upstairs. It will feel like a jail sentence as long as I am here.

I wonder, when I do eventually leave the flat to see my dear Pippa, if he will hurry upstairs and come in, changing the locks, and I will return to bin bags and cardboard boxes on the doorstep. I believe this is a man who, despite what he says, has no respect for the law and operates outside of it.

IT IS LATE NOW, tipping from midnight into the early hours of the morning. I tried to have as normal an evening as I could, eating my microwave meal in front of the television, reading my library book, doing a crossword puzzle to keep my mind active and sharp. But I was on edge right through to going to bed at 10.30pm, part of my brain listening out for what was happening around me.

But it has been quiet, at least from downstairs. I fear the landlord's son and what he might do next. He is down there right now, plotting against me. I have no doubt about that. The oddball upstairs is clumping about in his heavy-footed manner, but he is not trying to annoy me, to make sport of it, tonight. Mr Grunt and Mrs Groan are loud as ever, going about their business as thoughtlessly as they always do: the TV is blaring, doors are slammed, they shout now and then. I try to block it all out.

Sitting quietly here in my bed, I return again to writing my notes up into a readable form in last year's desk diary. What with one thing and another, I have not been as dutiful as I should have been at turning my spidery scrawl of thoughts into something resembling a proper, neatly written memoir. It has been an age. As my bedside cabinet clock's numbers turn to 00.01, I start what might be called 'my translation of rough notes to tidied memories.'

My mother saw me as a nuisance when I was a child, tying me to the bedpost when she went out at nights. As I got older, I made her money, her gentlemen friends making me do whatever it was they wanted. This went on until I was fourteen and strong enough to fight them off. Some of them, anyway. I left school at sixteen and went through all sorts of short-lived cleaning jobs whilst my mother lay at home, drunk most of the time. Those gentlemen friends eventually stopped calling. The stink of her was repulsive.

I killed my mother when I was eighteen. I came back earlier than usual one night from yet another temporary job cleaning offices — sacked because I wouldn't let the boss have his way with me — and found her drunk and sprawled on the carpet. She struggled to her feet, ready to start an argument about this or that, as always. Then she slumped down, her head tipping back, mouth open. As she

*did so, she went to vomit, and something inside me
snapped — years and years of abuse and degradation —
and I stepped forward and pinched her nose and pushed
her mouth shut. I have always had a terrible, instinctive
temper.*

*I held her like that, nose and mouth clamped tight, for
many minutes. Maybe longer. Hours, I don't know. It was
as though I were in a trance. I let go eventually, expecting
her body to fall forwards or backwards. But she just sat
there upright and perfectly still, which made me laugh
aloud. I gathered up my belongings in a rucksack to go. I
then hesitated, gently tipping her back so she was laid flat,
vomit in her nose and mouth, surrounded by empty
bottles. I don't know who found her nor when. It may
have been weeks, months or longer. I just walked and
never looked back.*

*I made my way — hitchhiking from London to Brighton
to Plymouth to Exeter to Manchester, a blur of places —
as best I could over the years, going from one grim cash-
in-hand job to another; from one hostel — and, occasionally, a run-down bedsit — to the next. Eking out my cash
week to week. I lived on the streets, doing this and that,
pickpocketing, stealing, whatever, on and off, for years. It
was not so bad in summer, although I had to hide somewhere I'd not be uncovered by a dirty old man or younger
men full of drink and egging each other on. The winters
were the worst of times.*

*My life steadied by my mid-twenties, as I got a proper job
— they needed anyone they could get — working as a*

home help for old people who weren't well enough to get out and about, but weren't so bad that they had to go into a home. I made friendships, and a little extra money, in different ways, but they'd all go in the end, of course, to homes or their graves.

I did that, all in all, until I was forty. Lived in a bedsit. Had a normal life. Had friends, close women friends, four in all. But none of them stayed long. I was damaged in so many ways. And I had the most awful temper. I may write about them another time, but not now.

I had, over the years, bettered myself, learning to drive and getting a little runaround car. I studied Maths and English GCSEs at evening classes. I read everything I could lay my hands on — encyclopedias mainly — to expand my knowledge. And finally, I did an Open University degree in creative writing. I thought education was the best way to change my life. And it was, in a way. I was a voracious reader. One day, I saw an advert for a lady's companion in a posh magazine in the library. It was placed by my soulmate, Monica. Soulmate-to-be anyway. For a while.

I remember driving in my battered red mini all the way from Rustington in Sussex to Fakenham in Norfolk. It was a bright and sunny Friday morning in early spring. I was full of hope and expectation, having had a very pleasant conversation with Monica on the telephone a few nights before. (I took my belongings with me in two suitcases, just in case.) She was the same age as me and had never married. She had family money from a trust fund. She seemed to have a range of physical and other issues, arthritis and fibromyalgia in particular, and wanted, as she put it, 'to live life to the full before retiring to my wheelchair.'

And she — we — did for the next six or seven years. I moved into the annex — a classy, one-bedroom-kitchen-living room apartment — that same day. I began as a live-in companion and, through such happy times, trips to National Trust properties, evenings at the theatre, days at home reading and listening to the radio, I — we — became lovers. And I was truly happy for the first time in my life. I thought it would last forever. But then, over the following two or three years, her physical disabilities and early onset dementia brought her low. Her brother, a barrister in the city, was granted power of attorney, and my days were numbered.

I killed Monica on her fiftieth birthday. By then, she was in a wheelchair, and, with money so tight, there was little to spend on anything to make her life, and mine, easier. She was sullen as I spoon-fed her porridge for breakfast, then insisted on drinking her tea herself, spilling it over her legs. And she soiled herself profusely. As I helped her into the bath, she slipped beneath the water with an indignant cry. It was this, the sound of ingratitude, and the thought of another twenty years of this with nothing at the end of it, no home or money, that made me snap. I held her head under the water for ever so long. Until she was dead, I suppose.

I stop there. I cannot write about Monica or the inquest and what the coroner said about the 'tragic accident,' and how the brother acted, putting me out on the street. Not now. Even ten years or so on, it upsets me too much. I will, at some point, write more about my life since then, here in Felixstowe. About Patricia. And perhaps even about Pippa, my new soulmate, and what might just be the happy-ever-after I have always longed for.

I put my notebook and pen and my neatly written desk diary into the drawer of my bedside cabinet. I dry my eyes with a tissue from the box I keep by the clock. I do not cry often — I am not that sort of person — but thoughts of Monica bring up my deep-down emotions. Perhaps that is what the GP meant when he once said how writing things down can 'cleanse the soul.' In truth, it just upsets me. And makes me feel dirty as well.

I turn off the lamp on the bedside cabinet and lie here on my bed. I see everything with such clarity in this instant. I am a sad and lonely woman with nothing to do, living in a horrid little flat that smells of dirt and damp. Even now, that vile man above is marching about upstairs, and the young couple are doing unspeakably loud things in the bedroom next to mine. All I have — my whole life hangs on this — is Pippa. Without her, I have nothing to live for. No future. No life at all.

———

IT'S THE NEXT MORNING — after another troubled night — and I wait, my head resting against my door, listening for sounds of the oddball and the young couple on the landing and stairs outside my flat.

Between them, they kept me awake most of the night, and, after a brief sleep from three am, again from just gone six am. Now, at eight thirty, the couple must be about to leave for work. The oddball sometimes goes out at this time of day, doing whatever he does. The supermarket. The launderette. Fiddling with himself by the graves in the cemetery.

I want to speak to them about the landlord's son and leases and the property sale and what they plan to do. I do not like asking for help. It is not in my nature. But I know that I cannot take on this callous man on my own. Not that I am happy here, but those alternatives — a hostel, the streets again, at my age — are so much worse.

The young couple come out first, I hear them opening their door, walking onto the landing, laughing about something or other.

I open my door just as they move towards the staircase, look out, and am about to speak my prepared words in a pleasant voice: 'Hello, have you heard the house is being sold?'

She speaks first, blunt words in her coarse voice. "Here she is, with her glass to the wall ..."

I am about to reply, to respond with a sharp denial, when he adds a comment, the first time he's spoken to me for ages. "Perhaps she wants to join us ... for a threesome." He laughs uproariously, this stupid, grossly disrespectful young man.

She pulls a face and makes an 'uurgh' noise in the back of her throat as though she is gagging. Then she puts the middle finger of her right hand into her open mouth and pretends to make herself vomit.

He stops by the staircase, tipping his head back and laughing again. I can see metal fillings on all his upper back teeth, this ugly man, this repulsive, moronic couple.

I control my sense of rising anger — my rage at the way

they are treating me, their contempt, their complete and utter disrespect. I speak as calmly as I can as they turn to go. "The house is being sold. Did you know?" My voice shakes slightly and sounds whiny, almost pitiful, as I ask the question.

He shrugs as he moves down the staircase, his back to me. "We're moving out, getting our own place."

She looks back up at me, before I can mask the despair in my face, and smiles brightly, but not in a nice way.

And then they are gone, laughing and joking — sniggering about me — as they get to the bottom of the stairs and leave the house. I feel violated.

In my fury, I walk down to their door at the other end of the landing. I kick it as though I am kicking her on the shin. I want my revenge for the way they treat me. I then shake the lock of the door and think that I will go back in later with the key I took from the landlord's flat.

I would like to go in and do something terrible. On the floor. Or even in their bed. But they will know it was me, and things could get very nasty from there. I will think of something else, some other way to get even.

As I stand there, calming myself, I hear footsteps on the staircase from the loft. I turn, and the oddball is there in front of me. He is a short man with little eyes in a round, piggy face, and gingery strands of hair above his ears and below his nose. He looks like a character from the Muppets, but a malevolent one. He stares intently at me, blocking his way on the landing.

He really is strange looking. His egg-head is too large for his body. His clothes are ill-matching: a black, old-man rain-coat with plum-coloured cords and white teenager trainers. He has a creepy look to him. This stranger in the attic.

He does not say a word, not even 'morning.' Instead, he moves to go by me, first one way and then the other. Like I am an inanimate object. I stand still in the middle so he cannot simply brush by me on either side. He stops then and looks at me in an irritated manner and says, "What?"

"Mr Vickers ... Roger, the landlord ... he's died, did you know?"

He shakes his head dismissively. Not to say no. But as if my question is a foolish one. That he knows already. Everyone knows.

"His son's going to sell up, did you know that?"

"Yes ... is that it?" He goes to walk by my right side.

"No," I reply, and, with my voice rising, I add, "His son is selling up, wants us all out. Is that fair?"

"Whatever," the oddball replies in a so-what kind of voice. I don't know what to say to that.

As I gather my thoughts together — am I the only one who worries about any of this? — he brushes by me. No, he pushes me aside and goes towards the stairs.

"Don't you even care?" I shout.

"I'll get another place." He shuts the front door behind him.

It's not the indifference to me, the callousness, that bothers me most. It's the manhandling me out of the way. It enrages me.

The oddball does not know, of course, that I have a key to his rooms. I can, and do, go in there from time to time when I know he is out.

Sometimes, it is just out of curiosity, something to do, as I sift through his wardrobe, drawers and desk; his clothes, too. Now and then, if I don't think they will be missed, I take a coin or two with me, and sometimes a note.

But, of course, I could go up whenever I want, really. I would like to stand over his bed whilst he is asleep. Watch his face as he awakes and sees me there, watching his expression change. And then I'd plunge my bread knife into him. It is a satisfying thought.

7

FRIDAY, 21 OCTOBER, LATE MORNING

I have felt, these past few days, that I have been a prisoner in my own home, my horrid little flat. I have spent so much time in bed, reading my book club book, and then library books, and listening to the landlord's son downstairs, moving about, opening his front door now and then, as if coming out, waiting for me to come downstairs so that he can berate and insult me.

There have been times when he came upstairs, and I heard him moving along the landing by my door and the young couple's, up the stairs to the oddball's door in the attic, and then down again, pausing outside my door. I always think he will bang on it. But he does not. It is this — the menacing silent movement — that spooks me so much.

Early this morning, I watched as he got into his car, his smart Mercedes, and drove away; whether he was going shopping or even back to London, I could not say. He did not have any bags with him, though. I took the chance to get out, to pick up milk and bread and suchlike, and to take my books back to the library.

I am here now, in the coffee shop, after my visit to the supermarket and the library. A coffee and a slice of cake to cheer myself up. I cannot really afford such luxuries on my meagre budget. But my mood has been so low, so close to despair for so long, that I came in for a 'pick-me-up,' paying with coins I'd taken from Mr Grunt and Mrs Groan's flat, including copper ones, much to the barista's disdain. 'Barista' is such a pretentious term for a skinny boy with a pustulant, oozing face. I said nothing about the revolting sight.

I am sitting here at this little table with its two chairs opposite each other, near the front by the door, watching the world go by. What a mistake. Elaine comes bustling along with her shopping bags. She sees me immediately and shouts, "Coo-ee," and I pretend not to see her. Then she comes in and calls my name, and I look at her as though I were in a world of my own. She walks across and puts her bags by the table. Neither a 'Do you mind?' nor an 'Is it okay?' The presumption infuriates me.

As she goes back to order her coffee, my foot catches one of her carrier bags. I watch as it tips over, and two or three apples roll out across the dirty floor. I shut my eyes and pretend not to notice until Elaine returns, huffing and puffing and picking them up and jiggling the bags about; then she is sitting there opposite me, all breathless and excited. She tips a sweetener tablet into her latte, stirs the glass and slurps at the foam on top. "That's better!" she cries, her voice full of exclamation marks as ever. "I needed that!"

I don't like Elaine. In fact, I loathe everything about her. At the moment, her big moon face, bruised forehead, still-broken front tooth and that grating voice are all getting on my nerves already. More than that, though.

She now has a line of foam from her latte on her top lip. Just like Pippa had last time I was here. But this line of foam is not dainty. It is thicker, like Hercule Poirot's moustache. It makes her look dumb. And me dumber, for being with her.

I could nod and gesture towards her lips. Or, if we were best friends, I could lean across and dab at it with my serviette. Instead, I just sit here trying to look interested in her babbling.

After so much mindless gibberish, she finally leans in conspiratorially and whispers to me in an exaggerated way: "Pippa!"

I nod, not sure what to say.

"I was going to text you, but I don't have your number and didn't want to ask Pippa ... and give the game away."

I stare back at her.

"I've been thinking that we, the three of us, could have a lunch together ... somewhere nice ... to cheer Pippa up. She's been working non-stop at her boutique."

I say nothing, wanting to shrug indifferently. I don't want to have lunch with Elaine. Then again, I do not wish to miss out on lunch with Pippa, even if it means dipping into my meagre savings. "Where were you thinking?" I ask.

"Somewhere over by the Quay at Ipswich," she replies. "Next Wednesday. She has a day off. I've asked her to keep the afternoon free. So she knows something's up!" I expect her to snort, but instead she slurps her latte, making her foam moustache even bigger. How can she not notice?

If I am brutally honest, I hate this stupid woman. The big, gormless look of her. The rolling gait. The excited shouts of a conversation. Pippa is far too sophisticated for this foolish lump. She can do much better. What Pippa really wants, needs I think, is a true friend. Calm and measured and thoughtful. Who has her best interests at heart. Someone who will be there for her with advice and a guiding hand, not a fat dollop offering excited yelps and sudden snorts. What Pippa needs is me.

I think, somehow, I have to remove Pippa from Elaine's sweaty embrace. I am not sure how I will do that. In the past, I have used a number of ways to dissuade others from getting too close to ones I have loved. Some of these methods have been direct, some might say, but they had the desired effect of removing them permanently. I need to think what I will do to Elaine to resolve this troublesome matter.

Meantime, I smile at her and say that would be lovely. I'd like to come along. So she offers to pick me up at noon next Wednesday from the top of Bath Road where it joins Brook Lane, and we will drive to Pippa's together, who will be waiting outside her house. "Hello!" we will shout as though the three of us are the best of friends. And off we will go to Ipswich, to have a jolly old time.

It does cross my mind that, when we are there, big lumpy Elaine might trip and stumble and fall off the quayside into the water. What a tsunami of a splash that would be.

As I finish my coffee and cake and say I must be on my way — "I've got to return something to someone" — an elderly busybody sort of man with ginger-dyed hair and white sideburns stops and points to Elaine, towards her frothy upper lip.

She is embarrassed, but laughs and dabs at it with her serviette. Then looks at me, ever so slightly flushed, and I can see her thinking, Why didn't you say something?

And I think back, Because I hate you, you big fat tub of lard, and I wish you were dead. But I don't say that. I simply say "Oops!" and make a little tinkling noise of a laugh. Then I turn my back on her and leave.

———

THE LANDLORD'S son has gone. Back to London, I think. I have not seen him for days. A 'For Sale' sign is now up outside the house. I know my time here is limited, and I am sick with worry where I will go. I realise from my days on the street forty years ago that I could not survive them now, in these harsher times. I'd be a target for feral teenage girls. Young men, with evil in their hearts, would see me as fair game for whatever they wanted to do to amuse themselves.

Various letters have been sent from the estate and letting agent. They lie on the windowsill, unopened. I know what will be in them. A legal document, giving me two months' notice. Carefully worded 'requests' to let would-be buyers view inside my flat in the meantime. My mood is at its lowest for as long as I can remember. I realise I need to talk to Citizens Advice, the benefits people and lettings agents. But I can barely summon the energy to get out of bed.

Today though, Wednesday, I am rallying for this lunch, putting on my best face to please Pippa — my one and only chance of salvation out of this hellhole. Even so, I know I am going to hate every minute of it, because of Elaine. I have to do something about her — getting between Pippa and me — and soon. A chance moment will arise, and I will be ready for it.

As I stand waiting on the corner of Bath Road, Elaine's car trundles into view. Toot! Toot! As she pulls up and I step forward, she puts her hand on the front passenger seat, for

Pippa, directing me to sit in the back. I smile at the rude woman.

She then gabbles away as we drive into Brook Lane and up Picketts Road, her words spilling out so fast and breathlessly I can barely understand anything other than "Pippa ... so excited!" If I stuck a pin in her fat backside, any bit of blubber, she'd go 'ppp ... fff ... ttt' and collapse like an overinflated balloon.

Pippa is smiling and gracious, Elaine hyperventilating, as she walks towards the car. She sits next to me. Elaine is furious. I can tell from her body language and her tight face in the rear-view mirror. Pippa and I share a secret smile, and she pats my hand, which Elaine sees in the mirror. What a face. Miss Piggy!

Elaine drives us to the quayside at Ipswich. As we go, and having read various newspaper headlines on my phone this morning, I try to engage Pippa in a meaningful conversation. I raise points about the current political situation, royalty, even a new climate-change report. Pippa smiles and is about to reply each time when Elaine jumps in with a stupid comment, over and again: "Same old, same old!", "Long live the king!" and even "Phew, let's not worry about a hole in the sky today!" And Pippa is distracted every time.

I've already had more than enough of Elaine as we get to the car park and make our way to the pretty little bistro. I am sick of her non-stop flurry of nonsense, her bounciness, the way she tries to push me out of the way and hog Pippa to herself.

There's an old saying: 'Two's company, three's a crowd.' And never has it been more accurate than this damned lunch as we work our way through starters, mains and desserts, each course cranking the levels of awkwardness ever upwards.

Elaine fawns — it is the only word for it — over Pippa at every opportunity. Each comment Pippa makes is met with an adoring response. Pippa shows photos of clothes she has bought for herself from the boutique, and there are gasps of admiration from you-know-who.

Elaine talks such nonsense about ... well, everything, really. Covid and face masks. The NHS and strikes. Children these days (even though she does not have any). Why she feels the need to raise such subjects, especially when she knows so little, is beyond me. I think she is showing off to Pippa.

I take the alternative view time and again, putting her firmly in her place. Elaine struggles to respond coherently, fading into silence. Pippa changes the subject to something light and frothy each time. And she gives me increasingly dark looks.

There is a moment, as our desserts arrive, when Elaine gives us her views on transgender issues. She is muddled and contradictory and concludes with the comment, "Just because a man puts on a dress and calls himself Karen doesn't make him a woman." She almost snorts, thinking herself so clever, as she spoons a dollop of ice cream into her big, fat mouth.

I respond by giving her what is considered to be the right and proper views these days. "Whoever you are, you can identify in whatever way feels right for you. So someone who is born a male can, if they see themselves as female, call themselves a woman. And vice versa, of course, should they wish to do so." I make myself sound calm and reasonable.

Elaine flushes, shakes her head, and gives a little girlish giggle as if I am talking the silliest nonsense. Somehow, it annoys me, and I respond with, "I mean, look at you. You're dressed like a woman, but you look like a man." I should stop there, but I can't help myself, adding, "Like a Felixstowe docker."

Elaine dips her head down, fighting back tears. Pippa is livid, mouthing, "Stop it."

As we finish our desserts without talking, Pippa asks the waiter for the bill. I don't think she wants us to have coffees, as I would have expected. Pippa then gets up and goes to the bathroom. She is so abrupt that I sense she is still angry. She is at least frustrated by the differences between Elaine and me. But she is too polite, too ladylike, to say anything more than she mouthed.

Elaine and I sit here in silence. I look at her, waiting for her to meet my eyes. She looks this way. And that. She simply won't look at me. Then, seeming close to tears again, she says, "Excuse me," and hurries after Pippa to the bathroom.

As the waiter returns with the bill, I get my notes and coins out of my purse, ready to pay my third of it. There is a long wait. The waiter comes back with a card machine. I indicate that Pippa and Elaine are still in the cloakroom.

A good five minutes later, they reappear. Elaine has clearly been crying heavily. Pippa does not look at me, but goes straight to the waiter and pays the whole bill on a card. We leave without a word. It's all rather awkward. More than that, it's incredibly tense.

THE THREE OF us return to the car without saying anything. Elaine stomps ahead. Pippa follows. I walk quickly to keep up. As Elaine gets to the car, everything is done with exaggerated good manners. Opening the back passenger door for Pippa to slip inside. Then opening the other back passenger door for me. She gives me such a tearful look. I smile sweetly. She then slams my car door shut, but I am expecting it. She does not catch my fingers nor my toes.

Elaine puts the radio on as she drives us to Felixstowe, jabbing her way through various stations, BBC Radio Suffolk, Ipswich Radio, until she finds one playing rock music. She turns the sound up. She then tries to change stations a few minutes later, when the song ends and the adenoidal presenter begins chattering away. She jabs and jabs and jabs without success, then turns the radio off, and puts on the air conditioner, turning it up so we cannot make conversation even if we wanted to. (We don't.)

Pippa smiles and says, "Thank you," to Elaine as she gets out of the car by her house. She glances at me, a noncommittal look, and I smile back pleasantly enough. And then she is gone. Elaine makes an aggressive three-point turn and drives me back, far too fast, to Bath Road, where the car comes to a sudden, grinding halt. She sits there with her back to me, and I wonder if she will drive away as I am half-in, half-out of the car.

As I hesitate, she angles the rear-view mirror and looks at me. She is breathing heavily. She is going to say something cutting. Moments pass, as though she is calming herself.

I look back, holding her gaze. I make no effort to disguise my contempt for her. My dislike of her has grown through book club evenings and coffee encounters to now and, finally, hatred.

"What's the matter with you, Sharon?" she says unexpectedly, a note of something close to anguish in her voice. I had anticipated something like, "You bitch!"

I was going to explain, ever so patiently, everything that was wrong with her. Why no one likes her. How she should keep away from Pippa.

I'd rehearsed the opening in my mind. "I feel sorry for you, Elaine, really I do." But her opening comment, spoken in a calm and sympathetic voice, throws me off balance.

"You need to talk to someone, Sharon. You have issues." She is still looking at me, and something in my face — surprise, most likely — seems to encourage her to go on, ever bolder.

"Anger management issues," she says, with growing confidence. I don't know what to say to that. "And other things," she adds ominously.

"I know you've never liked me. I don't know why; I've always been friendly to you at the book club, even when you've said nasty things."

I had not realised she had been aware my clever comments were directed at her.

"And you tripped me up, didn't you, the other week? I wasn't sure at first, but now I think you did. Didn't you."

I am not sure whether this is a statement or a question. I stare back at her, nonplussed for an instant.

"I invited you today as I thought the three of us could be such good friends ... lunches ... days out ... trips to London ... even holidays together ... it would be such fun." She hesitates now, a tremor in her voice, and glances away. I wait for her to go on.

"I'm sorry, Sharon, but I don't think we can be friends anymore." She draws in a long and ragged breath. "I don't want to be friends," she adds, as if for emphasis. As if I bloody care!

She sits there, the conversation, such as it is, over, waiting for me to get out of the car. All I want to say, to shout back, is, 'You? You! I don't care about you. I just want Pippa!'

But I do not. I simply give her a withering look as best I can, then open the car door and get out. She goes to say something: "Sharon, you need to talk to your —" but I slam the door shut and walk away.

My mood, as I walk to my flat, has been brought low by Elaine's unwanted 'pep talk.' I had, up to that point, been quite cheerful about the lunch, having scored several open goals, as Elaine put up such a poor defence of my counterarguments about Covid and masks and so on. Only Pippa's black looks worried me a little — that she may have taken sides with Elaine. And I also worry that Elaine might report back our one-sided conversation in the car just now.

I will have to make sure that Pippa takes my side against Elaine. I have one or two ideas that may help convince Pippa that I am her best friend — her soulmate — rather than Elaine. I will develop these and put them into action shortly. I do not know what I would do if I lose Pippa. It would be too much to bear.

As I return, I see the landlord's son's car, that smart Mercedes, on the driveway. My mood plummets even lower. I hurry up the path, expecting the net curtains to twitch downstairs as the landlord's son watches my arrival. I unlock the main front door, shut it behind me and, without hesitating, take the stairs two at a time in my haste to get to my flat.

I open the door of my flat, shut it and lie on the floor, crying. It is all too much for me.

8

WEDNESDAY, 26 OCTOBER, THE EARLY HOURS

I pass the evening in my usual dreary way — a microwave meal, a library book, a television programme — until I go to bed. It has been unusually, unexpectedly, quiet in the house. The lull before the inevitable coming storm. My mind is mostly on Pippa. I replay the lunchtime conversations over and over and wonder whether she will ever speak to me again.

I text Pippa as I get into bed, suggesting a coffee the following morning. She texts back ten minutes later: 'sorry — at the boutique the rest of the week.' I wonder, with a tightening feeling in my chest, whether I have lost Pippa, if she is siding with Elaine against me. In years gone by, I would have texted, emailed or phoned incessantly, almost in a frenzy, all to my cost. I have done terrible things in a frenzy. These days, I bide my time. But I twist in agony inside.

It is now gone two am, and the landlord's son has his music on, loud enough to keep me awake and stressed, but not so loud that I could complain to the authorities. There is a telephone number to call out of hours. But they'd not do anything. So the music goes on and on. He has the bass turned up.

Boom. Boom. Boom.

I cannot sleep with this noise.

Boom. Boom. Boom.

I lie here in my bed, the noise coming straight up from the room below. It is aimed at me. I know that. He thinks that he can drive me out by making my life hell. He does not know it has been hell for years, and I have learned to live with whatever happens. I do not care at all. I do know I don't want to go, though.

I have to lie here, ignoring the noise and not letting him know it bothers me at all by pacing about or banging my foot on the floor. I wonder how long this will go on and who will break first. It will not be me. I suspect it will continue night after night whilst he is here. Until I go downstairs and beg him to stop, agreeing to leave. I will not do that.

I can only hope he will eventually give up and go back to his job in London within the week, two at most. I can last that long. Then again, these days, many people can work from home, wherever that may be. Perhaps this is his home now, at least until the property is sold.

Boom. Boom. Boom.

He turns the bass up. He is getting angrier.

Boom! Boom! Boom!

I have to endure this, no matter how long it takes. I do not know what else I can do. I signed a lease, and I have the right to live in peace, without being troubled or harassed. But I do not know where to turn to enforce this. I cannot afford a solicitor. There is a local Citizens Advice Bureau, but that know-all from the book club, Alan, rules the roost there and would offer poor advice with such certainty. And all with a smug, self-satisfied face.

I think the landlord's son has to give me two months' notice to leave at the end of the lease, but, as I only just renewed the six-month lease, that would be seven months away. I'm not sure of these things. They confuse me. He won't wait, though. He wants us all out so he can sell and bank the proceeds. He wants me gone as fast as possible.

I wonder how far he will go to drive me away. I realise that this loud booming noise into the early hours is just the beginning of his campaign. And that if I do not react tonight, tomorrow, next week, whenever, he will step up the campaign and do something else, even worse; that he will use physical threats to terrorise me into defeat. I imagine all the things that he might do, and I feel a sense of utter dread.

Boom! Boom! Boom!

Up the noise goes again. It's so loud that it throbs inside my head.

Boom! Boom! Boom!

He is sitting downstairs, waiting and listening for me to react in some way. He expects me to hurry down, to knock on his door, asking him to turn the music down. Please! And he would sneer at me. And it would be the beginning of the end of his campaign, over before it had really begun. Instead, I lie still as though I am fast asleep, untroubled by it all.

And up it goes once more, the bass, louder and louder. I wonder about the young couple and how they will respond. The man has a hair-trigger temper, I think, and she is full of herself and would be quick to bang on the door downstairs. But then I remember it is a Wednesday, and they are some-times away for a night midweek. I don't know why; perhaps they visit a relative. And the oddball in the loft probably cannot hear it, at least not as much.

And then, joy of joys, the music is abruptly turned off. It takes me a moment to realise, as the boom-boom-boom still echoes inside my head. I am shattered now — exhausted and depressed beyond words. Eventually, my head clears, and I lie here in silence with a sense of relief although it will be hours before I can fall asleep. Then, suddenly, I wonder why the music has been switched off — why it is now so unnaturally quiet — and what he is about to do next.

———

NOW THE LANDLORD'S son is on the landing just outside my door. I hear him creaking repeatedly on the floorboards and tapping on the door and rattling the handle; all quietly menacing in their way. You'd only hear what he is doing if you were awake and listening for him. As I am.

The door is locked, and, as I always do without thinking when coming in, I have left the key in place and pushed the bolt across the top of the door. I imagine he could smash his way in if he wants to. I doubt that he will, not now anyway, not with the oddball in the house. He wants to frighten, spooking me out of my home. I have my mobile phone switched on just in case, though.

I want to open the door and shout at him to go away. Holding my phone up and recording his reaction as I do so. But I fear what he will do if I force him into a corner. He would have to snatch the phone and stamp on it to destroy the evidence. Then what? He may just push me back into the flat, knock me down and stand over me. I don't know what he would then do in such a fury. As I wait, holding my breath, my mind reels back over the past ten minutes.

The landlord's son turned the music off. There was a full five minutes of silence.

Then he banged on the ceiling with what sounded like a broom handle. Three times.

To wake me up if I were asleep. An unmistakeable warning to me. That this was starting again.

Then three more times. Six. Nine. Twelve in all.

I heard his door open. It creaks loudly. And the slower it opens, the longer it creaks.

It creaked ever so slowly for ever such a while.

He was sending me a clear and threatening message, now that I was awake, that he was coming for me.

I heard his footsteps on the stairs. Slow and measured, full of certainty.

It is an old house, and pretty much every stair groaned or squeaked under his heavy footsteps.

And then he was on the landing, turning left, three more creaking steps to the door of my flat.

Now, my mind comes back to this moment — here he is, outside my door. Creaking and tapping and rattling, all to unnerve me. I ignore it, but it goes on. Creak, tap, rattle. Silence. Creak, tap, rattle. Silence. Creak, tap, rattle. Silence. I lie here in the dark of night just listening. It does not frighten me, this nonsense. If I am honest, it makes me angry that he behaves in this way, believing he can scare me out.

But then the noises change. The creaking stops. So too does the tapping. And the rattling. There is the longest silence. I think maybe he has gone downstairs and I can fall into an uneasy sleep. But then there is another noise, a different one — one that makes me sit up in sudden fear. It is the sound of a man with his shoulder to the door, pushing, pushing, pushing at it until it cracks and breaks open.

I open the drawer of the bedside cabinet, scrabbling for my Spanish paper knife, a long-ago keepsake of Monica's, that I sometimes use for opening letters. I get up out of bed, holding the knife in my left hand. He's about to break the door down, coming in to do God knows what, to attack me in some way. I am out of the bedroom across the living area to my front door. I unbolt it. Unlock it. I raise the knife, ready to stab him in self-defence. I wrench the door open.

I AM LYING in my bed again now. The knife is in the drawer of my bedside cabinet somewhere near the back.

I am going to try to sleep. It is quiet all around me: upstairs, behind, below.

I know that I will be exhausted by the time I fall asleep and that I will not rest easy. I am going mad.

I pulled the door open and lunged with the knife, but there was nobody there. I moved onto the landing and looked both ways. Then to the staircase, staring down. I even crept downstairs, one step at a time, until I was outside the landlord's son's door. I put my head against it and listened for minutes on end. There was nothing to hear.

As I stood there, with only the moonlight coming through the glass panels of the main front door and everything else in darkness, I realised I had tipped over the edge of sanity. That I was now imagining things to the point that I was hearing creaking and tapping and rattling when nothing was actually occurring at all.

My mind went this way and that, wondering whether

what I believed was happening actually was. That maybe the music — and it was definitely on so loud — was just him relaxing into the late of night. I wondered whether the noise going up and up and up was real or whether it was just happening inside my mind. And I bowed my head as I made my way back upstairs and felt that this was all too much; my mind was now splintering.

I turn on the lamp on the bedside cabinet and sit up. Something is troubling me. I'm not sure what it is.

My subconscious has noticed something odd, but it has not yet worked its way through to the front of my mind.

I think that I am about to be confronted by further proof that I am losing my mind.

Then I see it. I have one library book on my bedside cabinet. A pile of three other library books is on the chest of drawers on the other side of the bedroom. I usually lay the books on their side, horizontally, one on top of the other. I don't know why. Just habit, I suppose. Maybe I'm a little OCD. Now they are upright, leaning against the wall so that only the cover of the front one can be seen. I do not stack my books like that. Ever.

My mind goes back over everything that has happened since I got back from lunch. I went to make a jam sandwich. When I picked up the jam jar, the lid came off, and the jar fell onto the work surface. I am always careful to tighten the lid of the jam jar after using it. And it only registers now, when I went out to the toilet, the seat was up instead of down. I think I was the last to use it. I've never left the seat up.

When I am out, the landlord's son must take the set of spare keys his father kept for emergencies, and come up to my rooms to let himself in. He does not steal or damage anything. He does not go through the papers in my cabinet and throw them on the floor. Nothing so obvious! What he does is more subtle than that. He moves something ever so carefully in each room, nothing that I could go to the police about. Only I, so sensitive and in tune with my surroundings, am aware of it.

I realise then that I am not going mad, that this is a carefully orchestrated campaign against me.

The landlord's son must have heard me coming across to wrench my door open, and dashed upstairs to the attic. I never thought of looking up there.

And then, after I'd come back inside, he crept back down to his flat, leaving me tense and twitching. As I lie here now, I hear more creaking and tapping and rattling. And I feel lost and completely and utterly broken.

9

THURSDAY, 27 OCTOBER, THE EVENING

Today is the day of the book club evening, and I am in utter torment. I do not feel I can leave the flat in case the landlord's son comes up whilst I am out. I do not know what he will do next. My fear is that I will come back late, open the front door, do whatever I do, get into bed, and the bedroom door will swing closed, and he will be standing there.

I am spending all my time in my living area, listening for him downstairs and looking through the window — if he goes out, I can hurry to the supermarket to stock up on essentials. I cannot sit still and settle. He is downstairs all morning and just so quiet, and that, the eerie silence, leaves me on edge.

I am now, truly, a prisoner in my flat. I can only leave when he goes out, and quickly, before he returns and lets himself into my flat to play his mind games. I will have to order food to be delivered from the supermarket — the delivery charge an extra expense I can ill afford, but I have no choice. I will become a hermit, a recluse, until I don't know when. Until he either goes or, more likely, takes stronger measures to force me out. The thought of what those might be makes me feel sick.

Even worse, I think Pippa has rejected me. I do not know what to do. I lie here now on my bed, in the silence, worrying about losing Pippa forever.

I have texted her three times this morning. One email too. All jolly, silly messages.

I've not had a reply. I wonder if I should phone her. I do not think Pippa is run-down or ill. She is giving me the cold shoulder because of the fallout with Elaine. I fear this may be a permanent banishment.

By lunchtime, sick with worry about him downstairs, and Pippa, and just about everything in my miserable, rotten life, I get up and make myself a cheese sandwich and a glass of orange squash. The bread is stale now, and I put it in the microwave for a few seconds to freshen it up. I am almost out of squash and have a weak half-glass to make it last that much longer. I sit by the living area window, gazing out.

I am here for half an hour or more, my thoughts on my beloved Pippa and what the loss of her means to me. The end of everything. I listen for the landlord's son, but now, truly, in this moment, I don't care what he does any more, really I don't. My heart is broken into a million pieces without Pippa. I note that his car sits right across the drive so that no one else can park there. The back of it juts out over the pavement, and people have to walk around it. What a horrible, arrogant man he is.

The road is busy, with cars coming and going, and people, some stopping to have a conversation. Two middle-aged women, with loud and braying voices, stand below my window, and I can hear everything they say to each other, on and on, about mundane problems in their vacuous, middle-class lives. I just want to bang on the window and yell at them to go away. "Fuck off!" I'd like to shout. "Go on, fuck off, you dirty fuckers!" But I don't. Instead, I go back and lie down on my bed, thinking still about Pippa.

'Pippa,' I tap eventually into my mobile phone, 'I'm very worried about you.'

I go on. Picking my words carefully. 'Are you ill?' I hesitate, then add, 'I miss you. Love Sharon x.'

I reread the text and then press send. I hope it will work and Pippa gets back to me soon.

This afternoon is much the same as this morning. I lie on my bed, worrying about Pippa, my mind playing out all sorts of possible scenarios. I check my mobile phone regularly, but she has not replied. Even though I am in hell now, I will not text again. I wish to keep my self-respect. I have not always done so, and that, my neediness, my desperation for all to see, has made me act irrationally and then loathe myself at times.

I get off my bed now and then put my head against the carpet, listening for the landlord's son, working out what he is doing. I lie in different places, but there is complete and utter silence below, no coughs or creaks or anything at all. The silence torments me, as I wonder what he is doing. It is almost as if he is not down there. Yet his car remains on the driveway. He is sitting there waiting for me to crack and lose my mind.

As teatime approaches, and I am going through the motions of making myself ravioli on toast and a mug of tea, I hear the door downstairs being unlocked. I listen to him in the hallway. I hold my breath in case he comes up the stairs. But then he is opening the main front door and out to his

car. My spirits lift as I watch him reverse the car into the
road. He looks up at me standing at the window, such an evil
look, and, finally, the car is speeding away.

I text Pippa, 'Looking forward to seeing you at the book
club! Can't wait.' I'm going to go, taking my chance he is out
for the evening, or maybe even returning to London. I have
to know, to see, if she is there.

I sit and wait a while. Half an hour. To see if Pippa
responds. She does not. I wonder if maybe her phone battery
is flat or whether the phone itself may be broken and
beyond repair.

I set off just after seven o'clock for the book club get-
together. I hope to see Pippa there. I don't know what I will
do if she is not.

———

THE BOOK CLUB evening is a disaster. I leave at the interval,
having made an enemy of Alan. Everyone, really.

I don't care about Alan. Or Elaine. Nor any of the other
stupid people forcing themselves into my life. The landlord's
son. The oddball. The young couple. I hate all of them.
Every single one.

I care only about Pippa. She has not replied to my texts.
She did not turn up to the get-together. What's the bloody
point of it all anymore?

Just May, Alan, the sisters, Joanna and Moira, and I were
there. More fool me. May announced on my arrival that Paul
and Stephen had messaged to say they were away. Head
Down Harry, who turns up now and then, was in hospital for
an operation — 'down there' as May put it. She dipped her
head and said a prayer for him. We all played along,

although I don't think anyone was that bothered. I couldn't care less.

I was just sitting there, hoping that Pippa would arrive, late and hot and bothered and apologetic.

She'd look across at me and mouth 'sorry,' and all would be well again between us.

I knew in my heart that she would not, though. And why. And that I would never see her again.

The first half of the evening was much the same as usual. May began by giving a summary of the latest Richard Osman novel and offered her extensive thoughts on it. On she went. I did not think she would ever stop. The sisters nodded and smiled as though they agreed with everything. Alan tried to butt in with some comment or other, time and again, but May just raised her voice a notch and kept on going.

As she came towards the end of her speech and before she could invite comments, Alan started talking determinedly over her about the book and what he thought of it. Of course, May and the rest of us are just readers. Alan is a self-proclaimed 'fellow author.' He once self-published a book — an A4 booklet — mistitled *Felixstowe — The Roman Runs*, about the remains, the ruins, of a Roman village that is supposed to be close to the seashore. That seems to give him carte blanche to read any book and tell us precisely what is wrong with it.

There was plenty wrong with this book, according to Alan. The story was 'too obvious.' He then used two words to describe it that I had never heard before. He stumbled over both of them, and I wondered if he had searched for clever words online before coming along. He could also see the twists and turns 'a mile off.' He added, "I don't know if" —

he waved his hands around dismissively — "if others see this ... or it's just authors." He then laughed. I told him to shut the fuck up, and there was a silence.

All I could think about was Pippa and how everything has been ruined. I miss her so very much.

What's worse, I knew I would never see her again. There is nothing I can do to change that.

The stupid lump Elaine ruined my friendship with Pippa. And I truly hate her for it.

May was the first to react to my instinctive response, the thought that was in everyone's mind. "Um," she said, looking at Alan's angry face and then my own bland one. "That was, er ... I think you should apologise, Sharon." She had her head down, not looking at me. I kind of sensed that inside she was cheering that someone stood up to the stupid man at last. Neither of the sisters said anything. I felt that they were on my side, too. Alan sat there, pumped up full of righteous indignation.

"No," I said quietly. I did not add anything to it, and just sat there looking across the table. Neither May nor Joanna or Moira met my eye. Alan was all stiff-backed and affronted. It was as though we were all holding our breath to see what he would do.

Alan breathed in deeply, the pompous little man, put his hands together and sat up as tall and straight as he could. "I'm sorry, May," he said portentously. "Joanna. Moira." He nodded towards them and sighed. Far too theatrically for my liking. "That is not acceptable." I thought he would turn to face me, but the cowardly man did not. "Either Sharon leaves now ..." He paused for effect. "Or I do."

I'd had enough by this point, and got up and threw my book on the table as my final gesture. It knocked Alan's half-empty cup of coffee over and into his lap. He yelped. Not that I imagine he has much use for anything down there these days.

One of the idiot sisters — I did not know which simple Suffolk voice was which — said, "Good riddance." The other added, "Hear, hear." I told them to fuck off, too.

As I left, I struggled to get my coat off the stand, pulling hard. It went over, sending coats and bags scattering. May burst into tears. I told her to fuck off as well.

———————

I WALK BACK to my flat, head bowed, through a constant drizzle of rain. My mind has gone now, flitting over those moments of my life that brought me here.

But it keeps coming back to one thing. To one person. All I can really think about — all that truly matters — is Pippa and the certainty that she has finished with me.

I know, as I stumble along, close to collapse, that this is it, that my life, such as it has been, is over, to all intents and purposes. Without Pippa, there is nothing left for me now in this world.

As I get to the house and lift the latch on the gate, I look up and see the oddball in his room in the loft, standing there gazing down at me. He will be stomping about all night.

Alerted by the noise at the gate, the landlord's son pulls back a curtain and peers out. His prey, me, has returned, and he will soon start his stupid mind games.

In the morning, I will awake to the sounds of the young couple tormenting me, then sit there on my bed, waiting for them to leave. For what? Another long and endless day alone with my thoughts.

I turn, instinctively, and walk back along the path and out through the gate, shutting it behind me. I do not look over my shoulder. I will never see this house nor these despicable people again.

I make my way along Bath Road towards the sea, my mind deciding what I am going to do. Deep down, I already know.

And so I am now standing on the corner of Cobbold Road. I look at the big, familiar face of the moon. Then turn again, so I am looking at the cold dark sea.

I take out my phone to text Pippa, at home with her faithless husband and stupid son. I should be there with her, not them. Just Pippa and me.

I tap in, 'I'm going to Cobbolds Point. I've had enough of this life.' If she comes to me, I will stop and step back from the sea.

If not, I will end my life, walking into the water and then swimming for as long as I can. I click send.

Five minutes on, and I am now standing, waiting, on the pebbly beach by the shore at Cobbolds Point. I am looking out to the North Sea. Everything — my life — hangs in the balance.

It is a clear night, with the moon and the stars and the drizzling rain on my face.

Due east from here is Holland. Amsterdam or Rotterdam, I think. I read somewhere once how far it was. Holland. I forget the number of miles though. I wonder if I walk into the sea now, how far I could swim.

There is someone behind me on the beach. I hear their heavy footsteps crunching on the stones. It is not Pippa. Too soon. Too heavy-footed. Whoever it is stops, and there is a silence other than the crashing of the waves.

"Are you alright?" An old man's gruff voice. A dog walker, most likely. He sounds worried. About me or him, I'm not so sure. Nobody wants to see someone take their own life. Nor do they want to get involved.

"Yes," I call out in a firm enough voice. Then, dismissively: "Thank you." I hear him pause, hesitate, before replying, "Well, if you're sure." And then he is hurrying away, relieved he has not had to get involved.

I am in the sea and edging forward. The waves lap against my feet and then my ankles and now my thighs. I stop for a moment, wondering if I will hear the screech of a too-fast car coming to a halt. Then the sound of Pippa running, calling to me.

But all is quiet. I do not think there is anyone out and about, as it is so late and dark and cold and wet. And I am a little way in and dressed in dark clothes. Nobody will notice me, not unless they are looking.

The water is close to my shoulders now. I just need to keep moving, starting to swim, a slow and steady breaststroke, for as long and as far as I can. Until eventually, I slip under.

I turn around one last time to see if Pippa, anyone, is there on the promenade or in a shelter or coming down the road from Brook Lane. Someone who might see me out here.

But there is no one in sight. I am sobbing now. I am about to push off and start swimming. I do not know how long I will swim before cold and fatigue set in. I do not know what it will be like to drown. I hope it will be fast.

All I can think of is my text to Pippa. 'I'm going to Cobbolds Point. I've had enough of this life.' She has not come. So now, I will swim away. It's 178 miles to Rotterdam. I've just remembered.

PART II

HAPPY TOGETHER

10

FRIDAY, 28 OCTOBER, EARLY MORNING

I awake, disoriented for a moment, and then sit up on my elbows and look around. There is an illuminated clock on the wall, and it shows the time is 6.53am.

I am in Pippa's art studio, the garage extension, on the couch with cushions behind my head and a brightly coloured quilt over me.

I pull back the quilt, and I am wearing one of Pippa's silk nightdresses with nothing underneath. It feels soft against my skin.

It all floods back: last night. Pippa came for me as I began to swim, crying out, "What are you doing? My God, Sharon! What are you doing?" Before I could respond, turning and shouting back at her, "I'm okay, I'm okay!" she was already wading into the sea after me. She wrapped her arms around me and said, in a cracking voice, "You're safe now, Sharon. You're safe."

I let Pippa walk me back to the pebbly beach, her arm across my shoulders. I tried to speak, to say something to her, to explain myself. All she said was "Hush ... hush." As though she were saying, "There, there," to a sobbing child. I felt a sudden surge of anger, but stifled the urge to say something to her. Instead, I let her guide me to a shelter out of the sharp-as-ever wind.

She asked what had happened, and I told her, in fits and starts, what things were like at my flat and how I was at the end of my tether. I did not say anything about her and how thoughtless she was. How uncaring. I then said I was alright now and would be on my way. She sounded horrified and replied I must come back to hers, that she had some sweatshirts and jogging bottoms and other clothes I could have. She added that she could take care of me until I felt better. I said, no, I couldn't. She insisted. And I relented.

I get up off the couch and walk to a radiator, where my bra and pants and other wet clothes are hanging, now almost dry. I should go back to the flat, at least to get some more clothes, but I simply cannot face it.

I dress in a navy sweatshirt and matching jogging bottoms from a pile of clothes that Pippa has left on a chair. Then sit and slip on a pair of sports-type socks that probably belong to the boy. My canvas shoes, stuffed with rolled-up newspaper, are drying by the radiator. I put them on; I can wear them well enough.

I look around the studio, at the abstract art — amateur daubs — and think that, really, I could be very comfortable here, although I'd need to go into the house to use the bathroom.

I am not sure whether to wait here in the studio for Pippa to come to fetch me, or if I should make my way to the house and go inside, introducing myself. I imagine entering through the patio door and into the living room and the three of them — Pippa, the husband and the boy — all turning to look at me. The astonishment on the man's and the boy's faces as Pippa strides across and says to them, "This is Sharon, my friend." I must try hard not to look triumphant.

But it may be better if I wait here, for the husband to go to work and the son to leave for school. And then, once they have departed, she will come into the studio and hurry across and hug me when she sees I am well. And we will sit next to each other on the couch, her arm around me and my head leaning on her shoulder, taking in the scent of her perfume and the touch of her skin. And we will do this for ever such a long time. She may even stroke the back of my neck or the length of my arm to comfort me. Nobody has done that for such a while.

I decide, finally, to go to the house, not least because I need, sooner rather than later, to visit the bathroom. I find a mirror in a chest of drawers and check my appearance, tidying my hair with my fingers and wiping away a smear of dirt on my cheek. I look clean enough. And so I make my way out of the studio onto the patio and then walk up to the patio door. I hesitate, as I can see Pippa inside, facing out towards me. The nasty man and the boy have their backs to me. I have interrupted an argument.

"It'll only be for a few nights," I hear Pippa saying in a raised voice, as though she is tired of arguing. She is clearly talking about me. She sounds as though she is asking for permission.

Before the man and the boy can respond, Pippa looks away from them and towards me on the other side of the glass.

They turn at the same time too, and I can see the

husband and son both mouth the same word: "Fuck." They recognise me.

————————————

LESS THAN HALF AN HOUR LATER, I am back in the studio, on the couch, and Pippa has one arm around me and her other hand on my left elbow.

I am rather tearful, and Pippa is consoling me.

She leans into me so our heads are almost touching, and I can feel her sweet breath on my cheek.

Neither the man nor the boy said anything as Pippa pulled back the patio door and gestured for me to come into the living room. I did, keeping my head slightly bowed so that I did not look defiant to them. I waited for one or other of them to say something to Pippa. But what could they say? The boy, "I spoke to her when she walked by the house, and again when I was being chased." So what! The man, "I once saw her by my car." Who cares!

"This is my friend Sharon," Pippa said to them. "She's going to stay for a while ... in my studio ... until she's back on her feet." She was very matter-of-fact about it; this was not up for discussion. Then she did the introductions, "Peter, this is Sharon. Sharon, this is Peter ... Dom, Sharon; Sharon, Dom." I looked and smiled in turn and put out my hand. The man's touch was cold and limp. The boy's hot and sweaty. I shuddered at the thought of what he might have been doing just before he came downstairs.

Neither of them spoke much beyond brief greetings. I waited for either of them to say something about our previous encounters, but I noted, with some satisfaction, that both held their tongues. I smiled at them. I did it for Pippa's sake. And possibly my own. To establish myself here.

Then the man and the boy both turned to go, to get ready for work and school respectively, and Pippa and I sat down in the kitchen for breakfast. After that, once the man and boy had left, I used the bathroom. And very nice it was, too. And then I went back to the studio, Pippa following me.

I want to stroke Pippa's arm, encouraging her to stroke mine, too.

I know that one day, soon enough, that will happen, and more. But not now. It is too early.

I wait, enjoying the moment, until Pippa stands up and walks up and down, telling me the 'ground rules.' She seems embarrassed to use the phrase.

"You're welcome to stay ... as long as you need to." She gesticulates wildly with her arms, as though she is unsure how she feels about that. Then explains that 'Peter and Dom' are both 'set in their ways.' So, although I am welcome to have this studio ... and can come in and use the bathroom when 'the boys' are out ... and the downstairs cloakroom — the toilet and washbasin — are 'of course, all yours whenever you need them' ... I'd best view this as a self-contained bedsit.

Although she does not say it out loud, in so many words, her meaning is clear — you're here in this studio, but you're not to come in for meals or join us in the evening; you are not part of the family. I know that this is not Pippa speaking, but her cruel husband and thuggish son. I did not hear what they said before I went into the living room, but I can imagine it well enough. "We're not feeding her," the man would have said. "And we don't want her sitting here in front of the telly. Fuck's sake," the foul-mouthed boy would have added for good measure.

"I think you have everything you need?" It's half a statement, half a question. She glances at me. I look around. It's just a big room, really, a converted back of a garage that's been extended, with windows and radiators put in and a couch and cushions and a quilt and a chair and a couple of storage units — chests of drawers, really. And stacks of art equipment and paintings. It's not a proper bedsit, is it! I want to shout. There's no kitchen sink or fridge or toilet or shower or television — just a room with thin carpet, a bit of warmth and no little niceties.

And then Pippa is saying goodbye — "Chin up" — as she leans forward and pats me on the arm. No hug or kiss, nothing.

"I'm off to Ipswich ... running late," she says, turning away. She is off to work at this boutique. She does not say anything else. She does not even tell me when she will be back.

As she is leaving, she turns suddenly and says, "We've our old microwave in the garage. I'll get it for you later." She then takes a key from her pocket and hands it to me. "For the patio door ... in case you need to, you know."

And that's it. She is gone. And at that moment I think, I would like to you know right in the middle of her living room carpet.

I AM in the house and have looked around downstairs. To the back of each cupboard and drawer and down the side of every chair and sofa, even underneath. I want to see — to know — everything about Pippa's life. The whole place is perfectly co-ordinated and pristine — and ultimately empty and vacuous. These people have more money than sense, with their ridiculous paintings and pieces of artwork and nonsensical bits of equipment in the kitchen.

I used the cloakroom to have a wash and a you know, as Pippa calls it. A you know this and a you know that, actually. Even the cloakroom — 'toilet' to the likes of me — had a lump of hand-carved artwork on a shelf. A twisted and stretched vine of black grapes on a plinth, by the look of it. I'm not sure what else it can be. As I go to the stairs, the dog, lying in its basket by the fireplace, lifts its head lazily, looks at me, and then goes back to sleep. A typical Labrador.

I am now in Pippa and the husband's bedroom at the front of the house. Judging by the personal bits and pieces on the bedside cabinets, they sleep together in the huge grey bed. But I see no evidence from the drawers or the bed or the duvet or even the sheet that they are having sex. A marriage of convenience, for sure. They share the same bed after all these years out of habit, perhaps to protect the feelings of the yobby son.

He should not be here. The adulterer. Carrying on as if he has done nothing wrong. Not just once. But twice. Maybe even more. A string of affairs! He has been forgiven once. He should never be forgiven again.

As Pippa's friend — her best friend, now — I want her to be happy and treated properly. To be loved and respected. He offers none of that. I can deal with this. I have the photos of him with that student. If Pippa were to see them — when — it will be enough for her to send him packing.

But these are incriminating, not conclusive. I need more than that, ideally. I want hard evidence of his repeated wrongdoing. So that she is driven to fury, demanding he leave this house forever. Just leaving Pippa here with me — and the son, at least for now.

I look around this bedroom, not sure what it is I am searching for and doubting that there will be anything in plain sight. I check the three drawers of his bedside cabinet. Perhaps for a pocket-sized diary or notebook that might have a series of codewords or symbols that represent illicit meetings and sexual encounters. But there is no diary or notebook or anything out of the ordinary there. I check under the bed and behind the bedside cabinet without success.

One of the two built-in wardrobes is full of his suits and jackets and trousers. I put my fingers deep into pockets to see what I can discover. I had hoped for a folded-over scrap of paper with a phone number on it and a 'x' for a kiss. I find tissues and pens and chewing gum, but nothing much else. I search the arty-farty books on the shelf above, flicking through page by page, hoping a telltale slip of paper will fall to the carpet. But nothing is there. Even his slippers and trainers and shoes at the bottom of the wardrobe are empty of anything other than fluff and, in one, a jagged piece of toenail.

Of course, if there is something conclusive of his wrongdoing, it will most likely be on his mobile phone or a laptop. He will keep these with him, taking them to work. I will never get near those, let alone have a chance to get into them with passwords I could never guess. And then I recall where some men hide things they don't want to be seen: in the loft or a shed or the garage. Places wives don't usually go.

I go through the kitchen into the utilities room and on to the garage, checking shelves, inside tins and cases, everywhere. There is nothing hidden away here.

I take a stepladder from the garage to the house and up
the stairs to the loft. There is no shed — no man cave — in
the garden, so this is the only possible remaining hiding
place of the secrets of his other life. But other than empty
suitcases and boxes of Christmas decorations, there is
nothing here, either. They've not lived in this house long and
have not had time to fill the loft with junk, as most
people do.

I return the stepladder to the garage before heading back
into the house to search the dirty boy's room. For the father, I
will have to plan his downfall with the photographs. I dare
not got back to the university to try to take more.

The boy's bedroom smells of sweat and deodorant spray
and something not quite nice. As boys' bedrooms do. There
is a single bed with a Crystal Palace Football Club pillow
and duvet. Football posters on the wall. Clothes on a chair
and across the carpet. A chest of drawers and a wardrobe
and a desk and another chair complete the furniture. I am
looking for something incriminating here, too. I'm not sure
what it is, but I will know it when I see it.

In the old days, of course, there would be dirty magazines tucked out of sight. As a former cleaner, I know where
people hide intimate stuff. These days, that sort of thing is
all online. And Pippa is a modern woman who would just
laugh at such things: "Boys will be boys!"

It needs to be something that would offend her 'woke'
sensibilities. Perhaps he is circulating photos of a naked girl
from school. That would cause a rift. But that would be
through his phone; there won't be anything lying here
waiting to be uncovered.

I check all the usual places and more. Between the
mattress and the base. Behind and beneath the chest of

drawers and wardrobe. In-between the pages of schoolbooks
and football magazines. I go through drawers, one by one,
my fingers probing and pushing to the back and along the
undersides. Then to the wardrobe, running my hands
through shelves and boxes and into the pockets of trousers
and tops. And, at last, the clothes on the carpet. There are a
few coins in a pocket, and a stuck-together tissue, which I do
not wish to examine closely, and that's it.

I then look around the bedroom one more time, in case I
have missed something obvious. When I used to clean for
fading old men, they'd hide coins and tobacco in rolled-up
socks. But the boy has nothing in any of his socks.

Old women were craftier. Most of them knew their
cleaners were as likely to steal from them as not, and went to
some lengths to hide their money. I tug at carpet edges, but
there is nothing tucked underneath.

There, on top of the desk is what I really want — his
laptop. I open and turn it on and try 12345678 and qwerty123
and other possible — most likely pointless — passwords,
until I turn it off and slam it shut in frustration.

And then I see it, plugged into the side of the laptop. A
USB stick. I am not sure if this is something innocent or if it
might be more sinister. Perhaps topless or naked
photographs of young girls from school. He is seventeen
years old — it may be that a girlfriend is fifteen or fourteen
years of age. This might be something I can use to my advantage — the possibility of his coercion of her.

I hesitate for a moment or two, listening to the silence in
the house and the quietness of the outdoors. I am deciding
what to do. I need to see what is on this. Innocent or guilty. I
must know the truth about the boy. I do not know what to do
with it. I can only think of walking into town, to one of the

computers in the library, where I will see what is on the stick.

If it is all innocent, I will hurry to plug it back in before anyone returns home. The boy and his father will return later this afternoon. Pippa could be any time. But she would not notice it was missing. And I could put it back by saying I needed to pop upstairs to the bathroom to wash my hands. I hope there is something on the stick that will leave the boy at my mercy.

11

MONDAY, 31 OCTOBER, MID-EVENING

I t is Halloween, a cold, crisp evening. I have the door of the studio extension open for fresh air, and I sit here, listening to young families, groups of children, and boisterous teenagers going up and down the road outside. Teenage boys are wild and do not adhere to society's laws, neither written nor unwritten.

It has been many years since I came face-to-face with teenage trick-or-treaters. When I last had a ground-floor flat, I put up a polite handwritten sign 'No Trick Or Treaters — Thank You.' I should instead have just left all the lights off. The next morning, I went out to find broken eggs all over my windows and a bin bag of rubbish tipped onto my doorstep.

I got my revenge the next year by inviting younger children to help themselves to my tray of long-out-of-date wrapped sweets. I smiled at the thought of them being opened. I toyed with the idea of offering teenagers my home-made toffee apples and cupcakes with added ingredients, but feared their reprisals. I am scared of teenagers.

I am so full of anger tonight. I can feel myself brooding and my fury coming to the surface.

The sounds of teenagers running amok on the road, provoking bad memories, is part of it.

But there is more to it than that. Much more. I am so resentful of how I am being treated here.

Four nights on from my arrival and I am still alone here in the extension. Pippa has given me their old microwave and some pillows and a duvet and some more clothes. Not that much, really. Stuff she doesn't want. And she puts her head round the door mornings and evenings, asking if I am okay and whether I need anything.

'Yes!' I want to scream at her. 'I want to be indoors with you!' But I smile and say, 'All's well,' and sit there with my resentment and anger building. I see more of the dog when they let it out to do its business all over the garden.

One day soon, she will ask quite specifically, as though it has just occurred to her, is no more than a passing thought, if I've found somewhere else to live. I don't know what I will say or do when she does.

They — Pippa, the husband and the boy — are in the house now. I step outside my doorway, and I can see all the lights are on. But the kitchen blinds are pulled down, and the patio curtains are drawn, so I can only see cracks of light at the top and sides. I cannot see indoors.

I do not think they are taking part in Halloween. I can hear the front doorbell ringing, but have no sense of it being opened. There is only further ringing and shouts and noises from teenagers on the driveway. I imagine the three of them with their heads down, eating at the table in the dining room, ignoring what is going on outside.

This is an unhappy household. More than that. A house

full of strains and tensions, ready to spill over into arguments, perhaps even violence. The husband and wife keep up the pretence of a happy marriage for the son. He will have picked up on this and, as many teenagers are prone to do anyway, could explode at any moment. It is a potent mix.

I hear girlish noises, screams and laughter, to the side of the house, coming into the garden. I cannot believe the nerve of teenagers these days, walking into someone's back garden uninvited.

Three teenage girls, maybe fifteen or sixteen years old, if that, stop as they see me watching them. They go quiet, looking curiously at me. I step back inside and push the door to, listening to what they do next.

This is not a home where outsiders, young teenage girls, whoever, are made welcome. Invited in to share whatever the family is eating, to be offered a drink.

This is a household that scratches and shrieks in pain — a marriage about to implode, a son full of teenage angst and fury.

I wonder if these silly girls might pull open the patio door, and what might then happen.

There is a long silence, and then they are banging on the patio door and giggling and joking. One of them shouts, "Dom! Dom!" Then another. And the other.

I move to the window of the extension, opening the top a fraction so I can hear more clearly. The girls are calling repeatedly to the boy, knocking on the patio door and whistling. I wonder what will happen, whether Pippa will come to the door, all placatory. Or if the husband will wrench the door open and send them packing.

I can hear a commotion indoors, the sound of raised voices, and the girls stepping back, a moment's silence between them, and then a round of uncontrollable giggles. They look at each other, not sure what to do. One pulls another's arm, wanting to leave. The other, the boldest girl, not only stays put, but steps forward and rat-a-tat-tats on the door again. There is another round of giggling.

A long silence from indoors. Then, all of a sudden, the patio door is pulled back, and the boy, putting his jacket round his shoulders, comes out. He stomps round to the front of the house and away, followed quickly by the three girls. There is silence again, other than shouts and screams from the road. And I am alone once more and go and lie down on the couch, wondering what will happen next, now that the boy has gone and Pippa and the husband are alone together.

LYING HERE ON THE COUCH, ignoring the never-ending shrieks and yells from the road, I feel an almost over-whelming sense of rejection and a rising feeling of resent-ment. I must not allow these justified feelings to turn into uncontrollable fury, which could ultimately spoil everything for me.

I do not expect much from Pippa, and I do not ask for anything. But I would have thought by now, on my fourth full day here, I would have been invited into the house at least once to have a meal with the family, or to watch televi-sion with them. I am treated as a pariah.

I know that things are horribly difficult for Pippa right now. The husband having an affair with a student. The boy up to no good, one way or the other. She may even be protecting me by not inviting me in and having to endure the tense atmosphere. Even so, I am disappointed with Pippa. I expected so much more from her.

I came here full of hope, but it has been thrown back in my face, all of it. And so I have been making my careful plans against the boy and the husband. I want them gone. The boy will probably leave home in eighteen months or so anyway, to university. I can wait for that if I have to. But I'd like to see the cheating husband out long before that. And I'll then be invited in by Pippa, and we'll be as cosy as can be together.

On Friday, I took the USB stick from the boy's laptop into town with me. I used the computer in the library to try to open it. I expected to see so many secrets, so much guilt, in the files within it. Things I could use when the time was right. But I struggled to open it. I asked the young man behind the counter, and he looked at it and said it was a dongle to access the internet. I felt so stupid, so ignorant, that I just took it straight back, smiled briefly and left immediately. I don't like looking a fool.

After returning the wretched dongle to Pippa's, I went out again. I sat on a bench between the local school and the house and watched a while. Not long after, I saw the boy on his way home, walking alone on the other side of the road. He did not notice me. He was in a world of his own, and I had a *Daily Mirror* I'd found to hold up as necessary. As he drew opposite and I raised the newspaper, a car, a black Nissan Qashqai, pulled up alongside him. He stopped and peered in through darkened windows. A back door was opened, and he got in, and the car drove away. I had just enough time to lift my phone and take two or three photographs.

When I got back, I expected to see the black Qashqai on

the driveway; relatives up for a visit from London, I supposed. One of the uncles, maybe. But the car was nowhere to be seen. I puzzled over this — the Qashqai stopping, the boy getting in, the driving away — for an age, wondering what it meant. I did not see the boy over the weekend — other than when I passed through to and from the cloakroom — and did not get a chance to search his room, for money or drugs, until this morning, Monday. There was nothing incriminating there.

My hatred towards the husband grows stronger by the day. On Saturday, I went by him twice on the way to the cloakroom. I smiled at him on both occasions, but he just looked straight through me.

On Sunday, I went to smile and say something to him, nothing of consequence, about the weather being dry and bright, but he turned away. He just stood there, his back to me, using a remote control to change the channels on the television.

Early this Monday morning, before they all went their different ways, I came through the kitchen early, having something of a tummy upset, and, as I left five minutes later, he gave me such a look of contempt. I did not respond, but that man will pay dearly for the way he has treated me.

I have struggled with my feelings for Pippa. As I searched the house on Friday, I noted the spare bedroom needed little more than a dust and a polish and fresh bedding and assumed she would soon invite me in to stay in that room. But she has not. Nor has she made any suggestion or hint that I ever will be. In fact, she comes and goes, to check I am well and if I need anything, with such a look of long suffering on her face at times that I wonder if she really wants me here at all.

I thought perhaps, on Saturday or Sunday, when I went through all my usual dreary doings — the town, walks, the library, taking bits and pieces from shops without security cameras — that she might pop in and suggest lunch or even a day out, just us girls. She did not. It would have been such fun. I felt so let down. More so at Sunday lunchtime, when I heard the unmistakable toot-toot of Elaine's car horn outside the house.

I got up and went into the garden, to the far side, walking and stretching my arms and legs as though exercising. I saw Elaine standing by her car, all red-faced and excited, and I felt such outrage. She did not even acknowledge me, so, equally, I pretended not to see her and turned round. I glanced back at the sound of girlish voices and laughter and saw Pippa walking towards Elaine and hugging her. Off they went for lunch and an afternoon together. Pippa returned late and did not bother to come and see me. I felt physically sick — so betrayed — and have been unhappy ever since.

And so here I am now, Halloween night and full of hate. It is quieter now that all the teenage trick-or-treaters have come and gone. There is no sign of the dirty boy returning. I wonder what he has been getting up to with those young girls, who all looked under-age to me. There is a storm brewing around that boy, and I hope to be there when it finally explodes.

I open the door to the extension again, and I can hear voices, loud and angry, coming from inside the house. With the boy out, Pippa and the nasty husband are arguing, and from the sound of it, this is about to turn ugly, perhaps even violent. I have a terrible image in my head of the man throwing Pippa downstairs, and her lying at the bottom with a broken neck or a fractured skull.

Despite how I am feeling about Pippa right now — her indifference towards me, her affections for Elaine that upset me so much — I could not stand by and see her harmed. I am not as shallow as that. When I love someone — my soulmate — I love completely and forever. That will never change. I certainly will not let that horrible husband get away with anything.

I pull the door of the extension closed behind me and walk towards the patio door. I hesitate as there is a sudden silence, wondering for one dreadful instant if he has knocked her unconscious, maybe even worse than that. But I pull back the patio door and step inside. I will act normally and see what happens.

I STAND IN THE KITCHEN, my right hand on the half-open patio door, my head tipped at an angle, listening. My left ear hears more clearly.

There is a lull in the shouting, and I wonder if one or other of them is coming downstairs and will see me standing here, so obviously eavesdropping. I feel sick at the thought, especially if it is him.

I pull the patio door to and walk slowly, naturally, into the living room, as though heading for the cloakroom. I am so tense, not knowing what to expect.

As I move through the living room, the daft dog lying there and ignoring me as always, they start up again. But they are quieter now, more reasonable with each other. It is as if the storm has blown out. I stop to listen.

I suspect she has accused him of having an affair. Asked him — yelled — why he leaves for work earlier than he used to do. Gets back later. Why he is so reserved and distant with her.

But he has given well-rehearsed answers that she finds believable. Maybe he said the job is more demanding and the hours are longer and there are more meetings. And he is taking time to settle. He has talked her down from her anger.

"You promise?" she says in a clear voice.

"I do," he replies simply. What he is promising — that he's not having an affair or will try to be a more attentive husband — I'm not sure.

There is silence. I get the sense of an embrace.

He is a liar. And a cheat. She is naïve. And gullible. He has fooled her and will continue with his affair, albeit more carefully, at least for a while. Until she forgets and he can slip back into his old ways.

I despise him for doing this. Running two lives along parallel lines. He will keep going until his student lover demands more from him. And then he will dump her and take another. He will string Pippa along endlessly.

I put my hand into my back pocket, touching my mobile phone and thinking about the three photographs that show him to be a shameless adulterer. I will go somewhere in the morning and get them printed off. I will send them to her anonymously. As though they are from an outraged colleague. It will get this matter out in the open once and for all.

I turn to walk back out of the living room into the kitchen and beyond, making my way to the extension, where I will zoom in and out of the photographs for the best effects and then save them. What a shock she will get when she sees them!

I stop, as there are noises upstairs, sexual noises, that

make me feel revolted. I did not ask Pippa about her physical relationship with him when she revealed her fears to me. I would not dream of doing such a thing. But I assumed they were no longer intimate. And had not been since she suspected this second affair.

I jump, startled, as their bedroom door slams shut. They've closed it in case the boy returns, most likely, although I feel it signals more to me: the end of my dreams. For now. I cannot wait to post the photographs to Pippa. Having lied and then having had sex with her again, Pippa's response may be to finish with him once and for all. And I will then step forward.

12

TUESDAY, 1 NOVEMBER, ANOTHER EARLY
MORNING

I am at a store in the nearby town of Woodbridge, somewhere I go to from time to time when I have found a little spare money to spend. I enjoy the bus ride and a walk around a different place and a sit-down by the river, watching the boats. Anything posted from here, of course, will have a different postmark than Felixstowe. I now have my phone in my hand, standing by a machine that allows me to print off photographs.

A spotty posh boy, 'Henry' on his name badge, is showing me what to do. He is not good at his job. He has not seen a phone like mine before. It is old. It does what I need it to do. But it is not what he is used to, apparently, this marble-gargling private schoolboy. He looks confused. I wait, nothing to say, and he stands there through the silence until he starts sweating and eventually calls the manager.

She comes bustling over, with her blonde extensions and rubbery lips and short black skirt, and sighs as she takes my phone and huffs and puffs and gets it to work — such a huge drama! She looks at the photographs on my camera, probably expecting to see snotty-nosed grandchildren with their dribbly smiles. I point to the three photos I want printed off, and she gives me a peculiar look before passing me back to the spotty boy to complete the transaction. I take three copies of each photograph.

The first photo is of the horrid husband and the student by his car. He is smiling broadly at her. Their arms are almost touching. Certainly, they are close in the sense that they are at ease with their bodies brushing each other's.

The second shows the husband's arm on the student's back. It looks more intimate than it actually was. I zoomed in a little, which helped. It is still not decisive, but it certainly looks incriminating. Why else would this predatory man be doing that?

The third photo shows the student getting into the husband's car. It looks, from this angle, like the husband has his hand firmly on the student's bottom. Almost a grope. This was taken at a fortuitous angle. It is the clincher.

After paying, I make my way to the library. I find myself a tucked-away corner where I can sit at a table and do what I need to do.

I take the photographs from a pocket of my jacket — Pippa's jacket, which I have borrowed from her wardrobe. She does say, repeatedly, 'help yourself to anything you need.' So I have. From the other pocket, I take envelopes from a cheap packet that I bought from Poundland in Felixstowe.

Then I check I have the book of first-class stamps that I purchased from the post office in the little supermarket here in town. I have it. Finally, I walk over to a desk in the library and borrow a cheap pen from a pot there.

I have given this matter — my plan to get the husband

out — considerable thought. When I moved into the studio, I was happy to just do my thing, building my friendship with Pippa and being on amicable-enough terms with the husband and son. If — if! — they had treated me properly. They have not. I have been there four nights so far. And this is my fifth day. Neither of them has spoken to me at all — even my broadest smile gets little more than a cursory nod at best. More often than not, I am ignored as I go to and from their cloakroom. I get more attention from the sleepy-headed dog.

They have not invited me into the house to join them for breakfast or an evening meal or to watch television. They have not reached out in any way. Each night, I have sat eating an out-of-date sandwich from the supermarket and reading a library book late into the evening, and my spirits fall until I am close to desperation. I resent them so much. They have not even stopped by once to see if I am well, that I am comfortable and happy, and whether I need anything. It would not take them more than a minute or two.

Pippa is little better. She has popped in mornings and early evenings to ask if I am okay and if I need anything — but she flutters about, straightening this and pulling that into place, as though I have messed everything up on purpose. whenever I try to say anything to her, she responds, "If there's anything you need, help yourself!" like it's a catch-phrase, as she hurries away. What I need, Pippa, is warmth and love and affection, not to be treated like I am a bloody nuisance.

The final straw was last night. Not just hearing them beginning to have sex, but after that. In the early hours of the morning, I needed to go to the toilet rather badly. I had eaten something that upset my stomach.

I pulled at the patio door handle and felt as though I had almost ripped my arm out of its socket. It still aches, even now. I realised that someone had locked the door from inside, so I could not get in to use the facilities. I wondered if the husband had heard me creeping about earlier in the evening and this was his revenge.

I ended up crouched over a patch of soil behind the studio, digging a hole with my fingers and then covering it up with more soil afterwards. It was this, such utter degradation at my age, that has made me absolutely determined to not just destroy him with Pippa, but to ruin him completely.

I glance around to make sure I'm not being watched by anyone in the library. I am not, so I take one of each of the three photographs — side by side, arm on back, hand on bottom — as I think of them. I turn them over, ready to write. I take the pen in my hand, thinking about the handwriting. Mine is neat and tidy. I will make my writing larger and looser. There will be spelling mistakes, too. I take an envelope. I put a first-class stamp on it.

Even now, pen in hand, I am not sure who to send these to: Pippa, for certain, so that she can see the extent of his lies. He sweet-talked her last night. Back into bed, too. She will be so livid — and humiliated — when she sees these photos, she will order him out of the house immediately. I write on the back of the first photo, in a sloppy and unfamiliar hand, 'This is your husband's lover.' The next, 'He can't keep his hands off her.' Then, 'The Dirty Barstard.' (I spell it wrong on purpose.)

I have two other sets of photographs to send. I sit with my phone and Google for ages, looking at people I can send them to at the university: a head of faculty, perhaps, and the head of the students' union, maybe. Eventually, I find names and write the same on each photograph. First, 'Peter Kelly and his student lover.' Second, 'He sleeps with so many students.' Third, 'He gives them top marks.' And that's that. I seal and address the envelopes, pack everything away, and walk out of the library. I smile to myself as I post the envelopes in the letter box. I am well and truly putting the proverbial cat amongst the pigeons!

TONIGHT IS my fifth alone in this studio. And usually by this time, just gone six o'clock, I am wallowing in misery after another dull and forgettable day. All my fury and envy and hate come bubbling up.

Not this evening, though. I am, in fact, almost beside myself with glee at the thought of what the next day or two might bring. A ferocious row between Pippa and the husband, ending with him and his bags being thrown out into the street. I could almost clap my hands with joy.

Pippa will then be here, in the studio, weeping on my shoulder. The evening will conclude with me tucked up snug as a bug in a rug inside the house. Maybe even in the same bed as Pippa, if she needs extended comforting.

Pippa and I will become soulmates. I know it in my heart. And, after Monica, Pippa will be my last-ever soulmate. Until death us do part. I wish I had my desk diary with me to write about Patricia, a woman I befriended between Monica and Pippa. She broke my heart. I suddenly want to write about her to rid myself of my negative feelings. Instead, I think things over.

I met Patricia almost ten years ago now, here in Felixstowe, the two of us sitting on a bench at The Dip, looking out to sea. We got talking, about the weather and the containers coming in and out of the port, and she offered to buy me a cup of tea from the nearby hut. I said yes, please and thank you when she returned and handed the mug to me. We sat there for ever such a while in a companionable silence. I don't think either of us wanted to get up and go first!

Eventually, as the rain clouds filled the sky, we both looked at each other and said the same words, "It's going to rain," at the same moment. We both then said, "Snap!" And laughed. Neither of us had said anything to each other about ourselves, other than our first names, but as we said goodbye and went in opposite directions, I felt sure we would meet again. More than that — I knew we would become, at least, the best of friends.

Patricia and I met again the same time the next day at the bench by The Dip. I was already there and waved at her as she came along. "Let me buy you a mug of tea!" I called out as she approached. She smiled and said thank you. Neither of us said anything else for a few minutes as we sat there sipping our teas and watching a huge container ship crossing the horizon. I think we each knew the other would be there that day and time.

We chatted for a good while, talking generally at first about this and that, nothing in particular: the strong wind, the choppy sea, the Great British weather. As we relaxed in each other's company, we talked a little more: where we lived and what we did and how we liked the town of Felixstowe. We had so much in common. Both single ladies — a widow doing charity work, a spinster always between benefits and low-paid work — and in our early fifties, at that time.

Patricia lived on a housing estate further out in Old Felixstowe towards the ferry. She had spent her life at home caring for her disabled mother, who had died recently. Patricia was now 'deciding what to do.' She walked every morning and went up the town, or into Ipswich, or Colchester, or Bury St Edmunds in the afternoons, alternating with her charity work. I summarised my life, making it sound nice and happy. I said I cleaned offices late at night and early mornings, which I did at that time. When we parted company, we were friends.

Patricia and I were the best of friends for twelve weeks, that glorious summer. It began so well. We would meet most mornings at The Dip. That then rolled into the occasional lunch at Greggs the baker's. And afternoons out now and then. I remember happy times walking around the castles at Framlingham and at Orford. She had more money than I did, and would not take petrol money from me, for example. But money was not why it all went wrong.

I fell in love with Patricia, this mirror image of me in many ways. We were so close that on two occasions, at a café in Ipswich and a garden display in Orford, we were asked if we were sisters! We could have gone on as we were, with our lunches and our afternoons out, for ever. But I wanted more, and one morning on the bench at The Dip, my courage rising, I tucked my arm into hers. We sat there happily enough. Becoming bolder, I then stroked her bare arm with my fingers. A funny tickle, really. I wish I hadn't. Almost instantly, I felt her stiffen, her whole body tightening, She moved her arm away — quite forcefully — and got up to go.

I think, if I had left it at that, with maybe a quick, 'Sorry, what was I thinking!' we could maybe have continued as we were with our happy friendship. But I wanted more, so much more. I wanted love, both emotional and physical. I had been starved of the human touch for so long. So I did exactly the same thing again, when we met the next morning at The Dip. She gave me the chance to pretend nothing had happened and continue as before. But I could not help myself. And Patricia pulled away angrily this time and snapped, as she got to her feet, "I'm sorry, Sharon. I don't want to see you again." And she walked off.

With Patricia, I should have watched her walk away, just let her go. But I could not. I turned up at the bench — our bench — the next day at the usual time. She did not come along. I walked around the town centre. I did not see her there. I did the same the next day without success. The day after that, I plucked up the courage to walk by her house, quite casually, even though it was at the end of a cul-de-sac.

She was at the living room window as I arrived. I watched her dusting knick-knacks until she looked up and saw me. I went to wave, but she put her hands on her hips and stared back at me. I stood there a while longer, until she came out through the front door. I went to say something nice, but she shouted, "Go home! I don't want to see you." There was, I can now admit, something of a scene with me on my knees, holding on to her legs as she struggled to go back indoors. It was only when she threatened to call the police that I eventually relented, after much sobbing and hysteria on my part, and went away.

I sent jolly texts, suggesting a walk or lunch (on me!) to clear the air. I emailed her every day, more than once, for weeks. Just general chit-chat. I wrote letters to her eventually, begging her forgiveness. I added I was on medication that made me act like that, but I was not taking it anymore. She never replied.

I started going to her house again. She called the police after another scene where I got my elbow stuck in her letter box. The police said she would go to court to get a restraining order. I stopped then, full of heartbreak and impotent fury. Patricia sold up and moved away. I stayed here, full of sourness and hate. But now I have, or will soon have, Pippa. I must be careful with her.

As I lie here, working through what happened and making sense of my thoughts, there is a tap at the door of the extension. Pippa is here! She walks straight in without waiting for my response. "Come and join us, Sharon ... something to eat. Eight o'clock. Nothing fancy ... come as you are." She smiles warmly at me.

I smile and nod and say yes and thank you although I can barely get the words out. I am so pleased and astonished. Stunned, really. Perhaps their rapprochement has triggered this offer. That won't last long, of course — a day or two at most, until the photographs arrive. I will sit there at the meal anticipating the break-up. Then Pippa is gone, just as quickly as she came, and I get up and start getting ready.

I sit here now, on the edge of the couch, looking at my watch. It is five minutes to eight o'clock. I have changed into some fresh clothes. Cleaned my face and hands with wipes from my handbag. Put on fresh make-up and a dab of lipstick. I am excited and worried, too. I do not know what the evening holds in store. The husband and the boy will be there as well, of course. And the more-welcoming dog.

———

I sit opposite Pippa at the dining room table. The filthy boy is next to me. The cheating husband is opposite him. To be frank, it is all rather mannered and tense — nobody really wants me here except Pippa.

Pippa is smiley and polite as she spoons spaghetti Bolognese onto our plates, starting with me. She tops up my just-filled glass of red wine. Her smile is a brittle one. Truth is, she already knows this was not a good idea.

The man and the boy are now silent, as they largely have been since I arrived ten minutes ago. The man asked how I was, on my arrival, but turned away as I began my answer. The boy just glanced at me and grunted, as teenage boys do. I tried to start a conversation about the heavy fruit bowl, the centrepiece of the table — made by Pippa, I'd assume? They just nodded, and that was that.

Pippa raises her glass and says, "Cheers." I raise mine and clink it against hers. She smiles widely and turns towards the husband, who clinks his glass with hers but says nothing. I see him glance at me. It is not a nice look. I am not welcome here. He is barely civil. The boy already has his head down and is shovelling away. "Oh, Dom," says Pippa in an exaggerated, long-suffering voice. He raises his head, reaches for his can of Coca-Cola and dinks it against Pippa's glass.

As we eat our 'spag Bol,' as Pippa calls it, she asks me how my day has been. I smile and say, "Good, thank you." She nods her head encouragingly as if to say, 'Go on.' I hesitate and then lie, saying I had a walk down as far as the Martello tower 'for a change.' The man looks up at that and asks which one. I reply, the one down towards Felixstowe Ferry. He adds that there is another one at the other end, beyond a playground towards the town's refuse tip. I nod, and then Pippa asks what a Martello tower is.

The man takes over, saying how they are small forts built across Britain during the French Revolution in case of attack. On he goes, loving the sound of his own voice. The boy perks up as the man stops speaking. The boy adds, "They are all along the coast." (Like they'd be miles inland.) The man gives him an irritated look. The boy goes on without noticing, saying there are, "Loads here. Four or five. We done it at school." The man now seems angry, as though in some way he has been made to look foolish.

"Did you have a nice lunch?" Pippa asks, reaching across to top up my glass of wine again. It is, I think, a reflex action when she is nervous. I did not. I sat on a bench with an out-of-date tuna and sweetcorn sandwich and a cheap bottle of fizzy pop, watching the world go by. I did not say that, though, and just replied, "Yes, thank you." Pippa looked at me almost in desperation, as though she were keen for me to go on, to keep this conversation going as we finish our main course.

After more agonising chit-chat, we do finish, and Pippa takes the plates into the kitchen. They clatter together as though she is nervous, but that might just be my imagination. The boy, reading something on his phone, suddenly gets up and says, "Got to go," in the vague direction of the man. He replies, "Say goodbye to your ..." But the boy is already out through the patio door. Pippa then comes back with a raspberry pavlova — supermarket, not hers — and plates and spoons. She puts them on the table just before she drops them. The man watches but does not help. They look at each other, some unspoken thoughts between them about the boy.

As Pippa cuts the pavlova and puts the portions onto plates, she suddenly seems sweaty and horribly vulnerable, and I realise that this meal is a test of sorts. I know the man does not want me here in their home, or even the studio. They are — just about — being polite. I am not sure that

Pippa really wants me living in the extension, either. But she has given me a place to live, and I think she is now hoping I will repay that by showing the husband how nice and friendly I am.

I still do not know why I am sitting here, having this meal. I had hoped, or at least it had crossed my mind, that they maybe wanted to integrate me into the family in some way. An honorary aunt, perhaps. A surrogate mother of sorts for Pippa. But I can tell, from the man now, the way he sits, how he glances at me, the way he speaks — bored of idle chit-chat — that this is about as far from reality as it could be.

Pippa and I talk superficially, with me making up more nonsense about my lunch and my afternoon walk around the town, into the library and the charity shops. I try to make it sound as interesting as I can. The man now has his head down eating, shovelling in the pavlova with a fork. Other than a sudden cry — "I forgot the double cream!" — and a dash to the kitchen and back, Pippa keeps the conversation going. She replies to my comments, saying what a good library it is, friendly staff, and how you can get some smashing bargains in charity shops these days.

As we finish the pavlova — the man has not spoken, nor even looked up, for some time — Pippa clears the dishes, all emptied, waving away my offer of help. She goes to the kitchen. The man turns to me at last, not a particularly pleasant look, and is about to speak when Pippa calls out, "There's fruit in the bowl if anyone wants to help themselves? And who wants coffee?" The man and I both reply, "No, thank you," at the same instant. And that, as I get ready to get up and say thank you and goodbye, is pretty much that.

Apart from one last thing. "Um," he says, and I know, near enough, what he is going to say. I sit there with a blank expression. "You're Pippa's friend ... I suppose ... and we want to be as supportive as we can ... to her friends. But, ah, it can't go on indefinitely. All of us living like this. You need to, you know, sooner rather than later. This month, ideally."

I get up and nod, just before I go and say farewell to Pippa, and reply, "Yes, of course, it will all be resolved soon ... the next few days, actually." He seems surprised and rather pleased with himself, as though, by speaking up, he's sorted everything out. In a way, he has. I posted those photographs in that Woodbridge postbox late yesterday afternoon; they will have been collected this morning, and are now winging their way here to Pippa. Yes, it will soon be resolved — but he'll be leaving, not me.

13

FRIDAY, 4 NOVEMBER, THE MIDDLE OF THE
EVENING

I t is another cold but crisp night. I am sitting in the
extension with the door open again, at eight pm or so,
hearing fireworks from back gardens, and an organ-
ised display, and maybe even from over at the docks. Not that
I am listening to those. I'm waiting for explosions inside the
house.

Unlike my early nights here, I am so happy. I am full of
anticipation, bubbling over, really. I believe this is the night
everything changes for me for the better. So, so much better!
A complete turnaround in my fortunes, you might say.

I go over what happened again, in my OCD way, almost
drooling with delight. I posted the incriminating
photographs to Pippa on Tuesday afternoon, and they would
have been picked up by the postie on Wednesday morning. I
went into the house on Thursday, several times, checking for
their delivery, but the envelope did not arrive until late this
morning, lunchtime really, Friday.

I've been beside myself ever since, sitting here for hours,
knowing everything could unfold very quickly. Even now,

after such a long wait, I am still almost clapping my hands with delight.

Looking back, I heard someone in the house at about two pm and thought it might be Pippa. I hurried in as if going to the cloakroom. But it was the boy, who was in and out quickly, with a football under an arm and a sneer for me. The dog ignored me today, its back leg up, cleaning itself with a horrible chewing noise.

I knew the boy would come back later and just go about his business. The horrible husband would probably return at about five or six pm. He'd just put the post for Pippa on the shelf in the hallway. And then she'd return and open it.

All afternoon, I had anticipated — hoped, if not longed for — Pippa to come home early from the boutique. Some days she has come back at four pm if it was quiet at work. I imagined so many times how it would unfold in my head. She would go into the kitchen, the envelope in her hand, and pour herself a refreshing glass of Prosecco, then sit down on a bar stool. She'd look, puzzled, at the envelope and the unfamiliar handwriting before opening it and taking out the photographs.

Her mouth would fall open as she flicked from one photograph to another, seeing her filthy husband's arm around the student, on her back, and a hand on her bottom. This — the latest betrayal — is what she believed was taking place all along, so she would simply take the photographs at face value, as proof that he is having another affair. She might, later, puzzle over who took the photos and sent them, but she will conclude, most likely, it was an outraged colleague or a disgruntled student. Who cares!

In my daydream, Pippa would come stumbling out through the patio door, shaking and sobbing, and calling to me in despair in a broken voice: "Sharon! Sharon!" And I would rush out at the sound of her distress, and she would fall into my arms, hugging me tight. I would guide her to the couch in the extension, and as we entwined, Pippa would sob out the news and show me the photographs. Later on, I would march into the house with her. He would be told to get out. And, joy and wonder, I would be asked to move in. Just the boy to deal with, then.

But here I am at eight o'clock or so, and I am sad it did not happen like that. I hung around just outside the garage, hoping. The boy came back once more, returning with the football at about four pm. I went into the cloakroom and spent some time there, not doing anything, just sitting and holding my breath, wanting to be present when Pippa returned.

The boy left just as I came out of the cloakroom. I did not feel I could stay there any longer. He was outside, as though waiting for me. I smiled at him. He did not respond, but said something under his breath. Weirdo, I think. He does himself no favours. He will pay for these slights and insults. Every one of them.

I then hung around outside the garage for a while longer as it got dark. I don't think anyone indoors could see me there, looking out from light to dark. I saw the husband moving about the kitchen at half-past five, six o'clock. I wonder if anyone at the university has approached him yet about the photographs they've received. I suspect not; they will take soundings from colleagues first. Anyway, he made himself something to eat, then wandered off to eat it in the dining room. But there was no sign of Pippa. I thought perhaps she must have gone out with work colleagues for drinks.

It is well gone eight o'clock now, but I can wait all evening. Pippa will return. She will open the envelope, take out the photographs, and everything will transform in that instant. I lie on the couch with the window open. If the husband is there when Pippa comes back, I will hear them shouting at each other. I want to be nearby — just going through to the cloakroom — to flash a smile as she sends him packing. My delicious revenge.

If he goes out, for whatever reason, before that — to see his lover, most likely — Pippa will come straight to me just as I imagined so often all afternoon, and she will gasp it all out, and I will sympathise and hold her tight in my arms. And we will be there together, beside each other, the best of friends forever, all our differences forgotten, as our new life together begins.

So I will now sit back and wait, revelling in the joy of what is to come. I will be with Pippa. In that lovely house. My new home. A wonderful bedroom of my own. Perhaps more than that in time. Sharing a room, a life, our love together. The boy will have to go too, of course. But I will attend to that once I am living indoors.

I HAVE ALREADY LAID the groundwork with the boy, having been out and about early on Wednesday and Thursday mornings and later in the afternoons, being there as he walked to school and back home again. He never saw me. Sitting with my newspaper on various benches, unnoticed and overlooked. But I saw him every time, walking alone, slight and slender, head down, in his own world. I watched and waited for him to be chased by schoolboys or picked up by whoever was in that car. But nothing happened.

I was convinced the boy is up to no good. I thought he was chased by that gang of boys because he did something, physically or mentally, to a younger girl, perhaps a sister of one of the pursuing boys. I had no proof of this, not yet, but it was such a strong feeling I had. My instinct. It could have been that he was dealing in drugs, whoever picked him up in that car being the supplier. There have been no signs of drugs or cash in his room — I looked everywhere — but he may have hidden them elsewhere. Whatever it was, I knew there was something rotten about the boy.

And then, quite by chance this Friday morning, I uncovered what I need to know to bring down the boy.

I was at a bench, with a *Daily Mail*, and I saw the boy hurrying along to a smaller boy, ahead of him, perhaps thirteen or fourteen years old. The dirty boy came alongside, and after a glance around, he put his hand on the boy's back in what looked like a friendly gesture. The younger boy stopped, and there was a conversation between them. By their body language, I could tell it was not a pleasant talk. It ended with the younger boy handing something over — I could not see what, perhaps all his cash, and the dirty boy then crossed the road and strolled on. The younger boy looked distraught.

Pretending to check my make-up — even an old woman wants to look presentable — I took photographs of all of this: the hand on the back, the conversation, the handing over of whatever it was and the upset younger boy standing there afterwards.

Like the photographs of the husband, they will be useful to me at some stage. They are not as incriminating as those of the husband. And Pippa might dismiss them as some-thing and nothing.

But if there were a time when the boy and I had to have a little chat, about why he might want to leave home, perhaps to go and live with his father, or head to university asap, showing him these photographs might be decisive.

I have also been out and about addressing the issue of the troublesome Elaine. I had hoped that after our lunch at Ipswich Waterfront and subsequent falling-out, Pippa would side with me. I had assumed that was the case. But last Sunday's afternoon out for Pippa and Elaine, and their giggling and waving at each other on their return, suggests otherwise. That makes me very angry.

I have not dared raise the matter with Pippa. She is in and out so fast with me, and not at all attentive. That will come with the husband's downfall. I don't want to mention Elaine yet and perhaps unwittingly force Pippa to choose between us. I fear she would pick Elaine. I have been torn, deciding what to do. One way or the other, nuisance Elaine has to go. Emphatically and permanently.

I have been walking near Elaine's house. Hoping to bump into her and have a conversation, to get a sense of how things are between Pippa and her. I could not bring myself to go to her front door, the need for an apology to be invited in being a step too far. But when I have gone by, and her silly little car was not on the driveway, I have been up her path, through the gate and into the back garden to have a look around. I have done that twice now.

Her black cat came up to me the first time, and I stroked and befriended it. The next time, as I stood there deciding what to do, it weaved itself between and around my legs.

Following that, I took little bits of chicken with me, left-

overs from a packet meal, and fed it to the cat. Nuisance
Elaine's dear little friend. I then came to a decision. A plan
that would lead to Elaine leaving Pippa alone forever.

As I begin to work through this plan in my head, I hear
noises from the house. Raised voices. Pippa has returned
and opened my envelope and seen the photographs. She is
now screaming at him. I chortle with happiness. It is all I can
do to stop myself running as fast as I can to the house to be
there at the denouement of their marriage.

I AM in the cloakroom at the front of the house, just as I
would normally be, so innocently, at this time of night.
Washing my face. Cleaning my teeth. Using the toilet.
Getting ready for bed. If I am honest, I've hated coming in
here each and every evening. Like a thief in the night. It is
demeaning and degrading for me to be treated in this way.

When they were in the living room watching television,
I'd smile as I went by. Pippa smiled back. He usually turned
as I came through the patio door and had a face like thunder
until I crept back out behind them to leave. I'd hear her
admonishing him as I closed the patio door. I got more of a
response from the sleepy dog, looking up, hoping for food.

Tonight, they are not in the living room as usual. They
are upstairs in their bedroom, still arguing with such fury
that I'm convinced it will end with savage violence. With the
cloakroom door half-open, I hear each word and every yell
clearly. I do not think they know I am here, listening to it all.

"You promised!" I hear her shouting, a whining,
desperate tone to her voice.

He does not answer.

"You said. You said!" she shouts, for emphasis.

Still, I cannot hear him replying, but then she screams so loudly at him, "You shit, you fucking shit!"

That's better, I think, stand up to him. I hate the idea of her begging him, imploring him to give up his lover, going down on her knees before him. He has cheated on her, not once now, but twice. At least! She said she forgave him the first time — once too many, in my opinion — but twice? She should stand tall and strong and tell him to go.

I jump, startled, as the dirty boy suddenly appears in the hallway, dishevelled and with bite marks on his neck. He must have crept in through the patio door behind me. "Can you hear from there?" he sneers as I push the cloakroom door closed rather too late. I think he might bang on the door, even barge in to threaten me, but I hear him going up the staircase two steps at a time.

He makes a clattering noise somehow, loudly announcing his arrival. He must know they argue, will have heard them before. This racket he is making is designed to tell them he is back, that they should start behaving themselves. As he gets to the top of the stairs, I hear Pippa's door being slammed shut, followed, a moment later, by the boy's. I imagine he is putting his headphones on and then fiddling furiously with himself.

I hear stomping back and forth in Pippa's bedroom, drawers, cupboards and the wardrobe being opened in turn. Things being packed. Ready to go.

"Liar!" she yells at him. "You fucking liar!" Such fury in her voice.

"She has mental health issues ... anxiety." He is quieter, but angry too. "I was acting in loco parentis."

A likely story, that.

My heart soars with joy. That this dreadful man is leaving now. All I need to do, in a second or two, is to slip out of here, through the living room, opening and closing the patio door, and go back to the studio. I then simply wait for everything to change.

I'll dab a little perfume behind my ears. Pippa will come rushing to me. We'll embrace. And she will pour out her troubles. I'll pat her back and nod and gasp and make appropriate noises as she replays the shouting match for me while I comfort her. Then she will ask me to come into the house, perhaps even to her bed, to keep her company.

Once the appalling man has left, never to return, I will take my place at the heart of the household. I will cook in the kitchen, put my feet up on the coffee table in the living room and use the bathroom whenever I wish for as long as I want. I will come and go as I please! And we will be happy. Pippa and I. And loving. Maybe more, once the boy has gone.

"That's it!" she shouts at him, one last time. "It's over. I want a divorce." I hope she means this. I must make sure she keeps to it.

There is a long silence. I imagine, with a delicious thrill, that he is on his knees, quietly begging to stay, and she is rebuffing him.

Eventually, I take my chance to slip out of the cloakroom, along the short hallway and into the living room. To get back to the studio as quickly as I can to wait for Pippa.

As I reach the stairs, I stop and come face-to-face with Pippa hurrying down with a packed holdall. I can't believe it. She looks flushed and tearful, barely able to speak as she glances at me. "I'm sorry, Sharon, I'm so sorry." That's all she says as she rushes to the kitchen, grabbing her car keys, and then turns to go out the front door to her car and away. She does not look back.

I stand there, in shock, rooted to the spot. The horrid husband then comes down the stairs, all wild-eyed and spittle-mouthed. We look at each other, and I blurt out, "She's gone," and wish I hadn't.

He snarls, "I suppose you heard all of that?"

I do not respond. My mouth is dry; I fear him. What he might now do.

He goes on, "You don't fool me. This butter-wouldn't-melt act of yours. I see right through you." And then his face changes, to surprise and incredulity and finally back to anger again. More than that.

"My God," he says, such shock in his voice. "Those photos were yours." He goes to say more, 'bitch' and 'cow' and all the usual insults men hurl at older women. But I am already turning and walking away, refusing to be drawn into this horror. He shouts after me, as I open the patio door, "I'll have you. I'll fucking have you for this."

I shut the door behind me, my hands trembling, and rush back to the studio, locking the door behind me.

14

SATURDAY, 5 NOVEMBER, INTO THE NIGHT

I am now alone in this extension, with the husband still ranting and raving in the house. The son will surely hear him. When he does, the two of them will egg each other on. I am no longer welcome here. More than that, I am not safe.

I am in real and imminent danger. I know that. I have shut and locked the door of the extension. But there are no bolts on the inside. The husband will have a key somewhere in the house. He can let himself in whenever he wants.

It's only a matter of time before he comes here, telling me to leave, perhaps to physically throw me out. Or worse. I have been on the receiving end of men's fury before.

I text Pippa urgently, 'Where are you?' and, 'Are you okay?' and, 'What's happening?'

What I really want to put is: 'You've left me behind. Help! Come back and save me.'

I stare at the screen, willing Pippa to respond, telling me to hurry to the front of the house, that she'll return in her car for me, and we'll go away somewhere together.

I stand at the window of the extension, looking towards the house, holding my breath. All the lights are blazing away upstairs. I imagine the husband storming about in a fury. He'll be gathering up every one of Pippa's belongings and throwing them out of the house. It's the way of men.

Men are such vile creatures. Pippa is the innocent party. He is the guilty one. He should be the one who leaves. Yet he has obviously refused. Pippa is so upset, so beside herself, that she is not thinking clearly, and she has gone. What happens next is anyone's guess. I think the man is in such a rage that he will strip the house of everything of hers.

As his anger reaches a crescendo, he will storm towards the extension, blaming me for all that has gone wrong. At best, he will stand there shaking, yelling at me to go now. More likely, he will put his hands on me, on my shoulders, turning me around and marching me away. Perhaps I will suffer a beating or worse.

I stare at my phone, my hand shaking. There is no reply. Pippa is not coming to my rescue. She will not save me.

I have to go, just get out now, before the husband comes for me. Takes his anger out with his fists.

I am in despair. I have nowhere to go but back to the horrors of my old flat.

I hear noises from the garden. I turn around, looking across the room, deciding what to take with me. I panic, just grabbing for the old coat Pippa gave to me. Some warmth across my shoulders.

I move to the window, seeing what's happening outside. It is the man. He has wrenched open an upstairs bedroom window, which now hangs at an angle, broken in his rage. He is throwing Pippa's clothes out. The fool has lost his mind. He will come for me next. I suddenly notice a painter's pointed palette knife on the windowsill and pick it up for self-protection. It's not ideal, but it's all I have.

And I am out onto the patio, pulling the door of the extension closed behind me. I will return later, in the morning, when he is asleep, to collect my possessions, such as they are. If he is awake then, he will have calmed down. And he will just ignore me or look at me with contempt.

I look up. The husband is now coming through the patio door, striding across and stopping in front of me.

My hand tightens on the knife, ready to use it in self-protection. I will claim self-defence.

He looks into my eyes. I look back, holding his gaze, waiting for him to speak. I will stab him in the heart if I have to.

He breathes in deeply, as though calming himself. He is not going to attack me, nor strike me, not even raise a hand to me. I keep my hand tight on the knife, moving it carefully out of the pocket of my jacket, so it is easy to use but he cannot see it. I need that element of surprise. I stand up straight. If this man says the wrong thing to me, I will plunge the knife into him again and again until he is dead. I will say I had no choice.

He has ruined everything, not me. Pippa has gone and has left me behind. This man and the boy stay here, and I have to go. Back to where I came from. To the flat. To lick my wounds. Think my thoughts. Make my plans. To approach Pippa again. To hope we still have a future. If not, I will go into the sea. To end it all. I doubt I have anything to lose whether I stab him to death or not. I believe I have lost Pippa for good. I wait to see what he says — whether he is going to condemn himself in the next few words.

"You need to go." His voice cracks with emotion. "Now …

the photographs ..." He is breathing heavily, struggling to stay calm. "You evil bitch." He cannot breathe properly, and I wonder if he is about to collapse. I bring the knife out, but he is so distracted he does not see it. "Go now. You can collect your things tomorrow."

I lunge at him as he turns away, the knife just missing his elbow. He does not seem to notice as he walks back towards the house.

I could scream in anguish. I want to run after him, plunging the knife into his back, his neck, his head, again and again. But I stop. There is a chance Pippa may still come for me. Somehow, I control myself and watch him go into the house, pulling the door closed behind him.

He does not even look at me, and it is that, the dismissiveness of it, that enrages me so much. I will have my revenge on you, you bastard.

———

I AM SITTING on a bench in a shelter on the promenade, looking out to sea, my mind swirling with thoughts. On summer days, it is pretty enough here. At night, with spitting rain, it is an ugly place.

I should not have come here when I left the extension. I am cold, and I am now frightened. Young people, men and women, coming out of bars and clubs, go by. Most ignore me. One or two jeer. I am to be mocked and tormented. A figure of fun.

One drunk young man takes a handful of coins from his pocket and throws them at me. "Have a bath!" he shouts nonsensically. I dip my head down as the coins hit my head and shoulders. He runs away laughing.

I make my way to my old flat. When I get to the house, I see the landlord's son's car parked half on the drive, half on the pavement. The middle floor of the house and the attic are dark and silent. There is a faint, solitary light on somewhere inside the ground-floor flat.

I think nothing much of it as I approach the porch. It is lit, for the first time in years. Someone, the landlord's son, I presume, has fitted a new bulb. It is not strong and casts a dim, almost dirty, light. All the old landlord's potted plants and knick-knacks that had been on the porch for ages have been removed. I stand on cracked and broken tiles from a century or more ago.

I should realise, as I take my key from my pocket, what this tidying-up means for me. But it is only when I try to put the key into the lock that the truth dawns. I cannot even get my key in, let alone turn it. The landlord's son has changed the lock. As this sinks in, I kick the door in frustration.

Even though it is the early hours, I ring the doorbell and stand with a mix of emotions, mostly anger, that I am locked out. I feel fear, too, although 'trepidation' may be a better description.

There is no answer. I step back off the porch, looking up to see if any lights are being turned on upstairs. None are. I walk round to the back of the house for a clearer view of the attic rooms, but it is all just as dark from there.

I hesitate, not sure what to do, thinking my only choice, with the rain now falling harder, is to return to that shelter by the sea. As I trudge back to the front of the house, the landlord's son appears, standing on the path, blocking my way.

"What do you want?" he asks abruptly, pulling his dressing gown tighter, and pushing up the collar to provide some protection from the rain. "You moved out." He laughs before I can answer. It is a sour noise.

"No. No. I ..." I don't know what to say, suddenly feeling vulnerable. This late at night, out of sight and in front of an aggressive young man.

"Yes! Yes! You've gone," he adds. "Go!" He steps back, gesturing that I should walk by him, up the path and away. "Don't come back."

"I ... my stuff." I gesture up towards my flat, looking more desperate than I mean to. I want to say I have a lease. He has to give me notice. He can't do this. But, of course, he is. He has already.

"It's packed up. Three boxes. In the garage. You can come back in the daytime to collect them." He turns to go.

"I need a bed for the night," I call out, my voice not sounding as measured as I hoped. "And then I'll take my things and be gone in the morning." There is a long pause. "Please," I add finally.

He stops and thinks for a moment or two. Then turns and takes three strides towards me in an intimidating manner. As if he is going to push me over. Instead, he stands so close that I can smell his breath. It is all I can do to hold my ground and not step away from the stench of cigarettes and alcohol.

He smiles suddenly, unexpectedly, as though he is pretending to be jolly, and crooks his little finger in my face, gesturing me closer. I lean toward him instinctively. He speaks in little more than a whisper. Playing his evil game with me. He says five words: "I read your desk diary."

He steps back and puts his finger to his rounded mouth and goes, "Shh-shh!" He claps his hands together joyfully. Then, dropping the stupid charade, he spits out the words,

"Go! Come back for your things in daylight and then disappear." The words 'or else' hang in the air.

It is all I can do to stop myself reaching into my pocket for that sharp-ended palette knife. And if he turned and walked ahead of me in that instant, I would have done, plunging the point of the knife between his shoulder blades over and over.

But he stands facing me, a strange look on his face, almost of pleasure, like a cat toying with a just-still-alive mouse. I do not think I could pull the knife out without him stepping forward and knocking it from my hand. He is too young and strong; he would launch himself at me, pinning me down with one hand and using the other to call the police on his mobile.

So I walk by him, silent and fearful, my mind racing with thoughts about the desk diary. Fury at myself for my unthinking stupidity. Leaving my notes and the diary there. Writing anything in the first place. Not thinking he might read it. I go to ask him if I can have the notes and the desk diary back. But I stop myself. Whether he leaves them in the boxes or not, he may have taken photographs with his phone. He will forever have a hold over me. I will always fear exposure.

And so, now I am back in the shelter on the seafront, huddled on a bench in the corner, hiding from the wind and the rain and passers-by. I am cold, shaking really, and am unable to sleep. It's not just because of the notes and the desk diary. It's also about what happens to me next. I look out to sea and wonder if that is where I will be heading soon. Not just yet. By tomorrow night, though, I think that will be the only option.

I text Pippa again, once, twice, three times. I think each

message seems increasingly desperate. In the last, I ask her to contact me and end it with 'PLEASE!' My last chance, I feel. I press send and spend a restless hour looking at my phone, furious with myself, but also desperate for a reply. Pippa does not respond. It is as if she has vanished.

In the morning, I will go first to collect my things from the extension. There is a nice holdall in the corner, Pippa's, that I can use. I don't know if the husband and son will be there. Last Saturday, the husband did odd jobs in the garden, and the son went off with his football somewhere, the dog in tow for once. I hope whoever is there just ignores me. I will then go to the garage behind the flat and take what I can carry, and the notes and the desk diary, hopefully. I do not know what I will do from there. If I have not heard from Pippa, I will walk into the sea at night-time.

I SLEEP A LITTLE, maybe two or three hours on and off, waking as the sun rises and cyclists and dog walkers start appearing. I sit here a while, thinking my thoughts, feeling increasingly despondent. I have not heard from Pippa. I don't expect to now. What does that mean for me? Where does it leave me? At the end of the rope.

I drag myself up and walk — trudge, more like — along the seafront, by the theatre and the pier and the leisure centre, down towards the docks. There is a toilet block halfway along, where I wash and tidy and attend to personal matters. I then sit on a nearby bench, ignoring passers-by and their inane comments about the weather, and look out to sea for ages. I feel stiff and sore. I am too old for this. I have nowhere to go from here but the sea.

I will give Pippa one final chance. I will not text her again. And I will wait until six o'clock this evening to see if she replies. If not, that's that. Eventually, and I do it simply to pass the time, I make my way, mid-morning, after a cup of tea at Greggs the baker's, to Pippa's house to pick up that holdall and a few items of clothing. I keep thinking to myself, What's the bloody point? I feel as though I am on automatic pilot as I walk into the garden.

The husband is at the top of a ladder on the patio at the back of the house. He is wiping a bedroom window with a cloth. He's too mean to pay for a window cleaner.

He has earphones in, listening to music. He should be concentrating fully on what he is doing, really. Being so high up.

As I stand below, looking upwards, mulling things over, I can hear the faint buzz of music. I do not believe he knows I am here.

He leans to the left on the ladder, away from me, reaching into the far corner of the window, rubbing at some grime. He takes a while, and I watch him, weighing things up in my head.

If he were to fall off that ladder now, somehow, he would land on the studio roof. The fall would hurt him, maybe even break a bone or two. But it would not kill him.

He would lie there in pain, looking at me, standing there below, and I would smile at him in his agony and then walk away. Later, he would call the police and say I had pushed the ladder over, and they would hunt me down. I don't doubt that. But I will go into the sea tonight. So it does not matter. And I would like to see him writhing in pain so much.

But then I wonder, if he comes back as far this way and leans like that to the right, over the patio, and falls off, he might well land on his head on the concrete slabs below. And it would kill him outright. And that will open up all sorts of delicious opportunities for me.

I could phone Pippa: "Pippa, Pippa, come quickly! Oh my God, Peter's fallen off a ladder. I've called the ambulance, yes. Be quick, Pippa, come quickly!"

She would race back. And I would be here to console her. To move into the house to be her support, her best friend and, at some point, perhaps even her lover. I can see it all now in my imagination. And it looks perfect to me.

I gaze around as he wipes away, checking the houses to either side, seeing if any windows are open and listening for anyone in their gardens. But the windows are shut, and no one is outside on this dreary day.

He is oblivious to me. I turn my back on him and look towards the end of the garden, where a line of conifers provides privacy between the houses. I turn around and look up at him again. He still has not seen me. Nobody will see or hear anything if he falls.

If — when — he leans too far the right, stretching to rub the smut from the far corner of the window, he will be most at risk of falling onto the slabs of the patio. Off-balance and not hearing anything or anyone around him. Not noticing little old me.

I wait. I am a patient woman. Good things come to those who wait. All good things will come to me. Pippa will be mine.

He suddenly leans across to the right. I hear him grunt, straining to get that cloth into the furthest corner of the window to rub it clean. I step forward and to the side.

I pull the bottom of the ladder with all my might to the left. There is a split second's silence. I step further aside. He cries out and plummets headfirst onto the concrete slabs below. The ladder spins and crashes, landing next to him, beside his leaking body, I muffle my laughter.

I stand there in the silence for ages, waiting to see if there is any response, a calling out, a sudden movement from the houses to either side, or further away, to the front of the house. If there is, I will go into the studio, put on my earphones and pretend to be asleep.

But there are no sounds. He — the husband — lies there unmoving, and I smile to myself, reminded suddenly of the Humpty Dumpty poem we learned at school. 'Humpty Dumpty had a great fall. All the king's horses and all the king's men. Couldn't put Humpty together again.' He is dead, and stuff oozes from his nose and mouth.

It's a funny thing, killing someone. You never quite know how it will go. This was perfect. He never knew I was there. Did not see it coming. I would have liked him to. If I could be sure he would die. But of course, I could not be 100 per cent certain. I have, of course, killed before. Twice that I have written about. But never quite as perfect, as satisfying, as this. And, of course, it might just change my life forever.

15

MONDAY, 28 NOVEMBER, MID-AFTERNOON

Today is my birthday, and it is just the happiest day of my life. So far! I think there is a lot more to come later on. A lifetime of happy days.

We — dear Pippa and I — are on a boat trip on the River Orwell from Ipswich to Harwich. It's some sort of pre-Christmassy, jazz-and-drinks thing. Weather permitting, I suppose! And it is fine today.

We are having drinks on board. And chatting away to our hearts' content. Pippa is giddy — I think she is on and off medication since the husband's death. Sometimes she is desolate, other times delightful. Like today. Ding ding. All change.

She has dyed her hair dark and done something with her eyebrows so that they match and are a little like mine. It's something of a fresh start for her. And me, of course!

It was a complete surprise to me, this smashing treat. Pippa knocked on my bedroom door just after eight am and came through with a tray: croissants smothered in butter, just the way I like them, a cafetiere of my favourite coffee, a glass of freshly squeezed orange juice from our new machine and a bowl of her speciality, a granola-yoghurt mix. She leaned forward and kissed me on my proffered cheek and then said, "I have to pop to work for a couple of hours. Have a lazy morning ... but be ready for me to pick you up in the car at noon!" And then she fluttered away.

I had such a lovely time. I ate my breakfast, lay on my bed for a while, dreaming about Pippa, and then I had a leisurely bath and a hair wash. I dried my hair sitting at Pippa's dressing table, using her new hairdryer. I got dressed and looked through her wardrobe and chose a beautiful scarf to go with my own clothes; my wardrobe has expanded quickly in recent weeks with all sorts of gorgeous presents from Pippa. I've helped myself to this and that too.

Then Pippa texted, 'Be outside in 20!' And I was standing on the pavement, nervous and excited, as the car pulled up alongside me. "Jump in!" she shouted, winding down the window.

As we drove along, she gave me three guesses where we were going. The implication being that if I did not guess correctly, we would turn back. Ridiculous, of course. I played along happily enough though. "Give me a clue!" I said. "Um," she replied hopelessly. "Er, we start and finish by the waterfront." I knew immediately that it was going to be a boat trip; it could be nothing else. But I played dumb, and Pippa got more and more excited, especially when I asked for extra guesses. I got it on the fifth guess, and she clapped the steering wheel with delight.

The outgoing part of the boat trip has a commentary about the sights along the way. Pippa, who is a good, if rather cruel, mimic, gets the commentator off just so, but makes his self-important voice even more pompous as she adds funny comments.

Some silly old man with his camera around his neck, alone and listening to the commentator so seriously, tuts and hushes Pippa and me as we keep laughing between ourselves. We both have pre-lunch glasses of Prosecco, and they add to our merriment.

Then the boat stops — drops anchor or something — and we go up top to see Felixstowe Port on one side and the town of Harwich to the other. I think, given the time of year, this little trip — jazz and drinks — was meant to be held inside, but we are so lucky with the weather today. We move to the outside back of the boat, whatever that is called.

Pippa, loud enough for me to hear but nobody else, then starts giving me a running commentary of what she sees, in the deep voice of an old dog of a sea captain. It's all 'oo-arr, me hearty!' and 'splice the main brace.' Nonsense, of course. But it amuses me, and my laughter spurs her on to greater excesses. She puts her glass of Prosecco on the floor, picks up a boat hook from underneath a seat and starts jabbing at me. "You'll walk the gangplank!"

I adore you, Pippa. I don't say it to her out loud. It's what I think in my head. I've known it since I first met her. But now, in this silly moment when she is showing me such affection, I am overwhelmed by my feelings. I want you, Pippa. I want to spend my life with you. These thoughts bring me close to sobbing.

Then the silly old man with the camera is tutting again, being affronted on behalf of everyone else, whether they have noticed Pippa or not. He alerts two of the crew, who come across to us and ask Pippa to put the boat hook back. "Sorry, sorry, sorry," she goes, and then accidentally treads on her glass of Prosecco. One of the crew members clears it away whilst another fetches her a fresh glass. I put my arm around Pippa and guide her back to our seats inside.

The return part of the boat trip doesn't have a commentary. The captain announces over the tannoy that all the passengers are invited to relax and enjoy the cruise back. Jazz music is piped through. We are enjoying ourselves, Pippa and I, and it is glorious. I have never felt such warmth, so much love, in my life. Never. Ever. Ever.

Pippa sits next to me, her head on my shoulder, holding my hand. Such a beautiful and precious moment between us. It is perfect. Other than the old man with his camera giving us dirty looks from time to time. Like we should sit up and well apart! I smile broadly to annoy the prudish fool.

Then the boat docks and rocks wildly as we are getting off. Pippa goes first, in front of me, and seems terribly nervous. I put my hands around her waist to steady her, and that seems to calm her. We go and sit over at a nearby bar and share a half bottle of house red and watch the world go by. Funnily enough, this is where I saw the husband and the young female student. The car park is behind us. I can't help smiling to myself at the way things have turned out.

I let Pippa drink most of the wine. I think she is now ever-so-slightly tiddly. I beckon the waiter across and order a black coffee, giving him enough coins to cover it. I then hold Pippa's hand again, as though it is a perfectly natural thing to do. We relax a while. Then she sits up, her head rolling back with a jolt as if she has just woken up. She looks around, startled, and takes her hand away to lift and finish her glass of wine.

"What would I do without you, Sharon?" she says suddenly, her voice catching a little. "Everyone's gone," she adds sadly, and then repeats herself. "They've all gone and left me except you."

She thinks for a moment, swirling the wine around in her glass. "Mummy ... Daddy ... Pete, poor Pete ... whenever will they hold the, you know, the coroner's thing?"

I jump in before she becomes too maudlin and starts getting on my nerves. It's only been these past few days that she's seemed to have moved on from all of it: moping about the husband and how everything is in limbo until the coroner has dealt with matters. "Here's your coffee," I say as the waiter puts the cup on the table. We sit for ages. She sips at it, pulls an ugh face, and plonks it back down on the table. "Too bitter," she says.

"Come on then, let's be having you," I reply cheerfully, getting to my feet and reaching across to help her up.

I drive the car home, something I am doing more and more now, as I come into my own, taking charge of things, becoming the person I always wanted to be.

I will be with Pippa. Just her and me. Together forever and ever. I think it is meant to be. We will become lovers soon.

I am happy that, by and large, Pippa has moved on from the dead husband. The dirty boy and the stupid Elaine aren't around either, of course. They have all gone. It is just Pippa and me now.

I AM HAVING a lie-down on my bed in my room before we eat our evening meal. My birthday meal! After I came down-stairs after my usual, early evening bath, Pippa shooed me back upstairs, flapping cheekily at my bottom with a tea towel!

I think she is now drifting about indecisively for ages before eventually making something simple in her wok. Noodles and stuff. It is about all she can manage. Even then, the tea towel will probably get burned, and something will be dropped on the floor. "Five-second rule!" she'll shout, shovelling it back up.

Lying here, I think I need to nudge her again to give all of the dead husband's clothes from the wardrobe to charity. "You'll feel better!" I've said several times. "I know, I know," she replies, and, lately, "I will, I will." I want it done soon. It then gives me a better chance of moving into her room.

The husband dying is the best thing that has happened for me in my life. And it was a spur-of-the-moment thing!

Killing someone is not an easy thing to do. Planning it is so hard, so many things to consider; there are endless ifs, buts and maybes.

Doing it in the moment, without thinking ahead, is easier in a way. But then the niggling worries set in, dire thoughts that a mistake may have been made that will lead to exposure.

I worried and worried I had overlooked something with the husband, but it has all unfolded beautifully.

When I was sure he was dead on the patio, I slipped away and got the bus to Ipswich, where I did some window-shopping for the day. I tried to stay calm, although my stomach churned right through until I came back home. I returned late, noticing that Pippa's car was back on the driveway. I guessed — correctly, as it happened — that the boy had come back from playing football, had discovered Dead Dad and had phoned poor Pippa.

I slipped into the extension and spent my usual quiet evening, as if everything were perfectly normal. I ate my supermarket half-price sandwich (dry) and slice of cake (moist and fruity) and read a book. A Graham Greene, *The Tenth Man* (dusty), which I last read at school. I got it from a charity shop in town where none of the staff ever watch what's going on around them. I waited for Pippa to come to me that night. But she did not. I felt cheated in some way. I had been so looking forward to it.

She came in the next morning though, tapping quietly on the door and entering and telling me what had happened in a peculiar, strangulated voice. I gasped as if surprised — shocked — and said I was so, so sorry; I had been in Ipswich all day. I hugged her, a lifeless dummy, and watched her walk away, all crushed and broken.

I lay low for a while, through all that happens when something like this occurs. Police came and went. So did various official-looking people in grand cars. Pippa had to go out to register this and talk about that. There were interviews, I guess. I kept watch as best I could, walking outside from time to time, monitoring what was going on. I did not go inside the house, though. I kept out of it.

There will be some sort of hearing, with a coroner or someone, down the line. A formality, I suppose, followed by a story in the newspaper about people falling off ladders. I don't know. I don't really care. I'm not that bothered. I did not want anyone to notice me. And they did not. I kept my head down. It was as if I did not exist.

After a while, Pippa started checking on me as she had previously been doing, mornings and evenings, and I was as warm and friendly as I could be. Early on, she looked stunned. Wandering around as though in a trance. I was patient with her.

The husband's body was released, and then there was the funeral, where she clung to the dirty boy as if she were going to fall over. I knew nobody else there other than stupid Elaine, with whom I exchanged a few pleasantries, to be polite. Back home afterwards, the place was full of strangers. Pippa hugged me long and hard at the end. I knew then that I had got away with it, and everything good — so wonderful — lay before me.

And now I am here, waiting for Pippa to call me downstairs for our evening meal. We will sit at either end of the dining room table, facing each other. She will light a candle between us, saying it is romantic. She does not mean it that way; she just likes the flickering lights and the shadows. Pippa does not see me like that, not yet anyway, but our friendship has grown since that proper hug at the funeral. And it will grow ever further.

Once I knew I was safe from exposure, I started to go inside again to use the cloakroom and the bathroom, making myself more visible. Patting the dog, and for longer than I normally would. I'd ask Pippa how she was, and sometimes she would want to talk, and I would stop and listen. Then she'd come out and check on me more, lingering a while. And I'd be invited in now and again, and then more regularly.

Of course, it wasn't until the dirty boy and dumb Elaine had gone that I really came into my own, consoling and cajoling Pippa until I was fully ensconced in the house. Pippa is a woman who needs taking in hand and looking after. And that is what I have done. And everything is now just so and perfect. As she calls me downstairs, I suddenly wonder if she will have presents for me and what they will be. Something lovely, I'm sure. I'd expect nothing less.

As I walk into the dining room, with my carefully brushed hair, freshly applied lipstick and wearing clean and ironed clothes, I could almost weep with joy.

It's not the champagne flutes placed carefully next to the bottle of bubbly nor the three candles alight in the silver candlestick; I am already used to the luxury and wealth in this house. My home.

It is what is on my placemat: a cream-coloured envelope with *Sharon* written on it and a heart drawn next to my name. There are two presents there — small and dainty boxes covered with silver wrapping paper and bows. Classy presents, not some clunky box of cheap supermarket chocolates in saved and reused wrapping paper.

I sit, struggling with my emotions, my love for Pippa, as I hear her moving about the kitchen. There are clatterings and crashes as usual, but I resist the temptation to go in unless something catches fire and sets the alarms off.

Then she is coming into the room, carrying two plates. I look at her, my eyes brimming with tears, and smile. "Oh you!" she says, seeing my expression.

"Hot, hot, hot!" She slides the plates piled high with noodles and things onto our respective placemats. She sits down opposite me.

"Oh, Sharon," she says, looking at me and sounding emotional. "Come here." Before I can get up, she is on her feet and around the table, her arms opening wide to embrace me.

She hugs me tight, my face, at this height, pulled between her breasts. I breathe in the sweet smell of her skin, a dash of perfume from her neck. I put my arms around her, in the small of her back, and I am in heaven.

I snuffle and shake my head slightly, feeling the swell of her breasts at either side. It is all I can do to stop myself sliding my hands down from her back. But if I misjudge the moment, I might lose everything I have: my life here, my friendship with Pippa, our love.

She lets go, returning to her seat and sitting down, smiling so warmly at me. I don't think she has even noticed the closeness of our bodies, not like that, anyway. She is not aware of my feelings of desire. I don't think it would even cross her mind, such a thing.

"It should be me thanking you for everything!" she says, her voice full of gratitude and love. "Peter. The funeral. Waiting for the coroner. Where would I be without you by my side?"

She reaches across and takes my hands. She looks into my eyes, and I wonder if she is going to tell me she loves me. If she does, I think my heart will burst.

But she releases my hands and gestures to the card and presents in front of me. "For you, my darling Sharon."

I open them. The card, home-made, folded cardboard, sweet and simple, with a candle in a cupcake sketched a little inexpertly on the front. Inside:

Happy Birthday Sharon, Thank you for everything, Love Pippa x.

A nice card, although I might have hoped for more: *All my love.*

I then unwrap the two beautifully wrapped presents, and my heart breaks. The first, what must be an antique pair of earrings . Pearls, real pearls! The second, a matching, oh-so delicate necklace. These must be symbols of love. Our love, surely?

"I saw them in a darling little jeweller's in Bury St Edmunds," she says as she sees me drop my head and weep my tears of joy. "I thought of you straightaway. They are just perfect." I wonder if she will come and hug me again. She does not. I smile and nod and wipe my eyes.

Then, just as we are about to start eating, she gets up and comes back to me, lifting the beautiful earrings and standing there as I take my cheap old earrings out and slip them into a pocket. My hands tremble.

I put them in, my wonderful new earrings, and then Pippa reaches out and takes the necklace from the box and lays it gently around my neck, fixing the clasp at the back. Her touch feels so sensuous. I hold my breath, wishing she would stroke my neck.

But she steps away and looks at me. I feel suddenly that I am old and ugly. But not to Pippa, who gazes at me and my earrings and necklace and gasps out the word 'delightful.' And I blush and feel so happy.

We work our way through our meal. A main course of noodles, mushrooms and other vegetables, and a sweet chili sauce. Student fare, really. But hot and tasty. We look at each other now and then and talk of silly things.

Our dessert comes out of a supermarket packet — a tiramisu, which she mispronounces slightly, 'tiramirasu,' and I laugh. She asks why, and I tell her and offer the proper pronunciation. We chuckle together. Pippa repeats the word several times as we eat, and we smile and laugh time and again.

And then we have coffees, nice, milky coffees using her top-of-the-range machine. And we have a box of chocolate mints, freshly opened, that we work our way through. And it is bliss, utter bliss, and I really don't think things could get any better.

But, incredibly, they do. As we finish our coffees and put the box of chocolates to the side — one last one for each of us! — she reaches down and pulls out what looks like a bundle of holiday brochures from her bag. I see, as she puts them on the table, that they are print-offs of various website pages.

"I've always wanted to go on the Orient Express ... and to New York ... to Venice, too. And to spend the winters in Florida," she says as I clamp my hand to my mouth in anticipation. "Peter wasn't much of a traveller. And Dom wasn't keen. I've always wanted a companion. So next year, we'll go to all of these places together."

Pippa pushes the pages across the table to me, and I fight back more tears of joy as I flick through them. There are other pages, suggesting more places to visit, perhaps the year after — the Taj Mahal, the pyramids of Egypt and Jerusalem. I cry as I get up and walk towards Pippa, and we hug long and hard. I say, "Thank you," over and again.

Later, after we sat and listened to music and kissed each other chastely good night, we went to bed. And I lay awake for ever such a while, thinking my thoughts and enjoying my pleasures, knowing that this is the perfect happiness I have been searching for throughout my life.

I have it all. Pippa, my dearest friend. A beautiful home. Time and space to enjoy reading and listening to music.

Someone to look after me. To care for me financially. And so much to look forward to — lunches and days out and, now, trips abroad to all of the places I have dreamed of visiting, but have never been able to afford. The furthest I have been was a solo trip to the lochs of Scotland on a wet and miserable four-day coach trip, years ago. The man next to me was sick on my shoes. Inside my shoes, actually. I could feel the sticky mess between my toes.

Yes, I have everything. Almost. I don't share Pippa's bed. I do not kiss her as I would like to do. I cannot wrap my arms around her at night. I cannot stroke her face, her arms, her neck, her breasts, her legs. I cannot slide my hand, my fingers, between her legs. But I will do all of this. And more. Soon. Very soon.

16

TUESDAY, 29 NOVEMBER, THE MORNING

P ippa is at work all day today, and I am alone. In times gone by, a long and empty day stretching ahead of me would have seen my spirits plummet.

But not now. Not when these are the happiest days of my life and will only get better and better and better. Such days of joy and wonder!

After a lazy morning at home — a leisurely lie-in, a warm frothy bath and a continental breakfast — I make my way out of the house for a stroll around town. I am going to Elaine's house first.

Elaine is out of our lives. But I have not killed her. I did not need to. I did think long and hard about it for so long. So many mouth-watering ideas! But there was no obviously easy way to get rid of the stupid lump and — more importantly — to get away with it. I thought of at least a dozen ideas, but not one of them was sure to succeed.

My favourite was going to her house, late one night, knocking on the door and saying I had an important message from Pippa. She'd let me in, all worried and anxious. As she led the way, hurrying to the living room, I'd slip on my gloves, pick up something heavy like a table lamp and bludgeon her to death with it.

I quite liked the idea of hitting her in the face over and again with a hot iron, but thought this would be hard to do in practice. However I killed her, I would make it look like a botched robbery by a young thug, but felt that everything — her blood on me, my DNA on her, neighbours at their windows, CCTV — all made it so hard to be sure I'd not be uncovered. And, of course, I have much to lose — Pippa and my new life of luxury.

There was a spur-of-the-moment instant when I did come close to it. Pippa had scribbled a handful of thank-you notes after the funeral to local people who had written to her about the dead husband. She posted some to those people who live out of town, but asked me, the day she started back at work, to drop a few through the appropriate doors in Felixstowe. Book club folk. One for May. Another for dreadful Alan. The last one for Elaine.

I put the notes for May and Alan through their letter boxes — I did not want to stop and speak to them after what had happened at the last book club evening. But I went to Elaine's with the idea of handing over her note face-to-face, making a few comments about how I was now living with Pippa and we were best friends forever. I wanted to see the expression on Elaine's bovine face.

There was no answer to my knocking on her front door, so I went round the back and through the gate. Elaine was there on her patio, turned away from me, talking to her cat beyond her feet. As you do. I went to pick up a heavy-looking plant pot to cave in her head when — to my horror — a woman on the other side of Elaine, hidden by Elaine's great blubbering mass, suddenly began speaking. It was Moira from the book club. Elaine had not been talking to her cat. I simply thrust the note into her hands as she turned towards me, ignored Moira, and walked away.

As it happened, I did not need to kill Elaine to loosen her friendship with my beloved Pippa. Soon after I had dropped the thank-you note round, she turned up on our doorstep. I ignored the ting-a-linging bell and made myself scarce when Pippa went to the door and I realised who it was. I listened, from the top of the stairs, to Elaine's grating voice telling Pippa that she was going on a winter cruise, to Iceland, Norway and so on.

This 'trip of a lifetime,' as she put it, was something she and her husband had always planned to do on their twenty-fifth wedding anniversary. It would have been this year had he not died several years ago. She goes alone, as they did not have children. She has an inside-out womb or some such. And she has no real friends, as she does not work, never has done, and lives carefully — other than this trip — off his life insurance payouts. I think he fell off a crane or got his fat head trapped in machinery at work — something stupid, anyway — and, that being the cause of his death, there was a further payout.

And so Elaine has gone away. Pippa was put out, but did not like to say anything negative about Elaine to me — but I could see from her face she was disappointed and felt let down. Perhaps that she was not invited on the cruise. And maybe because Elaine did not hug or make a fuss of her. Whatever the cause, I could tell that this was the end of the friendship between Pippa and Elaine. If Elaine turns up again after her cruise, I am sure Pippa will send her packing. If not, I will get rid of her permanently. Since her departure,

I have come up with a plan, a fine-tuned version of an earlier one.

Meantime, here and now on my way to town, I let myself into Elaine's house with a key she gave to Pippa. She asked Pippa if she'd pop in twice a day to feed the cat. Well, if it were left to Pippa, the cat would starve to death. So I have been doing it. I love cats. Dogs. All animals, really. I would not hurt one.

I go in and have a look around, pocket an apple corer with a ceramic handle that takes my fancy at the back of a kitchen drawer, and knock over another expensive-looking ornament. There will be few left, if any, by the time Elaine returns. And the cat will be blamed for that.

Before Elaine comes back, I might borrow Pippa's car and take the cat in a cardboard box and dump it outside the Blue Cross centre in Ipswich or maybe further afield. It's a pretty thing, and someone will take it. But Elaine will be bereft. Welcome home, Elaine; welcome home.

I ARRIVE BACK HOME at lunchtime after a wander around the town. I bought myself a slice of quiche from the delicatessen, a newspaper and a bottle of fizz and a chocolatey dessert from the supermarket, and a loaf of fresh bread from the bakery. I have more money these days, now I am with Pippa.

Two surprises await me. One is a beautiful bouquet of flowers on the doorstep for me from Pippa. The note reads:

I forgot birthday flowers! Love you, Pippa xxx.

A mix of flowers. A winter bouquet, it is called. I hurry in to put them into a vase of water.

After that, I double back to the doormat for the post. I examine the four envelopes addressed to Pippa: two bills by the look of them, and two invites to spas. We will have a spa day soon. I have never had one, but it would be nice if someone were to scrape all the hard, dead skin off my heels. For me, post-wise, there is one envelope containing a credit card in my name for Pippa's account. I was expecting it.

I take plates and a glass and a knife, fork and spoon from kitchen cupboards, arrange my lunch, and then go and sit by the front window in the lounge (as Pippa corrects me whenever I say 'living room'), looking out into the bright sunshine. Such joy!

Not only do I have a lovely home, everything I could want in terms of clothes, food, drink, and luxuries too, but I now have spending money of my own. Pippa had mentioned a few days ago that she would get me a credit card on her account, in case I needed it. "So you don't run short!" she said. I look at it endlessly. I have never had one before, given my hand-to-mouth existence all my life.

I want a little runaround car of my own. I had hoped, and did hint, that I would like the dead husband's car to come to me. But she took it into Ipswich and sold it just after his funeral. Like she could not get rid of it fast enough. I imagined she had visions of her husband having sex with the student on the back seat.

I would also like more clothes of my own, a proper, four-seasons wardrobe. Not just odd gifts from Pippa and random borrowings from her wardrobe. I wonder if I can have all of that with this card.

I glance up, out into the road, and see a young, ginger-bearded policeman, an old-fashioned bobby on the beat, going from door-to-door, knocking. I stand up to see.

My mouth feels dry as I watch him go up one side of the road, talking to whoever answers their doors, and then moving on to the next house.

I think suddenly of the landlord's son, my notes and desk diary that he has read, and wonder if he has alerted the police, if they are now looking for me. Irrational though it is, I feel a stab of alarm. It is nonsense, but I cannot suppress the feeling.

The policeman is now crossing the road, up at the top, coming over and starting to work his way down this side. He will be at my door in minutes. I look at the dog in its basket, hoping it will not bark so that the policeman starts peering through the window.

If the landlord's son has talked, it would surely be passed to a detective. But they might ask the local police to knock door-to-door like this, with an old photograph of me (with Monica) from my belongings.

"Have you seen this woman?" the ginger-bearded policeman may be asking, door-to-door and also up the town, all over Felixstowe, really. Perhaps I dare not go out anymore.

He is now coming up the driveway, noticing me, or at least my sudden movement, as I pull back from the window. He knocks on the door and then calls out, cheerfully enough, "Hello, Hello?" as though he has spotted me. Like we are playing a game. The dog lifts its head, then lies back down, ready to sleep.

I stand here, out of sight unless he comes up close and peers through the window. I am sweating now and holding my breath. "Hell-oo-oo," he says again, louder, as though he knows I am there and that we are playing hide-and-seek.

I wait an age in the ever-extending silence. Him there. Me here. And then, as quickly as he arrived, he has gone on to the next house. And I sigh and feel fearful, unsure if I am being prescient or paranoid.

I settle back down after a while, doing some of my calming, breathing exercises, and then begin to eat my lunch, although I have mostly lost my taste for it. My mind, the rational part of it, goes through all the ifs, buts and maybes of writing notes and a diary and leaving them with my belongings at the flat. It never struck me that anyone would ever read them, let alone the landlord's son. I had so much on my mind when I left. And since.

I think he went through my things in a malicious way, expecting me to have a few sentimental trinkets of value that he could steal from me. To take his revenge, as he'd see it. But I have nothing like that. I have always been so careful and frugal, living my life out of two suitcases — one for each hand — ready to move on at a moment's notice. Habit, I suppose, ingrained over decades of misery. I imagine him gasping as he opened and read the key parts of my notes and diary.

I know men like that. I understand their hard and callous hearts. He will have taken photographs of what I wrote 'just in case' before tipping it, and everything else, into a skip. He has the photographs to show if I make a nuisance in any way: if I took him to court, for example. Otherwise, he'd leave it be — he'd not want to waste his time on it. So the policeman's visit is neither here nor there. A new bobby on the beat, introducing himself, most probably.

I spend the rest of the afternoon in a better, upbeat

mood. I have a tidy and a dust and a polish around and a vacuum, too. I don't spend long on this, as Pippa never notices anything. I think they had a cleaner in London, and she now assumes everything is somehow done by magic. She only notices if she cannot find something that should be immediately to hand. She's always losing her phone. And making me laugh, "Where's the toilet paper?" she'll howl. I hurry in and hand her a roll. Often, she is sitting there crouched forward naked, soon to get into the bath. To her, nakedness is neither here nor there. It's a pleasure for me.

Then I sit on the sofa and do a little Amazon shopping — Pippa has given me her Amazon Prime log-in details. I buy myself a faux-fur hat and matching scarf for when I go out and about, up the town. They will keep me warm and protect my privacy so I can move about, minding my own business. I buy some new underwear and one or two personal items relating to my undercarriage and feet. I spend £127, but I am sure Pippa won't mind.

I then go and lie back on my bed for an hour or two's sleep and pleasuring before Pippa returns home. She texts me as she leaves work on the dot of five o'clock: 'Need anything?' she writes. 'Stopping at Sainsbury's x.'

All I want, Pippa, I think, is for you to come straight home and get into bed with me. But that will come, I think. Not so long now. I have planned it all out. For now, I text, 'I'm happy. Hurry home. X'

I SPENT a lovely evening with Pippa. We made a spaghetti Bolognese together, hugging each other now and then for no reason other than it felt nice. We ate our dinner by candlelight, talking over our respective days. Pippa is attentive to me. We watched a murder mystery — a true crime drama — on Netflix and went to bed.

I think it was the wrong thing to watch, really, although Pippa chose it. She seemed to be withdrawn, turning in on herself and not doing what she usually does when we watch television: calling out inconsistencies, repeating key phrases and impersonating any characters with strong accents. I thought it was because she was thinking of Dead Pete.

It was as we were heading for the stairs and I was about to implement my plan for sharing a bed together for the first time, tonight, that she said, suddenly and quite unexpectedly, "I miss Dom." I did not know what to reply to this, so I hugged her, but she was all stiff and tense and tearful. So ungrateful for my warm-hearted gesture. I soon let go, and she brushed by me, whispering, "I'm sorry ... I'll be better in the morning." And so we went to our separate beds. I lie there, thinking things over.

I did not kill Dominic, the dirty boy. As with Elaine, I thought about it long and hard. And there were moments, especially after the funeral, when Pippa and the boy hung on so desperately to each other, such an irritating thing to see, that I could have done it quite cheerfully, given the chance.

As he moved about the house, drinking water straight from the kitchen tap, dropping his dirty tee shirts and pants in front of the washing machine, he seemed to get in my way at every turn. I could have taken him by surprise so easily, several times, bashing his brains out from behind with any manner of heavy household objects. But I held back at the last moment.

I knew I could only really kill him if it would look like an

accident. I daydreamed about it. I went into his bedroom
once, asked by Pippa to collect his laundry — pants and
socks, ugh — and his window was wide open. I imagined
calling him across to show him a bird on a tree, and then
pushing him out. I even followed him to school twice in
Pippa's car when she was lying in bed grieving. I waited for
him to cross the road without looking. He did once, but
there were too many people around. I dreamed of doing it,
though.

The truth is, I could not quite bring myself to. She would
have been devastated if the boy was killed. I know that. The
unbreakable bond of a mother and child is so different from
a relationship with a cheating husband. I am not stupid. She
would have been beyond inconsolable. It would have
destroyed our love before it even started.

And I knew the boy would be leaving anyway to university after his A Levels. Somewhere far away, with brief
returns to begin with during holidays. Then a part-time job,
new friends, perhaps even a serious girlfriend, keeping him
there during holidays. And finally, a full-time job somewhere, anywhere, and a new life far from here. I just had to
bide my time.

I realised, though, that sometime, somehow, I would
have to address the matter of his existence. That if Pippa
were to die unexpectedly, everything — the house, her
savings, her belongings — would all go to him. And I would
be out on the streets, back where I started all those years ago,
but now an old and vulnerable woman. I would, at some
stage, when we were lovers, ask her to make some provision
for me in her will. So that I would be safe. And the dirty boy
could live.

But then, after the funeral, an opportunity arose

whereby the boy might leave earlier almost straightaway. Peter's two brothers — the builders from south London — got into conversation with him, just within earshot of me, saying that if he ever wanted a 'change of scene,' they were always looking for a good apprentice. There was talk of money and becoming a partner, eventually, and the attractions of the bright lights of London. If West Norwood, Sutton and Croydon have such things.

I thought nothing much of it at the time — it was the sort of conversation you hear amongst far-apart relatives at funerals. But later, Pippa mentioned that her brothers-in-law had been texting her, asking if the dirty boy might want to come down and 'join the business.' She pulled a face, obviously preferring that he would stay with her — us — and complete his A Levels and go to university. But they'd obviously been texting him as well, as she said he kept badgering her about it. I decided to help him on his way.

One afternoon, when Pippa was at work and he was in his bedroom doing whatever dirty boys do, I clattered the letterbox and threw my photographs of him with the younger boy on the mat. I waited. He did not come down. I went upstairs and knocked on his door. He shouted, "What?" aggressively. I went in, handing him the photos, saying, "A man, looked like a teacher, just put these through the door for you."

I then walked out and away up the town. By the time I got back, he had gone, leaving a note for Pippa, stating he'd gone to stay with his Uncle James. She sobbed, but not for long. Whether the photographs did the trick or not, I am unsure. He may have been going anyway.

And then, just as I am about to snuggle down and go to sleep, there is a tapping at my door. Before I can call out,

Pippa opens it and stands there in her see-through negligee, hesitating. I swallow and am about to say something welcoming when she takes three, four, five steps to the bed, pulls back the duvet, and slips in alongside me.

I can scarcely breathe at this sudden turn of events. I had planned so carefully how we would spend the night together, and now here she is anyway. I lie here, waiting to see what she says and does next. I would be thrilled, for tonight, to have a cuddle and then to fall asleep together, my arm around her waist.

"I've been texting Dom," she says, like I want to hear. "He's well and happy, and Chris and James have offered him a job, a proper one." I hesitate. Then she adds, in a slightly wistful voice, "So that's good, isn't it?" It sounds more like a question than a statement.

Then, to my utter disappointment, she is up and out of my bed, leaving. "We need to get a good night's sleep. I've taken the day off. We're going out at nine am. My treat!" And then she is gone, just as quickly as she came. And I feel cheated in some way.

17

THURSDAY, 1 DECEMBER, EARLY MORNING

I am lying on my new, queen-sized bed in what was the spare room, but is now my very own bedroom. I am so happy. Just another of so many happy moments in my life. It's all been such a surprise.

The bed is luxurious, as is the furniture: a wardrobe, a chest of drawers, a dressing table, a mirror and furnishings — all new and top of the range. I've never had either before.

Pippa has made everything so nice and beautiful for me. She even got someone to paint, in delicate lettering, 'Sharon' on the door. It is a measure of how she feels about me, and an indication of my permanence in her life. How clever Pippa has been to arrange this.

We went out for the day yesterday. The weather was cold and crisp, but sunny. We took a stroll through Framlingham and then had lunch in ever such a pretty café, followed by a visit to the castle and a walk around the moat.

Pippa hurried me out of the house just after nine am, which was not like her, although I never suspected a thing.

And she kept looking at her watch after we'd been round the moat. "Let's do it again!" she cried. It never crossed my mind that anything was out of the ordinary, let alone that there were people at the house transforming this room — my room — for me.

When we returned, I still didn't catch on, even though there was a delicious smell in the air — fresh wood and clean linen and lavender. Pippa beckoned me to come upstairs, made me shut my eyes and led me to the bedroom door. I cried when I saw what had been done.

As I lie here now, the next morning, my mind is full of such joy. I cannot help but contrast my current, beautiful life with the horrors I have endured over the years. My earliest memory is sitting up in a cot in the corner of my mother's bedroom and being told repeatedly to turn away and go to sleep when she had a dirty man in the room. That memory, and everything that followed from it, has haunted me all my life.

Through adulthood, there has been a succession of mostly single beds in dreary rooms and bedsits, with damp in the air and mould on the walls. The pillows and duvets were always cheap and faded — second-hand and stained, as often as not. The dirty mattresses sagged in the middle. I always dreamed of a nice, clean, proper bed. What I have now is beyond my dreams.

In hostels, I lay on thin mattresses over hard metal, listening to shouts and shrieks all around me. I kept one eye ever open, awaiting an attack. I have spent time in hospitals, now and then. It was quieter there, although the risk of attack was ever greater. I have been beaten and cut at times; nobody in authority much cared. And now I have all this. I am safe at last.

We had a lovely evening last night, cheese on toast and a shared bottle of cider on trays on our laps. We binge-watched *Pride & Prejudice* on the television, and then we made our way to our bedrooms, Pippa kissing me on the cheek at my door. I hugged her long and hard.

Pippa is out this morning, until lunchtime, covering for a colleague who is off sick from the boutique in Ipswich. She has said she will be back by two pm and we can have lunch together. She will 'get some little treats' for us from the delicatessen three doors down from the boutique.

We will have a wonderful afternoon together. I can't stop crying tears of joy. I feel I am at home. At last. I am where I have always wanted to be. I lie back and relax.

I feel loved by Pippa. I have had very little of that in my life. My mother was a monstrous woman who offered me out to men when I was little more than a child. I had three or four fumbling relationships through my late teens and into my early twenties, all with women of my own age, give or take, but they all came to nothing. It was harder in those days, of course, to be out in the open about such matters.

Later, there were proper relationships, always with women, of course, but none of them stayed around for long. I had such anger management issues. I don't want to talk about them nor how they ended so badly. It was only with Monica that I enjoyed a long relationship, but even that soured eventually. And she died too. Other than Monica, there has been no one since; just a failed attempt with Patricia.

I do yearn to be with Pippa. Properly. As lovers. It is not just the sexual act that I crave. It is more than that. I want the physical intimacy of holding her in my arms at night, our bodies snuggled up together. I want to kiss her awake in the morning and last thing at night. I want to rest my head on her shoulder, watching television in the evening. I want to share a bath, washing her back and her scrubbing mine. And be together in every single way.

I lie here now, soft and clean in my silk pyjamas, sighing with delight. Eventually, I twist and turn in ecstasy. And then I lie still for ever such a while. Such bliss.

My mind, as it always does, soon turns to other thoughts and worries, the beauty of the moment spoiled by ideas of what might happen next.

I feel I am where I should be. That this is my home, my room, my own special place. But I must plan for the future. I want Pippa as my lover, my life partner. I want to live here with her for the rest of my life. I must have a plan.

———

AS I LIE HERE, mulling over my plan, I hear Pippa's car on the driveway. She is back already, much earlier than expected.

I get up and off the bed, reaching for my dressing gown on the hook on the back of the door; and then I am at the window.

I smile and wave at Pippa as she gets out of the car, shuts the door and fiddles with her keys to lock it. She does not look up, but hurries into the house.

I walk quickly down the steps into the living room. I stand there on the wooden floor in my bare feet.

I am bewildered. I had expected her to be here, arms held high, a brown paper bag of deli delights in one hand and a bottle of bubbly in the other.

But she is in the kitchen, opening and shutting the fridge

and cupboard doors. I wait for her to come rushing out. "Surprise!" But she does not.

I follow her into the kitchen and watch her.

She is by the sink, looking down at two tablets dissolving and fizzing in a glass of water that she's just poured from the tap.

She tips her head back and drinks the mix in one go.

Then she turns and stares at me, and there is such a look on her face that I do not know what to say. I cannot make sense of her expression. Fear? Anger? I'm not sure.

I am holding my breath. I think suddenly it is all over. Pippa and me. She has somehow discovered something about me and the son ... or even, to my horror, the husband. And she is about to tell me so.

I do not know what I will do, where I will go. At best, I will be on the streets with no money. At worst, I will be in prison. I move my hand casually towards the block of knives on the side, thinking such a terrible thought.

"I'm pregnant," she blurts out, her eyes flicking this way and that.

I laugh. I cannot help myself. It is an instant reaction, that's all. I can't believe it.

Pippa does not really hear me. She is already turning away and putting the glass back by the sink.

"How?" I say. "Why?" I add foolishly. I move towards her, not sure what to do.

She shakes her head, exasperated, not by what I say, but because she is unexpectedly pregnant.

"We'd only done it twice in ages — just before he died ..." She stops, and I think she is going to cry. She goes on: "And another time, a few months ago ... when Pete and I were trying again ... ridiculous, really ... I haven't had a period since ... I assumed it was because of Pete ... and the worry with the coroner ... and Dom leaving, of course. I've had so much on my mind."

She comes towards me, and I wonder if I should hug her, just put my arms around her, pull her in, and kiss her on the cheek, maybe rest my head on her shoulder.

But she is distracted, brushing by and going to the sofa. She sits there and turns towards me, expecting me to sit down, too.

I sit opposite her. She is all tense and edgy, and I do not want to try to comfort her physically. Not yet, anyway.

"I never dreamed ..." she says. "But I've been feeling ... I don't know ... odd ... and Yaz at work was talking about this friend of hers who didn't know she was pregnant until she was six months gone. We both laughed."

She stops and gathers her breath. "Anyway, it set me thinking ... I went to the big Boots up by the Sailmakers Shopping Centre and got a test. Went into the toilets at Sainsbury's on the way home. And ... bingo. I can't believe it. I don't really look pregnant ... I didn't with Dom until quite late." She laughs, all teary and snotty.

"I'm afraid I forgot lunch ... what with one thing and another." She laughs again, looking at me for some sort of encouragement. I cannot tell if she is sad or happy. Either way, I am full of dread.

Even so, I get up and go towards her, hugging her and then sitting beside her. She holds my hands in hers in an absent-minded way. It is nice, though. Very nice indeed.

I do not know, I cannot tell in this instant, if she wants this baby or not. I do hope not. It would ruin everything for us.

I will encourage her to attend to the matter quickly without making it obvious this is my preference. My insistence, really. If she does not, I will have to do something about it. The baby must go. Simple as that. I can't be doing with a baby.

PART III

TWO'S COMPANY

18

FRIDAY, 2 DECEMBER, EARLY HOURS

Pippa taps gently on my bedroom door. As if to ask politely, Are you there, Sharon? May I come in?

I am awake due to my insomnia and running out of tablets a while ago; I have not gone back to my GP for more medication. I don't want to feel drowsy half the time, not now I'm with Pippa. I turn to look at the alarm clock on the bedside cabinet. It is 1.07am.

I know if I do not respond quickly, she will go away. I do not want that. I'd love her to come into my bedroom. And my bed. Just like she did the other night. It's what I've wanted all along. Just not quite like that, when she was up and gone so quickly. I clear my throat, calling back, "Yes?"

"I can't sleep," she says, now standing at the end of my bed in her negligee, all bare legs and arms. More than that. Her body is silhouetted against the light from the landing. She's barely showing, tummy-wise. I take a deep breath.

Then she says, "Can I get into bed with you?" I nod my head, unable to speak. A dream come true amidst this sudden nightmare.

"I can't stop thinking about the baby ... what to do," she says, moving forwards, pulling back the duvet and lying there beside me.

I can hardly breathe.

Her closeness fills me with such excitement.

I can smell the fragrance of her body.

Pippa has no idea, of course. How I feel. For her, I believe this is like lying next to your best friend in the dorm at boarding school. After lights out. Bedding pulled up and whispering sweet secrets to each other, maybe about a crush on a blond-haired boy they saw in town on Saturday afternoon.

Pippa tugs the duvet to her chin and then kind of wriggles in the bed. "That's better," she says, after jiggling the pillow and puffing it up beneath her head.

She reaches her hand across to me, and for an instant I think she is going to put her palm on my tummy or even my breast. But she pulls and pushes, tucking her arm between mine and my side.

I have dreamed of this moment. Something much like it, anyway. For so long.

Acted it out so many times.

Finding pleasure in my thoughts and release in my actions.

"What shall I do, Sharon, about the baby? I've hardly any tummy. I showed so late with Dominic," she asks, inclining her head onto my shoulder.

I swallow, not sure what to say, or even how to speak in this instant. Her comments give me hope. That she wants to get rid of it before anyone realises.

"I'm too old," she adds. "I'll be almost forty-one when the

baby's born. And it might be … you know." Down's syndrome, she means.

"What do you think? What do you want to do?" I ask. I know what I think. What I want her to do. Just get rid of the wretched thing. So that Pippa and I can live as best friends for the rest of my life, maybe something more.

I don't want a baby, a toddler, a child, in our lives. Screaming and soiling itself. Demanding attention. Always being there, fussed over, lifted up and cuddled by Pippa. I do not want that at all. I cannot say it out loud.

"You need to work through the pros and cons of having a baby," I say, quietly and in a reasonable tone. I instantly regret my words as she turns her head towards me. I wonder if I have been too matter-of-fact. I look at her, trying to see her face clearly. It is as though her eyes are searching mine, to see my inner thoughts and feelings.

I could kiss her now. Just lean forward and brush my lips against her cheek.

See what she does. Whether she responds. But I hesitate, too fearful of losing everything I have.

And then she is pulling away, sitting up, head in hands, saying, "Aarrgghh," theatrically.

I realise suddenly that this … this show … this act … is simply a charade. That she knows what she wants to do. She intends to keep the baby, and this pretence is simply because she wants me to say, 'yes, yes, you must keep the baby!' and to sound thrilled to bits, over the moon, all of that, about it.

If I go the other way and suggest she is too old, that the baby may be deformed, or show any sort of negativity, Pippa will turn against me. If it is the baby or me, she will choose the baby, of course. And, at some stage, I will have to leave, and what will become of me with no money and nobody to care for me?

So I say, "You must have the baby!" What else can I do?

I watch her face transform. "You'd be a wonderful mother," I add. Her face beams with joy. "Dominic would be so proud of you." That clinches it. She turns and hugs me awkwardly, one arm around my shoulder, before eventually getting out of bed and walking happily back to the door. She turns back towards me and blows a kiss. "Thank you, Nanna!" she cries as she leaves.

And that, I think in despair, is the rest of my life here mapped out ahead of me.

Nanna. Nanny. Some stupid name from *Mary Poppins* or *Peter Pan,* I forget which. A dog, I think. Or the instantly ageing 'Grandma' or 'Granny.'

A name — a title — I don't want. I am Sharon. Sweet love. Soulmate. Not a grandmother. I must make sure it never comes to it.

———

PIPPA and I sit at the central unit in the kitchen over breakfast in the morning before she goes to work. We are eating and drinking our way through cereals and toast, a carafe of coffee, and a carton of orange juice. I'd be happy sitting here with my own thoughts, just looking out on the garden in the sunshine.

But no. Pippa is excited, jumping up and down to fetch this and that. And she gushes away about the baby and how she'll give up work next month and how I must come along to all the hospital appointments and the scans. She's getting all that sorted today. On and on she goes. Busy. Busy. Busy.

"And!" she exclaims, almost bursting with excitement, "You can be my birth partner when the baby is born." Like it's an honour. I try to hide my grimace of revulsion, thinking of staring at a gaping bloody mess, before the blancmange-like afterbirth slops out. I transform my face with a big fake smile. I'm not very good at smiling. Pippa does not notice though, gushing ever on.

She's getting on my nerves now. I want to screech at her, "Shut up!" But I cannot.

"Will the baby go in Dominic's old room?" I say, wanting to slow her down. I watch her face cloud over.

She stumbles over her reply. I retrieve the moment by going up and putting my arms around her to comfort her. She welcomes my warm embrace.

Then, when I think she might get ready for work and just leave, she is sat back down at the table, sobbing about the dirty boy and how could she be so happy after what has happened to the husband. I could just scream at myself in frustration for my mistake.

I do not know which is worse, the endless gabbling and bouncing up and down about the baby, or the way she sits there and sniffles and snorts about the boy and the husband. It would be nice if she just sat still with her own thoughts and left me to mine. She is all over the place.

If I do not do anything, she'll just sit there sobbing and being irritating. It is up to me to get things moving. So I stand up and do my no-nonsense routine. "Come on!" I say. "He wouldn't want this. Let's get you ready for work."

And she stands up, but then wobbles for a moment and sits back down, taking out her phone. "I must ask Dom to come home for a weekend visit ... so I can tell him face-to-face ... a little brother or sister."

I could cry out loud.

"And I'll text Elaine ... she'd want to know, too. Dear Elaine ... she'd love to be an auntie ... she's back from her cruise now. Last night!"

It is all I can do not to scream out loud. I also wonder how she knows that. Her memory is not that good. They must have been in regular contact.

Then she is up once more, all fluttery, hither and thither, confused and flustered, before picking up her bag, ready to leave for work. She is coming back for her keys ... her bottle of water from the fridge ... and to kiss me. Three times!

I watch as she finally has everything she needs and then comes over to kiss me again, as though she has forgotten she did it only a few minutes before. I hug her and whisper, "I'll look after you," in her ear. She seems tearful as she hugs me back tightly. And then, at long last, she leaves.

I love her. I hate her too. That she does not realise, does not understand, how much love I have, how special things could be between us. But now, as well as the baby, she is bringing the boy and Elaine back into our lives just when I thought they had gone forever. And I now have so much to do. Getting rid of the baby. I also have to plan how to dispose of the boy and Elaine as well. Probably in the same way I dealt with the idiot husband.

———

TODAY, now that Pippa has gone to work, is how every day should be for me. I go back to my bed for the morning, reclining in luxury, alternating between reading my book, the latest Rachel Joyce (rather a change of genre for me), and listening to music via Spotify on my phone. I have coffee and biscuits mid-morning.

It is a fine, sunny day, and I wish the sun would stream gently through the window on to my face so that I could fall asleep for an hour or two. But the sun shines into Pippa's bedroom in the morning and mine in the afternoon.

I move to Pippa's bed, sprawling across the middle, taking in the fresh smells of the bedding and the aroma of her body on the sheets. I lie there thinking my thoughts and bringing myself to ecstasy, not once but twice.

And as I reach that moment the second time, there is a brisk knocking at the front door. I hear Elaine calling out, "Coo-eee, coo-eee!" in her silly voice. She's back from her cruise, just like Pippa said. She must have got a text message from Pippa and come round. She'll know Pippa is at work, so I suspect she's gone straight up the town to buy a congratulatory card and a bunch of flowers, and is now dropping them off. I hate that stupid woman and what her return now means. That I will have to share Pippa, maybe even becoming the third person in the 'two's company, three's a crowd' saying.

Now she is here, expecting me to answer the door, inviting her in for a cup of tea, thinking she can build on our fragile truce at the funeral, having a chinwag about Pippa, agreeing on a surprise party. I lie here hoping the stupid great lump will go away.

She knocks again, louder this time, and still I ignore it. Then, I hear movement downstairs as she pushes at the front door and walks round the back to pull at the patio door. I am sure it is open. She must assume I am out. And she wants to come in. I don't know why. Maybe to put up a banner or something. And it occurs to me that I could put paid to Elaine once and for all.

I get up off Pippa's bed, tidy it quickly, and hurry to my room, where I snatch at a heavy, decorative paperweight on the windowsill. If I call out to Elaine and she comes upstairs, I could hit her hard with the paperweight, sending her tumbling back down the stairs onto the hard floor below. Who knows what might happen; whether she would survive the fall? If not, I believe I am strong enough to drag her, semi-conscious, back up the staircase and over the top of the gallery on the landing. That headfirst plummet would do it.

"I was in my bedroom," I'd say, when questioned later. "Listening to music." (So I'd not have heard her approach.) "I came out of my room, to go to the toilet, saw someone — a burglar, I thought — at the top of the stairs. I feared for my life and instinctively pushed them away from me." I'd not mention the paperweight; I'd just clean it and put it back on the windowsill.

But Elaine does not come into the house. The patio door must be locked. I felt certain it was open. Pippa locks it sometimes when she remembers, and she must have done that today during her flittering to and fro. Elaine will now be walking away, and I have missed my chance. I dash back to Pippa's room, standing behind the window blind, watching Elaine get into her car and driving off.

I go down to the front door, and as expected — the woman is so predictable — I pick up a card in an envelope and a flower arrangement with a cheap little teddy bear in cellophane on the doorstep. The card is only tucked into the envelope, which is not sealed down. I take it out.

Darling Pips. Congratulations! Can't wait to be a godmother! All my love, El xxx.

Pips? Really, I could vomit.

I read the silly note again, something about it making me feel angry. I'm not sure why. I see it straightaway this time though. The reference to being a godmother — I've not been asked — infuriates me beyond words. I wonder what Pippa must have put in a text — 'Be godmother!' — and why she did not ask me. I feel so let down.

I'd like to rip the flowers, the card and envelope and the stupid little teddy bear apart and flush the pieces down the toilet, as though they had never been delivered. But Elaine will expect Pippa to thank her. And when she doesn't hear from Pippa, she will come round and make a huge, dramatic fuss. I would say someone must have stolen them from the doorstep. "Not round here, surely," Pippa would cry. And Elaine would turn to me, all sweaty and teary, and point with a big fat finger. "It was you."

I have to get rid of Elaine as soon as I can. Now she is back, and Pippa has obviously welcomed her with open arms, it is only a matter of time before she ingratiates herself fully. She will be texting and phoning all the time. She will be here for lunches and evening meals. She will crochet things for the baby and pick up little jackets and booties from fancy little shops in Bury St Edmunds. We will never be free of her. And I will be pushed out. Sidelined.

I am not someone who makes friends easily, nor am I a group person — I am not 'one of the girls.' If there is a crowd, I tend towards silence and am ill-equipped to make jolly, off-the-cuff remarks. I sometimes prepare a few 'ad-libs,' but do not always get a chance to use them at appropriate moments. I know I am not a particularly warm person. People are never drawn to me. They don't want to be my friend.

I am at my best when friendship is one-on-one — as it was with Monica for ever such a while, and Patricia for a time, and now Pippa. I had thought that would stretch out for years and years, to the end of my life, really. But now, not only the baby has to go, but Elaine, too. As soon as possible, before she pushes and shoves her way into this happy home and I get barged to one side, and, eventually, out the door.

19

Pippa is thrilled by Elaine's flowers and spends much of the evening — as we eat, shower and change, and sit and watch the television together — just texting and checking her mobile, smiling and laughing and texting back. I am ignored, mostly.

By the time we go to bed, I am tense and edgy and make one or two sharp comments to Pippa, although she does not seem to notice. She is absorbed by the texts with Elaine. I am glad to shut my bedroom door, although I can still hear intermittent peals of laughter from Pippa's room. These enrage me and seal Elaine's fate.

My chance to deal with Elaine comes suddenly — right now, this next morning, as Pippa gets ready to go to work. She announces, before she leaves, that she will hand in her notice today and stay at home from next month. "Won't that be great fun!" she says.

I pretend not to hear her and busy about, hoping she'll just go. But she doesn't. Instead, she sits down on the sofa next to me, with our mugs of tea, and takes out her mobile phone. And everything changes with a stroke of good fortune.

Pippa losing her phone has always been something of a running joke since I moved in. She does it all the time. It's just not funny anymore.

"Oh God!" she says, retracing her footsteps. "Where is it?"

I echo, "Where is it?" in an exaggerated, wailing voice. Mocking her, really.

She laughs, not realising, and then replies, "Come on, Sharon, help me, pl-ee-aa-se." And I always do, with as much good grace as I can muster.

It is usually somewhere obvious — a windowsill, by the kettle, on the armrest of the sofa. Some stupid place.

We go through this charade once or twice a day when she is at home. And the joke wears thin very quickly. In fact, it has been making me angry for a while now.

Early on, I amused myself on occasions by moving the phone out of sight — slipping it down the side of a sofa cushion, for example. I was oh-so careful where I put it; it had to look as though it was there by accident.

"Oh, come on!" Pippa would shout in frustration to herself. I let her build from frustration to anger. "I've got to go to work ... I'm late!"

I'd make her go back time and again where she had last been — sometimes, she'd even get that wrong. Going upstairs and then running down, shouting, "I don't think I went up there!" She is such a fool.

Laughing inside, I'd then point to the sofa and say, "Could it have slipped ...?" She'd dart forward and discover it and say how clever I was, and then hug me. I liked the feel of her body against mine. It made all this silliness worthwhile.

So now we sit on the sofa next to each other, finishing our mugs of tea, before she sets off for work, and I see — at last — her entering the four-number security code on her phone. 4. 8. 9. 9. I have, on so many occasions, when she is in the bath or the garden, tried to access her phone and went through various combinations, birthdays and so on, without success. 4899 seems so random.

I look on as she checks her text messages and makes various replies. To Elaine, for sure. She smiles and laughs to herself several times, but does not share the joke. Then she goes to her email messages, reading some and deleting others. And to a WhatsApp page. She angles this so I can see. "It's for the girls at work," she explains, showing me a photo of some brainless young thing on holiday, holding two large glasses of orange drink, topped with bits of fruit on straws, in front of her bare breasts. "Gina. She's in Egypt. She's mad, she is."

Pippa clicks and clicks, checking the weather in Felixstowe and Ipswich, then the headlines of the *Daily Mail* and the local paper, the *Evening Star*. Finally, after finishing her mug of tea, she says, "Better go ... I'm running late," and gets off the sofa, leaving her mug and her phone on the armrest. I stand, too, expecting her to hug and kiss me goodbye. But she is in a hurry, dashing upstairs to get something, and shouting over her shoulder to me to 'have a hoover round' and 'don't forget the washing.' Like I'm her bloody servant.

Then she is back down, moving quickly to the kitchen for her car keys on a hook on the wall and to the cloakroom for her coat, and then back to the sofa. "Oh God! Where's my phone?" she cries, as per bloody usual.

Pippa hurries back up the stairs, her mind so fluttery that she thinks she took it with her. "I need it for work," she shouts at me.

And she comes back down, rushing here and there. "Where was I?" she says, half to herself, half to me. "Did I go in the kitchen with it?" And she dashes off to check.

Then she's back. "Have you seen it? Have you seen it?" Like the stupid phone is the most important thing in the whole wide world.

I calm her down, saying she'll be late for work, and we'll find it together when she gets home. She pulls a face of frustration.

"You find it when I've gone ... then text me!" We look at each other and burst out laughing at the same moment. Pippa is, as the saying goes, daft as a brush.

And then she is leaving. The last thing she says is, "I'm sure I left it on the sofa." A sudden moment of clarity, soon forgotten as she hurries away.

It's not there, of course. On the armrest of the sofa next to the empty mug. Nor is it down the side of the cushion. Not this time. I moved it the moment she walked upstairs. Her phone is now in the pocket of the dressing gown I am wearing. I'm going to take it to bed with me for the morning. Go through it. Check her texts, emails and WhatsApp messages, from beginning to end. 4899 unlocks all her secrets.

Once I have done that, and I have not fully thought this through, I am going to text Elaine. As though I am Pippa. I like the idea that, as Pippa, I will text and tell Elaine that the friendship is over, and that I — Pips! — never want to see her again. I can imagine Elaine's stupid fat face with her mouth hanging open. The thought makes me laugh out loud.

But Elaine may come round, tearful and begging, and Pippa would be horrified and realise it could only be me who sent the text, and that might make things ten times worse. I could, of course, text Elaine asking her to meet me, dear old Pips, somewhere quiet and out of the way. I could meet her there, and, as I crept up behind her and she turned to greet me, I could bash her brains out with a house brick. The idea thrills me. It would put paid to her once and for all.

———

WHAT I AM SEEING on Pippa's phone makes me angry. Very angry indeed. She did not want me here from the start, and I now feel I am being used to clean and tidy, keep things straight, and so on.

I had thought, assumed quite naturally, that my friendship with Pippa was special. And her friendship with Elaine was less so. That she had chosen me instead of her. This is not the case. There has been a constant stream of text messages between them from just after that first book club evening right up to today. Even to and from each other during the cruise! I had not realised. It's quite a friendship they have. I scroll back to when I first moved here, into the extension, and read through their messages, my heart breaking.

'Must do ASAP. So-oo busy! Every day. Chelsey away on holiday!' was one of the first messages from Pippa to Elaine, in response to Elaine's, 'We must have lunch soon!' I was pleased to read Pippa's response, as I thought it was her gentle way of putting Elaine off. That later messages would be firmer, if necessary. Something like, 'No, Elaine. I'm best friends with Sharon now.'

But they are not. Quite the opposite. In fact, they had that Sunday afternoon out a couple of days after that early exchange. In a later text message, Elaine asked about me in a derogatory manner. 'She still with you?' Who's she, the cat's mother? So disrespectful! I could not hate Elaine more than I do now, reading that. Worse though was Pippa's reply, it upset me so much. All she put was, 'Yes, sigh.'

I scrolled forwards through the rest of the messages between them, wiping tears from my eyes at times. Elaine once asked when I would be leaving. Pippa replied that she didn't know ('I don't know!!!'). 'Soon?' Elaine put. 'Hope so!' came the reply. It struck me that Pippa was just saying this to be kind to Elaine, but the last text from Elaine, yesterday, before the pregnancy announcement, upset me most. 'Lunch soon? Just us two?' And Pippa's reply? 'Yes! Just us!' I could have cried myself to sleep.

I go through Pippa's emails. Mostly with colleagues in the shop. Business matters. 'Can you come in half hour early?' 'Yes.' Hardly riveting. One or two people from her old days in London. 'Put some flowers on your mum and dad's graves today.' 'Thank you so much.' Who cares! There is nothing of interest. Nothing about me.

It is the same with WhatsApp. All nonsense messages and photos between her and her colleagues at the boutique. 'New stock in!' writes one, Ginny, and accompanies it with photos of fluffy bits of this and that clothing, all hideously overpriced for poor saps with more money than sense. Again, no mention of me at all.

I flick through everything as I lie here in my bed. Phone calls made and received. No phone messages left; whether there haven't been any or she has deleted them, I don't know. I go through all of her photographs — many of the boy, some of the husband, a few of all of them together in happier times. One or two of her parents; I zoom in on her mother; they are the spitting image of each other. None of me.

I hold the phone up, reversing the camera so that it faces me.

The camera adjusts itself to my face, making me look for a moment like some sort of monster.

I take the photo and then look at it. I am not beautiful or pretty or cute. I am not even ordinary looking. I am ugly.

Then I am drawn back to the texts and look through those with her horrid husband. Scrolling to the top and then down, many are mundane. She writes, '12 eggs, mushrooms, peppers, please.' 'Yes.' The abrupt reply. There is one long argument, almost nonsensical, as if picking up on something they had argued over before he left for work. 'Bastard.' She writes. No answer. 'Fuck you.' No reply. 'I want a divorce.' Eventually, a response from him. 'Let's talk later x.'

The texts between Pippa and the nasty boy are nicer, warmer, but mostly one-sided as Pippa texted him when he was here to 'leave in good time, the coach won't wait' (presumably for a school trip somewhere) and, on another occasion, 'Don't forget your packed lunch' and then 'I'm late tonight, can you sort yourself out?' He texts back with the equivalent of teenage grunts and sighs, all expressed with emojis and nonsense abbreviations. Nothing of much interest there.

I dig further, going through everything on the phone, again and again, until I finally find something about me. I uncover another batch of messages between the husband and Pippa on messenger. I overlooked the app first time round on her home screen. 'How long is she staying?' he texted. 'I don't know! Not long!' The reply. 'PITA,' he writes. I Google it: Pain in the arse.

On it goes, my heart sinking, to her final, devastating message 'What can I do?'

As I lie there, feeling utterly destroyed, the phone makes a pinging noise. It makes me jump. I am not sure what it means. This is a newer and more sophisticated phone than mine. I assume a text message, an email, a phone message or something on WhatsApp has come in. I fiddle with the phone, turning down the sound at the side. Then I look at the home screen and see there is a text message. It is from Elaine. I hold my breath as I click through, wondering what it will state.

'Mummy!' she has written, making me feel sick. 'Can you pop in on your way home — God-Mummy has some-thing for Mummy and Baby xxx' (the card and flowers clearly not being enough). I ponder, for ever such a while, thoughts whizzing through my mind. I can ignore the text and just continue with my day, giving the mobile phone back to Pippa on her return from work. I could delete Elaine's text so Pippa will never see it, and Elaine won't know what is happening nor what to do. That would be best.

Or I could do something else that will put paid to Elaine forever, going back to my original plan, but being extra care-ful. I still have a key to the back door of her house. And Elaine, I rather suspect, may go out at some point this after-noon, perhaps to buy some biscuits and pastries, if she thinks Pippa may call round later. I could keep watch from a distance, and when I see her car is gone, I can slip in the back, with my gloves on, standing behind a door until she returns, not imagining for a moment that anyone is inside her house. Afterwards, I will make it look like a teenage robbery gone horribly wrong.

'Yes,' I tap into Pippa's mobile phone. Then I add an exclamation mark, think for almost a minute, and change 'Yes!' to 'Yea!' as that is how Pippa writes sometimes. Like an overgrown teenager.

I think long and hard. The moment I press send, the die is cast. There is no turning back. I will have to do what I am going to do. Finally, I press send.

Then I delete the message. I must remember it will still be on Elaine's phone. I must remove it from the phone. Better still, I will take the phone with me when I leave. After all, it is what a teenage burglar would do.

I AM DRESSED in old black clothes from head to toe, standing in Elaine's kitchen, behind the open door into the hallway, holding a fire extinguisher in my gloved right hand. It is a small one that was next to the oven. I can only imagine that Elaine's cooking skills leave much to be desired.

The extinguisher is, despite its compact size, surprisingly heavy. As Elaine pushes the door open and staggers in with carrier bags of shopping in each hand, she will be at my mercy.

Her back to me, I will step out from behind the door and club her as many times as I need to. The first will knock her to the floor. The second will render her unconscious. The third, I think, will kill her. I will strike more blows as I see fit at the time. I may even enjoy the last two or three.

It has all been incredibly easy, and everything has unfolded exactly as I had planned it. I walked by the top of her road at two o'clock. Her car was parked on the road outside her house instead of the driveway. I don't know why. I strolled away and came back at three o'clock. The car was still there. At four o'clock, though, it was gone.

Checking all around, both sides of the pavement, up and down, and looking at all the windows of the nearby houses whilst pretending to shake a stone from my shoe, I could see it was all clear. No CCTV cameras either. I was good to go.

I strolled to the gate and checked around again before opening it carefully, my hand covered with a cloth from my pocket. I then slipped inside the garden, shooed the cat away — I suddenly remembered that I forgot to dump it at the Blue Cross — and pulled on my gloves before stepping into her kitchen. I had a good look around, upstairs and down-stairs — force of habit, I suppose — before taking my place here in the kitchen.

I wait, on and on, as the kitchen clock moves slowly to 4.25. There is a thin red hand, hardly noticeable behind the black minute and hour hands, and I watch it whizzing around quickly. Time passes at an agonising crawl.

I clear my throat, which seems to be full of phlegm, time and again, snorting and snuffling to myself, and then listen out for sounds — the arrival of Elaine in her car, maybe banging or knocking from next door or out the back somewhere.

It is so quiet, I cannot even hear a bird singing in the trees that enclose much of Elaine's garden. The endless waiting sets me on edge, and I need to go to the toilet badly, even though I went before I left Pippa's. It is 4.40 now, and I feel I have been here, crouched and ready, for an unbearable length of time.

And then it happens, almost so fast that I am taken by

surprise. I hear the key in the front door but do not register it straightaway. There are heavy footsteps in the hall, coming towards the kitchen. I just about brace myself, as the door swings open, but it hits hard, knocking me back against the wall. I drop the fire extinguisher and look up as Elaine twists round and stares at me, her mouth wide open.

Before she can speak, I am moving, picking up the fire extinguisher and swinging it at her head. Somehow, instinct, I guess, she pulls back, and it misses her by centimetres. I am suddenly off-balance, and she shoves me as hard as she can against the half-open door. I hit my spine on the door frame and cry out in pain. Then she is scrambling in her pockets for her mobile phone, struggling to pull it out. I am up and at her, and we push and pull each other in utter desperation across the kitchen.

She slams me against a row of kitchen cabinets, then steps back, breathing heavily, one hand on my chest restraining me, the other taking her mobile phone out of her pocket. "Stand there," she says, in something close to a growl. She takes her hand away, ready to press 999 on her phone. I turn and take a knife from the block by my side. I stab it into her chest one, two, three times. She stays upright, a startled look on her face, but drops the phone. I keep going until she falls to the floor, and then some more. To be on the safe side.

There is blood, quite a lot really, coming out of her and into a pool on the floor. Not as much as I'd have expected on me. There is some on my black clothing, but not my shoes. I take off my outer clothes and wrap them inside a carrier bag from under the sink. I take her phone and turn it off and put it in the bag too. I will have to destroy it later. I go upstairs, checking I'm not leaving a trail of blood, which I am not, and pick an old, nondescript coat of hers at the back of a wardrobe. I'll slip this on to go home.

I then hurry round the house, pulling open drawers and emptying bags and the like, as if I am a teenage burglar. There is little here that a teenager would want — most of her possessions are more than twenty years old. Her computer monitor is big and chunky. It's all like that. There is some jewellery and cash, and I pocket these to take back home and dispose of them. Lastly, I go through her handbag, wondering what a teenager might take. I slip credit cards and debit cards into the coat pocket.

I take a small hand mirror from the handbag to check Elaine is no longer breathing. Her body seems to be making gurgling and sighing noises, but that may be my heightened imagination. She is dead. I take one last look around. It has the appearance of a robbery that's gone wrong. Just as I planned. I pick up the carrier bag, taking the phone and putting it in one pocket of the coat with the jewellery and cash. I fold the bag, with my outer clothes, over and over, and squash it into the other pocket of the coat. I leave the back door open, as though the burglar has got lucky. I slip out the back gate into the darkening night. The cat saunters into the house as I leave, no doubt looking for something to eat. Elaine, most probably.

20

SATURDAY, 3 DECEMBER, THE EVENING

T he evening, back at Pippa's, is hellish. I go into the old extension when I return and put everything incriminating into a black bin bag: the coat, the carrier bag of clothes, phone and jewellery and cash, even my shoes — which, on frantic re-examination, are heavily spattered with blood. I hide the bin bag, for now, underneath the bottom drawer of the chest of drawers where no one would ever look.

I change into an old sweatshirt and jogging bottoms of Pippa's that I'd left behind when I moved into the house. Check my appearance in the mirror. Hot and sweaty. Blood splatters on my face and hands. I take tissues from a box on the windowsill, spitting and wiping myself endlessly. I stare in the mirror again. I look so guilty. I know I will have to live with this — the fear of being found out — forever.

Eventually, I go through the patio door into the kitchen, where Pippa, her back to me, is cooking spaghetti Bolognese (yet) again. Alexa is turned up loud, playing Vivaldi's *Four Seasons* whilst she is pretending to be the conductor. I notice

Elaine's bouquet takes pride of place on the central unit. Pippa's mobile phone, which I'd dropped by the side of the sofa for her to find when she returned home, is next to it. Pippa looks surprised as I brush by her. "I've been for a long walk ... having a bath!" I shout back over my shoulder.

I feel sick all evening, struggling to eat the Bolognese that reminds me of dead Elaine's oozing body. I swallow down the bloody-looking meat in fits and starts with the fizzy water we now seem to be drinking instead of wine.

Pippa is almost oblivious to me, babbling away endlessly although, thankfully, she does not mention the flowers nor Elaine. Instead, it is all baby nonsense. Half-listening to her, I learn that she has already spoken to or seen a private doctor, and all is well, and she thinks she is sixteen weeks gone. She is giving up work in two weeks, as she is owed some holiday time, and wants me to go with her to look at baby equipment somewhere in Bury St Edmunds.

"Sharon! Sharon!" she suddenly cries, grabbing my hand and making me jump. "You're away with the fairies. Saturday! Can you come with me next Saturday to Bury? We can choose everything and get it ordered for baby's room."

I look at her and do my best to smile at her warmly. "Yes. Yes, of course," I reply as enthusiastically as I can. I have a terrible headache and seem to be sweating endlessly. And I still feel nauseous.

"I don't feel well, Pippa," I say simply, swallowing a mouthful of the fizzy water. "I think I may have a bug or something." I just want to get to bed as quickly as I can, putting the horror of the afternoon behind me. As if I ever could.

"Go away! Unclean! Unclean! Go away!" she cries, comically waving her serviette at me again and again. It is all I can do not to burst into tears. After a while, jabbing listlessly with my fork at pieces of cut-up fruit from the bowl on the dining room table, I make my excuses and leave. Pippa hugs me. I go up the stairs in tears. She does not see. I have to scrub myself clean.

I lie in bed, awake for hours, listening to Pippa's overloud music downstairs. She turns it off just after eleven o'clock, coming upstairs closer to midnight. She pushes open my door and looks in, but I have my back to her and pretend to be sleeping, so she goes away. I cannot face her; that's the truth.

I agonise over what I have done, replaying everything I did at Elaine's, trying to see it through the eyes of police detectives when they uncover the body. It might be this week or this month. Today, even; it will happen sometime soon. I must be prepared. I staged it well; I am sure of that. And, of course, I have been going in and out feeding the cat anyway, so my fingerprints there, for example, would not be unexpected.

But there are things I will have overlooked and not thought of that might catch me out. When I was in her house, I thought that her blood was only on my clothes. Later, back here, I was horrified to see it was all over my face, arms and shoes. How could I have been so blind? I lie in bed, worrying myself into a troubled sleep.

Now, this next morning, I am physically sick, just after Pippa comes across and puts my favourite breakfast, a bacon-and-fried-egg sandwich, in front of me. I make a dash for the cloakroom. When I return, she asks if I might be pregnant, and I smile at her feeble joke as brightly as I can.

I pick at the sandwich, the undercooked bacon and the burst yolk of the fried egg making me feel I'll gag at any moment. I swallow as much of it down as I can with great gulps from my glass of water. I put bits of bacon into my pocket when she isn't looking. I hope that Pippa will be off to work promptly, ten o'clock to four o'clock today, so I do not have to keep up the pretence of normality — this endless jollity — for longer than I have to.

And she is so close to going. After the usual fuss and bother, over her bag, her keys, her mobile and bottle of water, I am sure she is leaving. I even breathe a sigh of relief. But then she picks up the vase with Elaine's flowers and tops it up with water from the kitchen tap. I think that's the last thing.

But she sits down opposite me and puts on her serious face. I look at her and hold her steady gaze. "Elaine," she says portentously. She then speaks as though she is a mental health counsellor. "I know you don't get on ... but ..." She pauses for so long, and I keep my face bland although I flush hot inside.

"I wonder if you can pop round today and see how she is." Pippa goes on, reaching out her hand to touch mine. "She dropped these lovely flowers round ... and I texted her several times last night and rang her when I got up this morning ... there was no answer, which is odd. So if you could ... I know it's hard for you. Pretty please?"

I hate that stupid phrase, pretty please, and I loathe the way she speaks to me as though I am an inmate in a mental institution. But I smile and say I will 'see what I can do,' and she leans across and hugs me. I feel hot and clammy, but she does not seem to notice. And then she leaves, and I lie down on the sofa for hours.

I am in a quandary. I spend so long twisting and turning over which way to go. I know I could go around and 'discover' the body and that this, with new fingerprints and foot-prints maybe obliterating evidence, might be the best thing to do. But I simply cannot face it. The endless questioning. Putting myself straight into the line of fire. I read somewhere that the first person to discover a body is always a suspect.

But if I tell Pippa I have not visited, I did not want to, she might be offended, upset with me, even. And she might hurry round herself. And she would wonder why, especially after uncovering the body, why I did not go. She might mention her suspicions to the police.

Eventually, I reach a decision. I take Elaine's door key, wrap it in toilet paper, and flush it away. "I couldn't find the key!" I'll say later. "And there was no answer when I knocked on the door." I feel I am only delaying the denouement, that we'll both be going round there, and in through that left-open back door, later tonight. I have a sudden image of the cat feeding on the corpse, and that this might obliterate any evidence. I think, though, that this may be too much to hope for. There's a lot for the cat to get through.

MIDDAY, and I am in town for fresh fruit and vegetables. As I hurry along, instinctively looking around me over and again, I feel stressed and tense and sick to my soul. It's the first time I've been to the shops for a while. It will be my last.

The town is full of police cars and police officers — I count four and eight respectively in the main shopping street, Hamilton Road, between the green in the centre of town and the bank further down on the corner as the road leads to the sea. The police officers are going in and out of shops, quickly, and in pairs.

I do not think this has anything to do with Elaine. Not yet. It is too soon. There must be some sort of incident, though, with so many police officers here and a sense of urgency all around. Doddery old sorts stand and watch. Children, young and fearless and egging each other on, follow the police into the shops. I keep my head down and hurry away.

Fear rises within me. I think that, somehow, the unexpected appearance of so many police is linked to me. That the landlord's son has reported me and showed my notes and desk diary — my confessions to murders — to the local police. I am somehow, somewhere, on a list, a file, a database, and a photograph of me, from my belongings, is with the police. And they are keeping watch.

I linger a while on a bench at the green in the centre of town, 'The Triangle,' as it is known, opposite the Tesco Express on the corner where I had ummed and aahed over my purchases. After buying this and that, I sat on the bench and, something in me, a streak of recklessness, madness even, made me smirk and wave at the CCTV cameras. It was a stupid thing to do. I forgot myself.

I am wondering now if somehow, the images from these cameras have been relayed instantly to the police headquarters over at Martlesham and a bright spark has put two and two together and made four. "Guv? It's that woman we're looking for. She's in the centre of Felixstowe right now." And here they come.

I turn my back to the shopping street, standing in a doorway of an empty shop, watching what's going on behind me in the reflections in the window. Police officers are rushing about, searching. They have not noticed me yet.

Then, one young policewoman sees me, my back to her,

and comes running across. I move round to face her, to fight her off as best I can. But as my face twists in fear, she rushes by me to a shop by my side.

She calls out, shouting back to the other officers, who follow her in. Three of them in all. The remaining four will be on their way in seconds, responding to her radioing for assistance. There is a commotion inside — teenage shouts and yells and bellowed police instructions. I take the opportunity to put my head down, my scarf tugged upwards, and I hurry away.

The experience unsettles me. I wonder if, one day soon, this is what will await me when I am in town. The thought overwhelms me, realising that my life, as I know it now, could be over in seconds if I were arrested by the police looking into my confessions of historic murders. There is no statute of limitation for murder. And once Elaine's body is found, I'd be connected to that, too. And then, maybe some clever dick of a detective would think about the man falling off the ladder and connect the dots. I would stand trial, and I do not doubt I would be sent to prison, to all intents and purposes, for the rest of my life.

I will stay at home from now on, as much as I can. I am so distracted, so troubled by my thoughts, that I stumble on the pavement as I turn left for home along Orwell Road. I drop my thin plastic bag, and my fruit — oranges and satsumas — roll away and into the gutter. I drop to my knees to gather them up and feel such a sudden sense of despair. Three or four people, white-haired and older than me, come across to help, mumbling words of sympathy and good cheer. I fight back tears.

I half-expect one of them to say, "Oh, it's you — that woman the police are looking for!" And then another will echo the statement. And another will shout, "Yes, yes it is!" And the last old fool will grab me, as though he were sixty years younger, and call out, "Police! Police!" I snatch at and push the fruits back into the bag, my head down, and then I am up and away, my head now at an angle, not looking at them, not saying anything.

I find myself, unthinking and out of habit, walking down Bath Road towards my old flat. When I realise, I cross the road so that I am on the opposite side as I pass by. I expect the house to have been sold by now, a mum, dad, three children, maybe even granny, moving in this side of Christmas. It could be a happy and joyful place. But the 'For Sale' sign is still outside. As is the landlord's son's car. And he is there, opening the boot, taking out bags of shopping.

I want to go up to him and demand that he give me my belongings — those notes and that desk diary — back. But I am scared of him and what he might say and do. And he will have long ago thrown most of my possessions away. He may have kept the notes and diary. He may not. If he has not, he will have taken photographs and kept them on his phone. He has me at his mercy. I sob quietly as I walk on by. I feel, one way or the other, that I am trapped like an animal in a cage, and I am tipping over into madness.

As I hurry by, along Bath Road towards Brook Lane, I hear the landlord's son calling out after me. "Hey, Mary, Mary West!" A tasteless, repulsive reference to the infamous murderer. I turn, and he starts walking towards me as if he is about to break into a run and catch me and perform a citizen's arrest. In tears again now, I drop my bag in the gutter, the fruit spilling out as I run as fast as I can all the way home. Bent double, wheezing and sweating on the front doorstep, I look back, and he is not there. I wonder what will happen next. The net is closing in on me.

"FISH AND CHIPS!" Pippa cries as she comes in from work. "Are they open on a Sunday? We'll get three portions from that place on the corner in town and surprise Elaine on the way back! We'll have a catch-up!"

She talks like that, Pippa, as Elaine used to do. I had never really noticed it until now. All breathless excitement and raised ends of sentences. It's as though she is asking a question and expects me to confirm, to agree, to whatever she is saying. And with gusto!

I've had a long afternoon, lying in torment on the sofa, and I have been anticipating this moment. "Yes," I reply as enthusiastically as I can, even though I am full of dread. As she goes upstairs to change and shower, I slip out through the patio door and make my way to the extension.

I sit on the sofa there, holding Elaine's phone and thinking to myself, worrying over my choices and what I should do. The door of the extension is ajar, so I'll hear Pippa if she comes looking for me. I daren't let her see me like this, holding Elaine's phone with its distinctive case of bright sunflowers.

I turn on the phone, checking through the emails, messages and WhatsApp chats. There are none of note. Elaine is — was — despite all the cheer and bonhomie, a lonely person with no close friends or family.

I decide what I must do. I have no choice. I cannot face the idea of going to Elaine's with Pippa, and all that will result from the visit. I just can't. I have to prevent it happening.

'Pippa,' I tap into the phone. Then pause and think over what I had decided to put. 'I've met an old friend from school. Sarah! Gone to stay with her for a while. She's just lost her husband. Love Elaine x.'

I study it, what I've put, and wonder if that's how Elaine would write. I look at the text messages between them to see. I notice that she rarely used full names or even complete sentences. Sometimes, it's Pips and El, and at other times it's P and E. I do it again.

'P, Met school friend Sarah. Just widowed. Off to Cotswolds. Speak soon. E xxx.' I find myself breathing heavily, agonising as I am over what seems like a trivial matter, but could be devastating if I get it wrong. I fear Pippa saying, "That's odd, it doesn't sound like Elaine at all."

I suddenly hear the patio door opening, Pippa's footsteps on the concrete slabs, her calling out, "Coo-eee, coo-eee," in that silly way of hers that she's copied from Elaine. She is seconds away from the extension door. I am moments from being exposed.

I panic, press send and go to slip the phone back into my pocket. In my haste, it slides by my pocket and falls onto the floor. I manage to turn slightly, both of my feet in front of it. As Pippa pushes open the door, I pray she does not notice it, recognising the big yellow flowers on the case.

"Come on," she cries. "Let's have a cup of tea and tell each other about our day." She clearly thinks I am still feeling down and is determined to chivvy me out of it. "I've got some more baby news!" she adds excitedly. And then, as she turns to go, "I've got the kettle on and some new biscuits ... two minutes!"

When she's gone, I pick up the phone, turn it off, and put it into my pocket. As I stand to follow her back into the kitchen, I start shaking and have to sit down quickly. A terrible sense of doom overwhelms me. I can't help but think that sending that message was a dreadful mistake.

It will stop Pippa going round tonight and perhaps for a week or two; maybe longer if she focuses on her pregnancy and baby things. But at some point after the body is found and everyone who knew Elaine is questioned, she will say, in that irritating way she speaks, that Elaine had gone to the Cotswolds. "Look, here, read the message!" And everything will unravel so fast.

Even if Pippa is not questioned, I am doomed anyway. The police, when they do their inevitable investigation, will wonder where Elaine's phone is. Someone will check her bank account and credit card statements and see she had one. They will contact the phone provider and get all the details. I wonder if they will be able to tell where the 'Cotswolds' message was sent from ... from here? I am not tech-savvy, have never needed to be. It worries me.

I get up and walk back across the patio to the door, standing there for a moment, watching Pippa floating about the kitchen. Such beauty. Perfect simplicity. Such a wonderful life. She shovels a tin of dog food from a can into one of the dog's bowls, and the dog, moving with a sense of purpose for once, comes in from its basket in the living room.

I wonder, here and now, if I should have destroyed the phone and disposed of it in bits, in bins and drains, just after I killed Elaine. And whether still having it may be danger-ous. That it could be traced here to me. I can destroy it at any time, but wonder if it is now too late. I must Google to learn more about such things.

Pippa turns and sees me outside, darts across and pulls back the patio door. She grabs my arm, all schoolgirlish excitement, and says, "I've got chocolate Hobnobs!" as if it is the most exciting thing in the world. "And something to tell you!" As she pulls me in, I try to smile, but my heart is breaking.

21

The evening is, I think, what it will be like every night from now on. Pippa all excited and gushing away about whatever comes into her head and straight out of her mouth.

I sit, picking at my dinner, then idly watching television, and finally, half-heartedly picking at chocolates, trying to be as bright and as jolly as I can. I nod and smile at what seem the most appropriate moments.

Inside, I am dying. I had everything for a fleeting time. Pippa and I and the chance of everlasting love. The whole wide world. Now, the landlord's son, the baby and, worst of all, Elaine crowd my thoughts. I am on borrowed time, especially when Elaine's body is discovered.

Pippa talks about the baby, who is never far from her mind, repeatedly returning to the subject so many times through the evening. She shows me pictures on her phone of various nurseries, pointing out colours and furnishings she likes. She ums and ahs over names. Oscar seems the favourite for a boy; she cannot think of a girl's name. She brings up a list of the most popular girls' names and notices 'Florence' is popular, her mother's name, and that makes her weepy. I go through the motions of consoling her.

At some point further on, when she has rallied, and I have been riled (so many times) by the endlessly repetitive, self-indulgent nonsense, I ask whether she thinks the baby will look like her or the husband or a bit of both, 'like Dominic.' That sets her off again, quite spectacularly, sobbing and dabbing at her eyes with a tissue that she keeps tucked up the arm of her cardigan (an affectation that has always irritated me).

She rallies once more and then goes on in her scatter-brained way, over so many baby-related thoughts. Breast- or bottle-feeding. Full-time mum or part-time mum (with Pippa working two or three days whilst I play 'Nanna'). I smile outwardly but grimace inside. She even starts talking about nurseries and independent or state education. "I'd always wanted to send Dom private, but Pete was a socialist and got very agitated about the idea."

At bedtime, Little Miss Butterfly-Brain suddenly remembers what it was she had to tell me that was so urgent. She pulls a goofy face and says, "D'uh. D'uh. D'uh. I've been so distracted. I meant to ask, tomorrow afternoon, are you free?" I say, "Yes," automatically. I am not sure what is coming next, but know it will be baby-related — as every-thing between us is going to be from now on.

"I called this private clinic in Colchester." I can see her face is full of emotion, and she does the lip thing she always does — the bottom lip coming up — before she is about to cry. "They do 4D scans of babies. Not flat like the NHS. And I'm sixteen weeks already, which is perfect. We should see features and ... you know. I've just bagged this slot for just after three tomorrow after work. A cancellation, so lucky! I can finish work early. Will you come if I pick you up … at two?" She babbles on to the edge of weeping, and I hug her, and she hugs me back. My mind is full of might-have-beens.

In bed, overnight, I am tormented knowing that, at this moment, I still have everything — just Pippa and me. But so much is crowding in — the landlord's son, the baby and Elaine — and I cannot breathe properly nor think straight. Happiness, ever-present lately, is now elusive and forever will be. It occurs that I could just go and disappear back to London or Brighton or elsewhere. But I have nowhere to stay, and I am too old to live on the streets with little or no money.

Next morning, Pippa is rushing around as she always does, picking clothes out of the tumble dryer, taking them upstairs and coming back down and forgetting what she is doing. She eventually darts over to the central unit with tea and toast that she has made in starts and stops whilst I've been sitting here waiting patiently. Then she sits down and reminds me to be ready at two. "Big day, big day, the first sight of Bump … I am calling the baby Bump for now." I smile politely.

We eat and drink for a minute or two, and then she gets her mobile phone out of her pocket and fiddles with it. I sense with horror, before she says anything, what is coming next. And I am correct. "You know, it's really weird." My mug of tea to my lips, I hold my breath, my shaky hands gripping the mug. "About Elaine, you know? I texted her, and she replied that she had gone to see a friend in the Cotswolds. Did I tell you?" She hadn't, so I shake my head as though I don't know anything.

Pippa scrolls up and down and then reads aloud what

she calls 'Elaine's text' — the one I wrote, of course. Then she looks at me and shrugs as if to say, 'What's all that about?' Then she adds, "I've texted her three times, and I've just called her ... no reply ... it's not like her." A long pause. "It's just so out of character. Going to the Cotswolds is one thing. But not replying to my texts is ..." She tails off, searching for the word. As she gets up to leave, she concludes, "I think something's happened to her between here and the Cotswolds."

Then, not noticing how devastated I must look, she is up and flapping about and eventually on her way, reminding me again, Little Miss Scatterbrain, to be ready for two o'clock. I wave merrily at her, my hand obscuring my face. If she sees my horrified expression, she might start putting two and two together. If not now, then soon enough.

After I've tidied everything up and done my various chores, I go at last to the extension and take out Elaine's coat, my carrier bag of clothes, the jewellery and cash, and my shoes from their hiding place. I have not been able to face them. But I look at them now, thinking things through. Finally, I put the coat back, not sure what to do with it. I push my clothes in the washing machine on the hottest wash, wrap the jewellery and cash in toilet paper and flush them away, and scrub at my shoes with soapy water and, finally, bleach. I leave them by the washing machine to put at the back of my wardrobe later.

I then go to my room and lie on my bed. I look again at Elaine's phone, noting Pippa's texts, which seem increasingly agitated, and listening to her message, which sounds almost hysterical. As though Elaine is — was — her best friend forever, not me. I feel a sudden flush of grim satisfaction that she has gone. I text Pippa, 'Sorry, grieving widow, speak soon xxx' and then turn the phone off and tuck it away and out of sight. The text will delay Pippa a while, but I feel more uneasy that I have used the phone again.

––––––––––

I AM GOING to spend my days at home, until Pippa stops work, lying in bed, tidying and cleaning, eating and drinking, reading and listening to music. These should be idyllic days of leisurely pleasure and endless enjoyment. But they will not be like that — they will be full of stress and almost unbearable tension, driving me ever closer to madness. With Pippa still working, I feel as though I am in solitary confinement, awaiting my execution. I do not know when it will be, and that uncertainty adds to the horror.

I'm no longer going to go up the town as I used to do so most every day for years. I have got it fixed inside my head that the landlord's son has reported me to the police — what I wrote in my notes and the desk diary haunts me forever — and they are now searching for me. The rational part of my brain knows that this is unlikely, impossible even, but I cannot seem to shake the thought, the certainty, from my mind. I will not risk going out and about here. I cannot relax, nor be at ease. The feeling is always there, nagging away.

I sit now in an armchair in the 'lounge', as Pippa likes me to call it, looking out the window. I read a book, have a drink and play some music on Spotify. But really, most of the time, I find myself gazing at the road, just watching the world go by. Waiting for something bad to happen, truth be told. Whenever I move away, I am drawn back by some sort of compulsion. The window is wide, without blinds or net curtains. People can see in, but the chair is set back,

and I think I must be in the shadows. From the pavement, I
don't think anyone could really see me unless I moved
suddenly.

This is a busy road, Picketts Road. It may sound like
something out of *Anne Of Green Gables* — the word 'Picketts'
making you think of picket fences and old whitewashed
barns and rolling fields. Some peaceful place for another
century. The late 1880s, the early 1900s, maybe. And, to be
fair, it is a nice road, with its wide width and pavements and
houses set well back and apart from each other.

When I was younger, living in seedy hostels and squalid
bedsits, a place like this — being here, doing as I pleased,
living a life of luxury — was beyond my wildest dreams.
Here and now, I don't feel happy at all. It is a gilded existence, for sure. But a cage nonetheless. I feel trapped here
and unhappy, as though I am waiting to be told when I will
be taken from here to a place of execution. It is how I truly
feel, and it is killing me.

There are constant streams of cars and people coming
from Old Felixstowe to go to the beach and the town and
beyond. And the postman makes his way up and down mid-
morning. Various Amazon delivery drivers pull up now and
then, dashing in and out of their cars and vans. And there is
a man with a baseball cap on back to front pushing leaflets
through the letterboxes.

And then, almost as though I had expected something
bad, it happens — the landlord's son walks by on the opposite side of the road, strolling, meandering, looking around
him as if out for some sunshine and fresh air.

It may be that he is walking from the house in Bath Road
to the Spar supermarket up the top of Picketts Road, and
some way along. But it is cold today. And it is a fair old walk

to that supermarket from his house. And he's not the sort to walk, anyway, not with his big, flashy car.

He must have followed me here the other day, or at least some of the walk. I don't think he knows I am in this house. He stops, looks across for a moment, scans up and down, and then wanders on to the top of the road.

I find that I have not been breathing, holding my breath, as I let out an almighty sigh when he turns right at the top and disappears out of sight. I had expected, when I first saw him, that he would criss-cross the road, ringing doorbells, knocking on windows, banging on doors, to uncover me, knowing I am here somewhere.

I imagined that he would have a photo of me, from amongst my possessions, and would show it to whoever answered their front doors, up and down the road. I have never spoken to any of the neighbours, let alone passed the time of day with them. But I have seen them in their front gardens from time to time and passed them by. Enough for one or two of them, if asked, to say, "Yes, that's the woman who lives there," pointing to this house.

It is, I think, rather like all those police cars and police officers in town, just a coincidence and nothing to do with me. I am becoming ever more paranoid. Stress and tension are playing with my mind. I am close to insanity. If he had known I was in this house, he would have come and rung the doorbell. If he thought I was in this road, even, he would have gone from door-to-door with my photo. My imagination is running away with me.

I sit here, with a fresh cup of tea, in my armchair by the living room window, waiting for the landlord's son to return, carrying a bottle of milk, a loaf of bread or a carrier bag full of shopping. To confirm that this is something and nothing that I am worrying without good reason. I think it will take him five minutes to get to the Spar, five to go around it, and five minutes to come back this way. It is the shortest route between the Spar and his house.

Fifteen minutes pass, then twenty, twenty-five and thirty minutes. I am ill at ease now, and sweating, all sorts of terrible thoughts crowding into my mind. That rational part of my brain says, in a calm but wavery voice, that he has gone another way home along the High Road or has walked further out, to The Dip and maybe even to the ferry. But it is still chilly and is becoming overcast now, and there is a sense of rain coming soon. The less rational part of my mind is screaming.

Finally, the landlord's son appears on this side of the road, at the top. I don't know where he has been nor what he has been doing. He looks exactly the same as he did forty minutes ago. He does not carry milk, bread or a carrier bag full of shopping. And he is doing much the same as when he went up. The only thing he does differently is that he stops outside my house and fiddles with his phone. He holds it up, and as I watch, transfixed, I cannot tell if he's taking a selfie or a photograph of the house. Eventually, he moves on. I am not holding my breath this time. I am crying with fear.

———

I HAD HOPED, although my mind has been elsewhere for a while, that Pippa would decide by herself that she would not have this baby. That she is too old. The baby might be deformed. She would have to bring up the child on her own. But she is further along than she thought, at sixteen weeks or so. And I think my presence — as 'Nanna' — has tipped the balance, encouraging her to go on. I am correct. The irony — the awful irony of it — is not lost on me.

I see now, this afternoon, as I watch her staring, fixated, at the TV-sized screen in this nondescript, office-type place in Colchester, that she is going to have this baby. More than that. She longs for it. Adores the idea. Cannot wait for the baby to be born. It is everything she has ever wanted.

She is transfixed as the baby's face emerges on-screen one last time from the murkiness of Pippa's womb — like some monstrous mud baby. The sonographer, rubbing this across Pippa's stomach, moving that to get a better view, clicks a button to take a photograph. Pippa turns to me, her face contorting with joy, gripping my hand tightly, and says it again, "Nanna." I try to look thrilled.

Driving home, towards the long A12 road, I have never seen nor heard anyone more excited about anything in my life. And she's not even on happy tablets anymore, because of the baby. She laughs, she weeps, she shouts with joy. "A girl! A girl!" she cries over and again excitedly, the car veering to the middle of the road, the driver of the car coming towards us honking his horn several times.

I rest the palm of my hand on her arm, to calm her, to steady her driving, but it makes things worse. She takes one of her hands off the wheel. And, clumsily, as our hands entwine, she puts it on mine. "Thank you! Thank you! Thank you!" She sobs out the words. The car veers over and across the middle of the road, and I pull my hand away and tug at the wheel. She kind of shakes herself, as if to say, 'Okay, okay, I'll be more careful.' A pause, and then she is as excitable as before.

"Florence Sharon, I'm going to call her ... Florence Sharon ... after Mummy and you." Just in case I hadn't realised. I think Florence Sharon Kelly sounds dreadful, but do not say. I have never thought Sharon was a pretty name, and it hasn't been popular for forty years or more. I smile encouragingly, though, and pull a face, as if emotional, when she turns to look at me.

We come off the A12 and go through a McDonald's drive-thru, Pippa so excited that she places the order in a silly and exaggerated South London accent that the young-sounding employee cannot understand. Eventually, we are served and go on, sitting in a car parking space, windows half-open for fresh air, eating burgers and fries and drinking milk shakes. Pippa is beside herself with joy, her mind going here and there, whatever is in her head coming straight out of her mouth, unfiltered. Babble, babble, babble.

The sonographer who did the scan was so-oo nice, really friendly ... it's a girl; I've always wanted a little girl ... I wonder who she'll look like ... we must get her room decorated; it must be pretty as a picture ... on and on. She does not mention the husband ... nor Elaine ... not even the boy. And that is a relief — a respite from the horrors that I feel are closing in around me.

And then she somehow lunges sideways, fries scattering everywhere, and hugs me. "Thank you, thank you, thank you," she repeats. I let her embrace me, my arms around her shoulders, for a moment or two. A gang of schoolboys, at an outside table nearby, see us and make mocking noises and unsavoury comments that we can hear. As we unhook ourselves from each other, we wind up our windows, but otherwise ignore them. I know we must not show signs of weakness, glancing at them, as it will encourage further verbal abuse. Schoolboys are animals.

Before we leave, we go into the McDonald's to use the

toilets. There is only one cubicle open. Pippa goes inside first. Listening to Pippa urinate feels so intimate, and, as we wash our hands side by side after I have been too, I have to fight the urge not to hug her again. Even though it is the closeness between us that moves me, I know that it would seem odd to hug someone in a toilet. There is rather a smell here, too, to be honest.

Back in the car, driving home, Pippa seems calmer somehow. She is still excited, but is more sensible, measured and thoughtful in her comments. She says, ever so nicely, reaching across to hold my hand, "Thank you, Sharon, I couldn't do this, any of it, without you. You're my rock. And I want you to be my baby's Nanna and be part of our lives forever." She squeezes my hand tightly, looking ever so teary-eyed, before letting go.

But that's not all. She begins a sentence, stops, thinks, starts again, stops once more until, finally, she says what it is she wants to tell me. "I want to look after you, Sharon, as you'll look after us." She thinks again, not looking at me, and then continues, "I want to give you more than a credit card. I have ... money. And I want to give you a nest egg, so you can ... be secure."

I say, "Thank you," not trying to disguise the surprise and delight I feel. We hold hands again briefly, and then, as it is getting dark, and the car lights come on automatically, she turns on the radio, and we listen to Radio 2 for the rest of the way home.

My mind races. I will have my own money — I don't know how much or how soon, but it opens up so much for me. A car? A static caravan? A small flat? Here or abroad? My spirits soar. As we detour — annoyingly — by Elaine's house, Pippa spots Elaine's car and says, "That's strange," but nothing more. I start to wonder, in my joyful mood, if I might just get away with Elaine. There is nothing obvious to link me to what happened. Pippa will flap and fuss when the body is discovered, but will get all her dates wrong about the Cotswolds. And maybe, just maybe, her phone will have 'disappeared' by then, anyway. I smile to myself.

Then we approach the landlord's son's house, and I see the 'Sold' sign up, and feel such a surge of overflowing emotions. He was, I think, just amusing himself by tormenting me when he saw me passing by, in following me and wandering up and down Picketts Road. My mind today, more rational and sensible than it has been, realises that he had nothing to gain by talking to the police about me. He would not want to become embroiled in any of that. And now that his house is sold, he will soon be gone and will forget all about me.

I am ecstatic, truly beyond words, as Pippa turns the car into Picketts Road and signals left, to pull onto the driveway. We're home! But then I look up, close to laughing with such overwhelming happiness, and my whole world comes crashing down around me. Dominic, the dirty boy, sits crouched on the doorstep, a rucksack by his side. He smiles at Pippa and then, as she glances away, sneers at me. I am so angry that I struggle to calm my emotions. I could kill him; really I could.

22

MONDAY, 5 DECEMBER, EARLY EVENING

Pippa is all over the boy, hugging, kissing him on the cheek, all of that. He pulls back as she goes to tousle his hair and cries, "Mum!" in an I'm-so-embarrassed-by-you, angry kind of way. He is not joking. He shakes his head as though that will put his hair back into place.

She does not take offence, brushing by him to open the front door. She leads the way; he follows without a backward glance at me — as though I am so far beneath him I don't warrant even the briefest hello — and I am two steps behind him. Then again, he ignores the dog in the basket, so maybe I'm level with the dog.

I am determined that Pippa and I will put on a united front — best friends forever, Mamma and Nanna, living together from now until the day I die, when she will care for me on my death bed. There is no room here for the boy now. Nor the baby, come to that. But that is a matter for another time.

We all gather in the kitchen, Pippa putting the kettle on to make mugs of tea. I fetch two mugs, put the tea bags in, reach for the packet of sweeteners and take the milk from the fridge, opening and sniffing it to check it is still fresh.

She leans against the cabinet next to me, waiting for the kettle to boil, watching him as he makes straight for the fridge. He takes a half-empty bottle of Coke Zero and goes to swill it down, like the pig he is. Pippa makes a tut-tutting noise, in a jokey way, and passes him a glass tumbler from the cabinet behind her.

He takes it, shaking his head and mutters, "For fuck's sake," as he pours the Coke Zero into the tumbler. He pours too much, and it froths up and over the edges. Pippa goes to the sink for a cloth. I say, "Oops-a-daisy," jovially. He looks at me like he wants to kill me. As I do him.

I wonder, as Pippa makes the mugs of tea, if she is going to announce that she is having a baby. She is sixteen weeks or so pregnant, of course, but with her baggy clothes, cardigan and wrap, it is not immediately obvious. I would love her to say it right now so I could watch the boy's face. I would laugh as Pippa spoke, as if delighted by the announcement, but he would look at me and realise I was laughing at him in a mocking way.

She gestures me towards the central unit in the middle of the kitchen, puts the mugs next to each other and says, "Sit down, Dom," gesturing towards the stool opposite. We sit beside each other, Pippa and I. She clears her throat, carefully preparing her words. I reach out my arm, close to hers, ready to hold hands in an encouraging way.

The boy sits on the stool and is obviously out of sorts. An angry misfit, as so many teenage boys are. Before Pippa can speak, he unleashes all of his grievances. A cascade of fury. How his uncle and aunt are 'so-oo strict.' He's not allowed to have anyone up in his 'fucking room.' How the two uncles —

the builders — treat him like a slave, giving him 'all the shit jobs.' He 'fucking hates all of it.' I would not wish to have afternoon tea at a hotel with this foul-mouthed boy.

Pippa glances at me, ashamed of him, not so much the swearing but the aggressive manner. It is as though, if Pippa says the wrong thing, he will launch himself across the unit at her, or turn and stomp off, pushing anything in his way over. I don't think she realises. Whatever she says, this will end badly. For her and him. Perhaps not so much for me.

"Well, come home, then, darling!" she cries, getting up and going to a cupboard, taking out and opening a packet of shortbread biscuits and spreading them out on a plate. She returns and puts the plate in front of the boy. Pippa thinks that a couple of shortbread fingers will smooth things over. She is so wrong.

"To Felixstowe?" he says. "Fucking hell. This shithole?" I can barely contain my delight. He is about to blow spectacularly. I dip my head down so I do not attract his fury. "What's here for me? The docks?" He shakes his head and goes on. "Living here with you and her ... fucking old dyke."

Pippa goes, "Oh, Dom," admonishing him, and is getting to her to feet to, I'm not sure what, console him possibly. But not me. He is already up, his face full of fury, and as they stand with only the unit between them, I think he might strike her.

She reaches across, for a clumsy, outstretched hug, but he knocks her arms away and is turning, picking his rucksack up by the door, and leaving. He does not look back. Pippa bursts into tears, and I dash to hug her, our bodies pressed tight together.

"He's so ..." She shakes her head, struggling for the words. "So angry. I expect he had to wait on the doorstep for hours." I think, but do not say, that the wait does not excuse his foul, ever-angry behaviour. Part of me hopes he won't come back, but Pippa goes on and confirms what I'm thinking: "I hope he gets something hot to eat ... he'll be back later ... at bedtime."

PIPPA and I are watching television, drinking mugs of hot chocolate and sharing a box of Maltesers with the *News at Ten*. She is distracted, though, no doubt by the boy's rudeness and storming out, and my gentle questioning has not uncovered all the reasons behind her current mood. I think there may be more to it than that.

I know she wants so much to tell the boy about the baby — to see the joy on his face — but needs to find the right moment to do so. It may be this that's on her mind now. But she has also been expecting to hear from Elaine and hasn't, and may be wondering why. She did say, "That's odd," when we passed Elaine's house. I fear Pippa digging about, going round there, any of that. But she does not mention Elaine.

The boy has been out all evening, doing God knows what. Pippa seems to be edgier the later it gets. And so I think — no, I am sure — that he, the boy, and telling him her news, is what occupies her thoughts so much. Then, I hear his key in the door and am proven correct. Pippa turns and, almost brusquely, shoos me upstairs — "Quickly, quickly!" — saying she needs to talk to him. I hate how dismissive Pippa is. It's not right.

Now, as I lie stretched out on the carpet in my bedroom, the door slightly ajar, I hear her talking to him in the living room.

"Please." She has a begging tone to her voice. She should not beg before him.

"What?" he replies, wanting to go to bed. I think he may have been drinking or taking drugs. His voice is slightly slurred and aggressive, even more than usual.

"Please sit down." She says it again, more placatory this time.

There is a silence. I imagine they are now sitting side by side on the sofa. Him huffing and puffing, wanting to go. Her desperate. The dog as indifferent as ever. She'll put her arm around him. He'll shrug it off. She'll be on the brink of tears, struggling to know what to say.

"What?" he says again. "What do you want?" He is belligerent, more obviously slurring his words. Hurry up! Get a move on!

"You're ..." I hear her choke on her words. A moment's silence. A tearful smile in her voice. "You're going to be a big brother."

There is another, longer silence. I imagine her so close to tears as she waits for her words to sink in. He'll be sitting there with his jaw hanging, mouth wide open.

I crawl closer across the carpet towards the door so I can hear more clearly. I touch the door, pushing it back, but it creaks, the noise sounding so loud in the silence.

They will know I am here listening. I don't care about him. What he thinks! Pippa will understand I am watching out for her, though. As best friends forever do.

"No!" she cries out. "No ... no, it's not." I did not catch what he said. Maybe he just made a dismissive or a disgusted gesture. I don't know.

She is so tearful. I imagine her standing up now, reacting angrily. "Lots of women my age do," she shouts defensively.

I hear sudden movement, as if he is getting up from the sofa and she is grabbing him as he tries to push by her.

"No, no. Stop." More movement, the sound of her being knocked back onto the sofa as he pushes by her.

I get to my feet, unsure how to react. I want to go and help. But the angry boy, slight as he is, has youth and fury on his side.

I dash to the windowsill, grabbing the heavy paperweight and then moving towards the bedroom door.

"You're old enough to be a fucking granny!" he yells, coming up the stairs two at a time to his room. I hear her sobbing downstairs.

Everything happens so fast. I come through the bedroom door and onto the landing at the same instant as he walks onto it from the stairs. He is wild-eyed, in a fury, and his arms are flailing as if he is off-balance. I raise the paperweight in my hand, above my head, ready to bring it down on his skull.

It runs through my head in a second. He'll tumble downstairs, breaking his neck as he lands, hitting his head on the stone floor. I will claim self-defence. Once it has all been settled, Pippa and I will be alone together here. The baby will be gone by then too, of course, one way or the other. Pippa's shock at the death of the boy might be enough to trigger things.

But it does not happen this way. As I raise the paperweight, he jabs his fist towards my face. One. Two. Three times. He is drunk. He misses. Three times. I move in for the kill as he stumbles back, confused, and teeters close to the steps. I raise the paperweight. But he sidesteps in time, and I feel myself falling forward and down the stairs.

I LAND HALFWAY DOWN, in a higgledy-piggledy way, my legs and arms all in a tangle. I am shocked, but have not fallen far enough to hurt myself. No broken bones or bruises.

I have my wits about me — enough to reach for the heavy paperweight on the step below and tuck it under my body. I do not want Pippa to see it and wonder. The boy will never remember it in his drunken state.

Pippa is at the bottom of the stairs, her hand over her mouth, her face full of shock. The boy pushes roughly by both of us and is out the front door and away without a word.

"I'm so sorry, Sharon, so, so sorry." Pippa comes up the stairs, then reaches down and puts a hand on my shoulder. "Are you hurt? Can you get up? Let me help you."

I get slowly to my feet, tucking the paperweight into a pocket of my cardigan. Pippa does not seem to notice. If she had, I wonder if she would realise why I had it. Then again, maybe not. She's not so smart.

She takes my arm, and I limp and wince my way up to the top of the stairs. I then stand there with a pained expression on my face.

Pippa asks me where it hurts, and I grimace and say all over.

She puts her arm gently around my shoulder — I recoil ever so slightly, as if I am being brave — and she guides me gently towards her bedroom; hers being here, and mine being at the far end of the landing.

She clicks on the main light and walks me to the nearest side of the bed, pulling back the duvet. She suggests I get undressed whilst she fetches my nightdress from my room.

As she leaves, I bend and slip the paperweight out of sight under the bedside cabinet, then get undressed and stand there in my bra and pants.

I notice, for the first time, that a nail on a toe on my right foot is long and yellowing, curling over like a claw.

And I've put on my old underwear today, without thinking. My bra and pants are stained and don't match. The front of my pants feels crusty. And my body is lined and saggy. I am a disgusting sight.

This should be a wonderful moment, the first time I spend the night with Pippa. And in her own bed, too. I move to the switch on the wall and click off the central light.

I hear Pippa in my room, then in the bathroom, cleaning her teeth and using the toilet. I like listening to these moments; I love the intimacy of them.

Then Pippa is back, clicking on a bedside lamp, handing me my nightdress and talking brightly, as if she doesn't have a care in the world. "Stay here tonight ... I'll look after you ... you can keep me company. Do you need to use the bathroom?"

I wince — no, not now, thank you — and then pull the nightdress slowly over my head. It is an old one, but is clean, give or take a stain or two on the front from when I had toast and marmalade the other night. I lie down on the bed, watching Pippa.

Pippa goes to a wardrobe, undresses and stands naked side-on to me, so slim and slender even with her oh-so-slightly swelling belly. I am entranced as she chooses what she is going to wear. There is not an ounce of fat on her.

She picks what looks like a simple black tee shirt. Then turns towards me so I see her fully naked. I have never seen anyone so beautiful as Pippa in my life.

She puts the tee shirt on and walks to the other side of the bed. The tee shirt is too short to cover everything that should be covered, front and back. It rides up a little. I cannot take my eyes off her. Then she takes a pair of lacy knickers from a bedside cabinet drawer and slips them on.

I lie here, wondering if this might be where I will sleep from now on, night after night. Pippa in next to nothing by my side. I do not know how long I can stand it, her alongside me like this.

"He'll be back in the morning. Dom," she says. "And he'll apologise to you. Don't worry."

It is all I can do to not reply, "I couldn't care less."

She asks where it hurts most, and I say, "My right shoulder," and she is turning, gently pushing me on to my side away from her. And she places the palm of her hand on my shoulder and caresses me. I can barely breathe. Despite everything — all the horror swirling about — this is the moment when all my dreams come true.

———

I LIE HERE NOW, on my back, next to Pippa in this lovely bed, so big and soft and sensual. I am close to tears.

She stroked my shoulder for ever such a while. And her touch, and the expectation of what might follow, brought me close to ecstasy.

But then, almost abruptly, she stopped and said, "Good-night," and rolled away onto her side, her back to me. I wondered if my body's reactions to her touch had given me away.

Pippa is breathing steadily, and she is awake, lying there with her tee shirt almost up around her waist.

I lie here in almost unbearable agony, wanting to reach out and touch her, resting my hand gently on her thigh before moving it to stroke her.

But the thought of her reaction — her shrugging me off, perhaps pulling away in disgust — stops me.

I love Pippa. I adore her.

More than anything else, I want her physically.

Now is my best chance. Of becoming true soulmates.

But if she reacts badly, pushes me away, it could be the end of everything.

Banished from her bed. This beautiful house. To the extension. Maybe even from there, too.

"I'm sorry, Sharon," she'd say, the horror plain in her face, such revulsion in her voice. "I'm not that way. I'm not bisexual. I thought you'd realised that by now."

Even so, I edge slightly closer in the bed, moving the duvet across my shoulders, towards Pippa.

I can smell the scent of her, see the softness of her hair and the shape of her shoulders, back and below.

I cannot help myself. I reach out and put my fingers on her neck, just below her ear, and gently pull her hair back. A sweet, comforting gesture, no more.

I feel her react, holding her breath, her body stiffening. For one glorious moment, I think she is going to turn, and we will fall into each other's arms.

But she does not. She sits up, turns on the bedside lamp, then gets up and says she's going to get a glass of water and a headache tablet. And, crushing me, "Do you need anything before you go back to your bedroom, Sharon?"

She is gone, and I slink — that is the only word for it — to my room, feeling rejected and angry.

23

TUESDAY, 6 DECEMBER, EARLY MORNING

I have the most restless night ever, tormenting myself with thoughts of Pippa's rejection of me. I wonder how our relationship will recover from it, and decide, eventually, as the sun comes up and my room gradually fills with light, that I can only go on as though nothing has happened. I hope it will be the same with Pippa.

I feel sick at breakfast-time, awaiting Pippa's arrival, so I just have a cup of tea. Other than the fact she has to be at work earlier today — "Stock-taking!" — everything is much the same as it ever was. I am as bright and as jolly as I can be. Pippa is perhaps brisker, more efficient, busy-busy-busy. I think we have tacitly agreed to not speak of what happened, and to move on as we were. I begin to feel better.

We have, as before, a last-minute panic as she searches for her phone as she hurries to leave for work. "I've been texting Dom!" she wails. "He hasn't replied." She dashes to and fro. Moving cushions, checking the sides of the sofa as per usual. "I'm hoping he's still here ... on a friend's settee."

Eventually, she goes, all hunched and heartbroken. I console her with kind words, without hugging her, not now.

Of course, Pippa's mobile phone is in my pocket. I need to see what she has texted to the boy. And if he texts back at any point, and what he says.

It is my hope that he has gone back to Norwood, West Norwood, whatever it is called, made up with the uncle and aunt and will stay there and not bother us again. He may not even reply to Pippa's text, or be blunt if he does.

It bothers me why he came all the way back up here in response to Pippa's request. It is a long journey by train, and costly, too. I can only assume he is so unhappy that, despite his angry words last night, he wanted to talk about returning here to live. Or perhaps he wanted Pippa to buy him his own place. That's more likely. With my money! I cannot have that.

Like most troubled boys of his age — uprooted, in a strange new town, his father dying — he is full of suppressed and often illogical rage against everything and everyone. Waiting forever for Pippa and me to return from Colchester saw that anger turn to boiling-over fury.

And, coming back late last night perhaps for reconciliation, Pippa's 'big brother' announcement was the last straw. Off he went, in high dudgeon, never to return. I could almost hug myself with glee.

I sit on the sofa and open Pippa's phone messages, six, no, seven, to the dirty boy. The first is calm and measured, but, from then on, as they go unanswered, they become increasingly anxious.

The final one, sent just before six am, shows Pippa close to hysteria, 'CALL ME!' and I laugh out loud. I cannot help myself. The boy has gone for good. I am sure of it.

From there, my morning picks up, becoming ever more

joyful. I start with a long and luxurious bath, laid out flat with the frothy water up to my chin. I spend ever such an age thinking all sorts of thoughts, some nice, others naughty. Only when I am done with all my imaginings do I get up and dry myself on Pippa's bath towel, my face in its softness, breathing in the smell of Pippa's body.

And then I make my breakfast, a cafetiere of coffee, two well-buttered croissants spread with strawberry jam and a plain yoghurt with one last blob of jam in it. I take everything up to my room on a tray and slide into bed, sitting up to eat and drink to my heart's content. I flick through my own phone, looking at the local online newspaper, reading about an old fellow in Ipswich whose body lay undiscovered in his bungalow for six years. I shouldn't, I know, but I laugh loudly.

I think somehow, from here on, life is going to be rather wonderful. The father has gone. The boy too. The landlord's son as well. Elaine's body may not be discovered for a long, long time. Six years, maybe more! If it is, it will be decomposed and all evidence turned to dust. I have Pippa, and that, other than her rejection and the baby, makes me so happy. And I will have money from her soon. So, if need be, I will be an independent woman. I could weep with happiness.

———————

WHAT I WANT, more than anything else in the world, is for this, my life now, to continue forever.

Pippa and I, living in this lovely house, spending time together, the closest companions — I will settle for that if I have to.

The baby will spoil everything and ruin this idyllic life. I will do something about that soon. More pressing for me right now is the dirty boy.

He stands in front of me on the doorstep, having just knocked on the front door. I was in the kitchen, loading the dishwasher, when I heard the knocking and assumed Pippa had come home early and somehow lost her front door key. Anything like that is possible with Pippa. I opened the door, saying jovially, "What a lovely ..." Then I see it is him.

I say nothing, simply shutting the door in his face, clicking the lock and putting the chain into place. It is an instinctive reaction, given what he did last night. I cannot take a chance. No one could expect me to. He has been outside somewhere all night long, most likely, then coming up the path to the door. Whether he came to see Pippa or what he wanted, I could not say.

I hope he will shout to say he's come to collect something from his bedroom, or that he wishes to apologise, or simply that he'd like to talk about Pippa and the baby. Something conciliatory. But he does not say a word. Instead, he puts one hand on the frosted glass and the other on the door frame and pushes it back and forth. The rattling and his anger spook me.

And then he stops, swears under his breath, and turns to walk back to the pavement.

I am about to turn away, too, walking by the dog in its basket to the kitchen to make myself another milky coffee before listening to the radio and having a clean and tidy around. But he is moving, running, to the right, across the garden, out of sight, going to the back garden.

I grab a knife from the block in the kitchen and just reach the patio door as he gets to it, clicking up the latch as he pulls the outside handle down to wrench the door open. He reaches for the latch to pull it down, too — a split second too late, as I lock the door from inside. He reels back in frustration and hammers on the door with his fists before stepping back into the garden and looking up at the windows.

I stand there watching, expecting him to see the bathroom window is open. After my relaxing bath, I opened it to let the steamy air out. For one glorious moment, I think he will, if I walk away now, imagine he has fooled me, that he has given up trying to get in. And he will, when I am back in the living room, go to the shed and get out the ladder, putting it up against the wall by the bathroom window, ready to climb up.

But I will be back in the bathroom by then, standing behind the door. And as he climbs up the ladder and pushes open the window and puts his knee on the windowsill, I will step forward and push him back out onto the patio below. That will put paid to him. It would be a rather fitting way to go. Like nasty father, like nasty son.

But he does not turn towards the shed, and I do not go upstairs to the bathroom. Instead, he stands there gazing upwards. I see his face crumple into sadness, and he dips his head down.

I think he has just remembered that it's from that window that dear old Dead Dad fell, and he's welling up. As he looks towards me again, I give him a sweet little smile. And pretend to rub my eyes, boohoo. I top it off by miming opening a window and then a diving motion — from the high board! — with my hands.

I watch the expression change on his face, from sorrow to disbelief and then to anger. He has put two and two together and made four. I expect him to run at me, battering on the door. I might even open it. I have a knife from the kitchen ready in self-defence. Instead, he turns and runs off. That, more than anything else, fills me with ice-cold dread.

I CANNOT LET the boy get away. I don't know where he's going to go and what he might do. He may run to the police station in town, spilling out his thoughts and ideas that, maybe, I killed his father. I curse myself for my mocking gestures, my desperate desire to hurt him overcoming common sense.

The police would send someone round, for sure, and they would talk to me. I might give myself away under clever questioning. At the very least, I'd be on their radar if or when Elaine's body is discovered. And Pippa would find out what I had done, and would look at me, puzzled, the cogs in her airy-fairy mind whirring slowly until she worked out the terrible truth. And the husband would, no doubt, come back from the grave to haunt me.

I cannot go after him now, on foot, as he will be too fast for me, wherever he goes. I wish I had a car outside the house. I would drive after him. In my head, I see myself spotting him on a quiet side road. I would rev up and accelerate fast, mounting the pavement and knocking him down, then racing away from his mangled body without anyone seeing. I feel a surge of immense pleasure at the thought.

Somehow, I need to reel him in, get him back here, kill him and dispose of his body. And I have to do it fast. What else can I do? The net is tightening.

I sit on the sofa, take out Pippa's phone, turn it on and click through. I must take control of the situation. My mind runs through what I must do, the order, and how to cover myself.

There have already been three calls from him, no voice messages, but there is a text message from him in teenage abbreviations. Three minutes ago. In essence, 'Where are you? We need to talk.'

I think quickly, knowing I have only minutes to retrieve matters before he heads for the bus stop and goes to Ipswich to see her. He knows she works in a boutique. I don't think he knows what it's called or where it is, exactly. But it won't be hard to find.

I text back, my hands shaking, trying to word my reply in Pippa's brainless voice. 'Yes! Let's talk!' I pause, thinking, and then add, to be certain, 'What about?'

I press send and sit back, waiting for a reply, working through various options in my head. I could text, 'Come home. See you there.' Then unlock the front door and the patio door and wait for him out of sight with the knife or a heavy paperweight in my hand. Knife, I think, so I can say he attacked me in the kitchen. It would be consistent with his behaviour last night.

The reply comes fast, and I don't need to translate teenage abbreviations. 'Sharon,' he writes, as simply as that.

I struggle to breathe. My instinct is to reply, 'What about Sharon?' But I know what the answer to that will be, and it might include, 'Now on the bus to you in Ipswich.' And all I could then do is to take as much money as I can find and flee Felixstowe for somewhere far away. Back on the streets at my age. I'd be dead behind supermarket bins before the spring. Recently, BBC News announced that this could be one of the coldest, hardest winters for years.

I hesitate, about to text him to come home as quickly as

he can, 'See you there.' But it suddenly dawns on me what I'll have to do. He is a slender boy, and, taken by surprise, I could kill him. But how do I clean things up, and where do I dispose of the body? There is nowhere in the house, the extension or the garden. I cannot dig and disguise a shallow grave behind the extension.

My mind, going here and there, comes up with a sudden plan that might just work. I need to stop him from doing anything, talking to, seeing anyone, until I have him with me. I need to be able to kill him. And I must, somehow, hide the body wherever I do it, with a chance that he won't be found, at least not for some time. The other side of winter maybe, when the animals have got to him first.

I text my first message: 'I know. I want to talk to you about Sharon too. Keep away from the house for now. Don't talk to anyone.' I press send before I change my mind.

Then the second: 'I'm at work at the moment. Then heading over to Bury St Edmunds to collect a puppy. A Jack Russell.' Again, I press send.

Finally, 'I'll be back at 5.00. Meet me at the car park at the Grove woods, and we'll walk Archie and talk about Sharon.' One more send.

I think quickly and then send a final few words, 'I want you to be happy. Decide where you want to live. And I will buy you a flat.' I can do no more.

I sit back, an agonising wait, wondering if my texts will do the trick, or whether he will realise these are not the words of his mother. He has no reason to suspect anything is amiss. Yet the thought nags at me.

I do not know if my messages will work — that he will somehow kick his heels all day, not talking to anyone, until five o'clock. If not, I will have to flee now, getting the bus to Ipswich and then the train to God knows where.

Then he replies, and it is full of abbreviations and emojis and other symbols and comments I do not understand. He is thrilled about the dog. And the flat. And talking about Sharon can wait until 5.00. He will go and see so-and-so ... visit the amusements on the pier ... 'see ya soon!'

And that is that. All I have to do now is to firm up my plan to kill him and dispose of the body where it will not be found for ages, if at all. It will take place at the Grove woodlands as darkness falls. I will have my trusty paperweight with me. And a kitchen knife. The paperweight will fell him; the knife will silence him forever.

I make two trips to the Grove, one mid-morning, the other early afternoon. Just an old lady having a morning constitutional and an afternoon stroll, a bracing breath of fresh air. Really, I am checking out ditches and looking at leaves and mud and branches that might make a nice, makeshift grave.

I check Pippa's phone now and then, just to see if he has sent any other messages, anything alarming that might need to be attended to. I even Google for photos of Jack Russell puppies and copy and send one to him. I write 'Meet Archie' and then '5pm!' A few minutes later, he texts back, the usual, mindless slang and emojis and 'Yea! 5,' sealing his fate.

FELIXSTOWE IS AN EVER-GROWING town with developers relentlessly filling every nook and cranny with new houses. 'For Sale' boards — profit signs for some — are everywhere.

There are few places where you can kill someone and dispose of them without being seen. One such area is the Grove: a vast expanse of woodland on the edge of town that stretches this way and that, shared mostly by dog-walkers, muntjac deer and perverted old men.

Even that is being encroached upon by developers, with more to come; there is talk of a huge housing estate and a leisure centre and more — so much development that there will be little here but bricks and concrete. Even so, it is the only place I have a chance of success.

I stand here now, all in black, beside a thick-set tree at the wooden gate by the car park at the edge of the woods, just out of sight, waiting for the boy. It is a cold late afternoon. There are only two cars in the car park — I watched as others left and these arrived separately. Both dog-walkers: one middle-aged woman with a black Labrador and an old, white-haired man with a mongrel. I waited as they disappeared in turn towards the adjacent fields and away. Dusk turns slowly to darkness as I wait patiently. The lights in the car park have yet to come on; when they do, they will cast eerie shadows.

The woods behind me are hushed. I glance backwards now and again, expecting a walker or a runner, somebody, to appear out of the gloom. But no one does. I pull Pippa's black hooded fleece over my head, just in case, and step further back into the shadows, anonymous. I hold Pippa's dog lead in my hand. If anyone passes me, they will think I am waiting for my dog to return from hunting rabbits. If they say something to me, I will nod, my head down, or make some sort of noise of agreement before turning away as though I am looking for my dog.

The Grove is a creepy place at this time of dusk into

darkness. Trees rising up, untended and often broken, towards the sky. Paths, sometimes dry, occasionally muddy, are overgrown with bushes and weeds and spreading tree roots. There are dried-up streams, and ditches, and smaller, uneven paths that lead into inaccessible dips and troughs. It is a place where bodies have been buried, I am sure. The stench of overturned soil and something rotting and dank water is forever in the air. I have walked here so many times over the years, idly identifying possible sites for developments and hidey-holes where bodies might never be found.

I suddenly see the dark silhouette of the boy, his unmistakable slight shape and striding walk, from afar. He is hurrying across the car park, right on time, moving towards where I am waiting. Out of sight, the element of surprise is on my side. It has to be. I must strike hard and fast and knock him to the ground before he realises what is happening. One chance, and one chance only.

I step back again, into the murky woods, so I cannot be seen, pull that black fleece around me, and feel in the left pocket for the heavy paperweight I'm going to use. There is nobody else about. is on my side. I take the paperweight out, ready to strike. I brace myself, counting down the seconds, imagining how long it will take him to get to the gate, the tree, the woods, and then go by me, standing back and hidden. At that point, in that instant, I must step forward and hit him as hard as I can, three times, on the back of the head. Then, after that, I will pull out the knife.

But, as I count to ten, twenty, thirty seconds, on edge, unable to breathe, my nerves making me tense and tight, he does not appear. I wait, shaking now with fear, holding the paperweight, expecting him any second. There is no one in sight in the woods. I can sense that it is just me and him. If I am fast and can fell him before he reacts, I can move in close and slam the paperweight against his head time and again. I have a knife, the one I used to kill Elaine, tucked inside my trouser belt, to finish the job.

Still he does not appear, and I am now sweating profusely. In my mind, I am cool and in control. As with the husband and Elaine, I do what I have to do, no more and no less, to be with the love of my life, my soulmate, Pippa. I hope it will give us time together, to live the life I have always dreamed of. Until the baby arrives, at least. Or longer than that if I have my way. I lean slightly forward so that I can see into the car park. The boy, the dark shape of him, stands in the middle, as if not sure where to go. As the lights start coming on, I take a torch from the right pocket of my fleece and flash it on and off towards him.

I stand back as he breaks into a run towards me, assuming I am Pippa with Archie the dog. I lift the paper-weight, ready to attack. I have to succeed. I will have to flee, if I can get away from him, if I do not. There can be no mistaking my intentions.

"I didn't know where you ..." He goes to say "were" as he runs in, but somehow stumbles and falls over tree roots in the darkness. And I am upon him as he sprawls, driven by fury and desperation. I hit him again and again, building to something close to frenzy.

When my temper has eventually eased, I stand there, panting and shaking, over his body, looking around. I have been so lucky. There is nobody in sight. I take his phone, in case it might be useful, and his cards and coins out of habit, and then drag him, stop-start, stop-start, over to a nearby ditch. I heave him in and cover the body in leaves. There, at last, I am done. And then I jump, so startled, as I hear a noise behind me.

I STEP BACK from the ditch, looking up and down the pathway through the trees and into the woodland around me. I have the strongest sense that someone is watching me, though that might be my nerves working overtime.

The noise, whatever it was — an animal, maybe a deer — spooked me. But there is nothing in sight, no one there to see. No movements. Lights. Nothing at all.

It is dark now, and I try to still my mind, fighting the urge to flee, to run away. From what might prove to be my terrible mistake. My undoing. But what else could I have done? He knew, or at least suspected, my involvement in his father's death.

My mind in turmoil, I go back down on my knees, tipping forwards, pushing my hands into the leaves, touching his still-warm body. I want to be sure he is dead. He is. I am certain of it. To be certain, I push the knife into him three times between his ribs. I wipe it clean on his jacket.

I glance round, still all clear, and push his mobile phone in one pocket of the fleece next to Pippa's; the cards, coins and paperweight into the other. The knife and the torch go into my trouser pockets with the dog lead. Then I stand up, ready to walk off.

I resist the urge to check the body one more time, to be definitely, absolutely, 100 per cent sure. I must go now. Every time I touch him, checking, and moving more leaves and broken branches for cover, the more I risk being interrupted. If I stay any longer, I will surely be seen.

What would I then do? Make polite conversation with a puzzled-looking dog walker wondering what I am doing here?

"I've lost my dog," I'd say, instinctively, pulling the lead out of my trouser pocket before turning and walking away. Hoping they did not notice my scared face or dishevelled and spattered clothing, and that they did not peer into the ditch.

But they'd remember it well enough when the body is discovered — tomorrow, next week, the following month — and a mock-up photograph and description of me will be all over the news.

And so I walk head down, my mind full of horror, along the path back towards the car park. I hear the noises of boys, young and carefree, playing football, calling to each other, on the pitches over the far side of the trees. I've never experienced much normality in my life.

I keep going, wiping my hands on the fleece over and again, as if the act will cleanse them. And me. I had thought there would be blood all down my front from where I caved in his skull in my fury. And later, stabbing him. But there is nothing there that I can see at the moment.

I just have to stay calm, act as though I am having an evening stroll, and no one will give me a second glance. Then I am out through the woodland path and on to the car park. The lights are now fully on, creating an eerie glow.

There are five cars here with old and young people, singletons and couples, and children and dogs, getting in and out. Some walk towards the playing fields, others towards the path I have just walked along. I am so lucky they were not ten minutes earlier.

I stand still for a moment. I can hardly breathe, the thought that these people, any of them, could still stumble across the body in the next few minutes. The ditch is barely off the beaten track, and the body is not buried as deep as it should be.

There will be no mistaking that this is murder, and my days will be numbered. Even if he is not found soon, some-one, a friend or family member in London, will check with Pippa, asking where he is. Thank goodness I have both phones. And Elaine's, too. I will have to live with the profound feeling of imminent discovery.

And then I feel a hand on my shoulder, and I squeal — there is no other word for it — and stumble forwards, landing on my knees.

I turn and look up, expecting to see a policeman there, someone who has followed me somehow all along the pathway.

But it is Alan, the stupid old fool from the book club, and his timid-looking wife with a yappy little dog on a lead, trying to be funny, to scare me.

He looks at me, pleasure at my expense on his face. I get to my feet, brushing myself down, expecting him to apolo-gise for making me jump and knocking me over. But he does not. He just asks, in his stupid voice, "What are you doing here?" And if he had left at that, I'd have said something about an evening constitutional and I'd have been on my way.

But he adds to it: "We've never seen you here before, have we, Christine?" He looks at the busybody wife, who shakes her head. We all look from one to the other. He thinks he's clever. She's no idea what's going on. I am scared. It will be Alan, when the body is found, who will turn to Christine

and say, "Do you remember when we saw that woman —
Sharon, her name is — at the Grove ...?"

I smile at them, trying to not look sour, and turn and
walk away. "See you soon!" he shouts cheerily, and I can
imagine him waving. He is the sort of man who has to have
the final word, the last laugh, whenever he can. I am in
torment.

24

TUESDAY, 6 DECEMBER, EARLY EVENING

When I get back home and have changed my clothes, hiding the dirty and bloodied items under the chest of drawers in the extension for now, I make my way into the house, heading upstairs to shower myself clean. I will scrub my skin for ages, over and over, before we eat.

Pippa is lying flat out on the sofa, head and feet on cushions propped up at either end, the soles of her dirty bare feet towards me. I wonder if she will sit up, asking where I've been, why I am wearing my old original clothes from the extension, and the reason I look so peaky. I will say I have been for a long walk — too far, too quickly — and have overdone things.

I sense her spirits are low by the way she is stretched out, her left arm across her head, a 'woe is me' position. I wonder if she posed like this when she heard me coming through the patio door. "I've left today," she says, in a close-to-tears voice. "The boutique. It's too much for me."

I'm not sure wafting about in an airy-fairy manner is that

hard, but still, that's what Pippa is like. I just say I am going for a shower.

She sits up and looks towards me, but not really at me, studying me, more that her head is facing my general direction.

"I've lost my phone." She stammers out the words. "I've really lost it this time. I've looked everywhere." She makes it sound such a tragedy. Like she's lost a child or something. Really, she is so self-absorbed.

I shrug, not sure what to say to that. Maybe get another comes to mind. I don't say it, though.

Her phone, along with the dirty boy's, is in the extension, under the bottom drawer of the chest of drawers. I see no advantage in giving it back this time. Along with the boy's cards and coins, I will dispose of everything first thing in the morning. Or at least I was going to, until Pippa announced she has left work and will presumably be here what people call twenty-four seven. I'm not sure how I feel about that. I like some time to myself.

"And I don't know what's happened to Dom. I called him from the landline when I got home, but it just goes to voice-mail. I'm going to phone my brother-in-law tonight, James, to see if he's gone back there. I worry about him. If he's not there, I'll call the police."

It occurs to me, and it makes me laugh inside, that Pippa may have been calling from the landline at the moment I was bludgeoning the boy. I imagine a ring-ring-ring in time with my arm rising and falling. Of course, the two mobiles, his and hers, hidden in the extension, are both turned off. I'd not want to be sitting here and one of them start trilling, only to be heard by Pippa, who'd recognise the ringtone and go towards the extension to investigate. Whenever I next get a free moment from Pippa, if she goes shopping perhaps, I will take the phones and pull them apart, stamping and smashing them to pieces, and then wrap them in toilet paper, flushing them away piece by piece.

"And Elaine," Pippa wails, such an annoying sound, as though she is going through every single bloody thing, one by one, to torment me. "I drove by her place on the way home. Her car's still there. That's so odd, isn't it? She said she was going to the Cotswolds. How would she do that from here without her car? I've called her from the landline ... I'm going to go round there in the morning. Then call into the police station up by the supermarket."

Elaine's phone — my little collection of phones — is upstairs hidden in my room, turned off too, of course. I am very careful. Otherwise, it would have rung as Pippa called it from the landline. She would have cocked her head to the side, heard the familiar tune of the *Neighbours* theme on Elaine's phone, dashed upstairs, and found it, holding it in her hand, puzzling, until she worked out what it really meant, being there hidden. As with Pippa's and the boy's phones, it will be destroyed along with any other evidence some time in the morning, hopefully.

"I'm going to have a shower," I repeat, finally heading by Pippa to the stairs. She is staring into space now and then starts sobbing uncontrollably. I imagine it's about the dead husband and the endless waiting for the coroner or what-ever; I don't get involved with any of that. I have to be honest and say that she is getting on my nerves. I just want to get myself clean.

She gestures me towards her, like I am her servant. I am loath to approach, as I feel I have the smell of the boy's flesh and blood on me. But she gestures again, more firmly. And so I do, reluctantly. She calls me her 'rock' and hugs me long and hard. Last night, the pass I made, seems to have been forgotten, or at least forgiven.

She smells ever-so-slightly sweaty, which is unpleasant for me. "Let's have your lovely omelettes for tea," she says, eventually letting go. She lies there grimacing as I go upstairs, realising she's going to be like this all evening, with me running round her. I wonder if this is how it will be all the time now she has stopped work. Right up to the birth. And beyond and forever, with the baby. I will be expected to be Mary fucking Poppins until the day I die.

———

I SHOWER for so long as I scrub myself endlessly, feeling I have the stink of the boy all over my body. I rub my hands raw. And I brush furiously at my nails, fearing there is evidence of the boy's skin beneath them. And, for some reason, I scour my face with a flannel, as though it is spattered with invisible blood.

In my mind, I go over all that I have done. The husband. Elaine. The son. And how I might have left clues behind that will lead the police to me. I think, once I have destroyed the phones and other evidence tomorrow, I will be safe.

But now, stopping work, Pippa is going over everything in her head, too. Making a call to the brother soon. Then the police. Visiting Elaine's house. And walking into the police station. I had not expected that she, my soulmate, might be the cause of my exposure. My downfall. It sets me thinking as I dry myself on a towel and then dress and leave the bathroom.

There is a moment. Now. As Pippa stands at the top of the stairs. And I am coming out through the bathroom door.

She is struggling with a pile of clothes from the wicker basket she keeps in the corner of her bedroom.

And she drops a bra and a pair of her little stripey socks on the carpet.

She is laughing, knowing that she has taken too many clothes and cannot carry them all in her arms.

She bends for the bra and socks and leans, off-balance, by the edge of the stairs.

She picks them up, but then drops a pair of knickers on to the first step down.

Leaning forward again, there is an instant when I think she will topple over and fall down the stairs.

I imagine her hitting her head on the wall, knocking her unconscious.

Then rolling the other way, hitting the banister rails.

Landing finally on her stomach on the hard wooden floor.

It strikes me, as I stand here watching, perhaps waiting, that this could mean that Pippa and I might be alone together for ever. If she were to take that fatal stumble down the stairs and land hard onto her stomach. But I also wonder, in that moment, if I actually want Pippa to die, too.

The thought shocks me. But it is now there. And it will grow. As it has done before. With Elaine and the boy in particular. I cannot stop my thoughts spreading. I will not act on them yet. I need to plan.

I could go through Pippa's things, her bank accounts and her cards, all of her money, and somehow take over her life, even accessing enough money to start a new life overseas. I must mull over my options.

For now, I dash forward, expecting her to stumble and tumble down the stairs. But she does not. Somehow, I don't know how, she regains her balance as I grab her, and all the clothes go falling down the stairs.

I dare not push her, not obviously anyway, as she might not be hurt that badly from the fall. And she would look at me, knowing that I had tried to harm her and the baby. And then what would happen?

I need to think things through first, if I decide to go that way, of course. I'd be happy to see how everything unfolds. But then I recall her intentions for later this evening, making calls and visits and more calls. I realise I need to think fast and make my decision.

She turns to me, flushed and alarmed, and puts her arms around me as if I have saved her life. Then she kisses me quickly on the cheek and says, "Come on." And we both go down the stairs to pick up the dirty clothes.

I could, even now, as she goes to take the first step, pretend to stumble myself, sending her tumbling down the steps, just to see what happens. But I do not. I bide my time for the right moment. It will be soon.

———————

WE SIT, face-to-face, at the dining table, eating the cheese omelettes I've made and picking at the rocket and tomatoes, drizzled with honey mustard dressing, on the sides of our plates. We drink from a jug of tap water tonight, as Pippa is on her 'no alcohol' regime for the baby. Me too, so it seems.

Neither of us speak much, just odd conversations about finding a nice frame for the baby scan photograph, and getting a new vacuum cleaner, as this one isn't as powerful as it once was. I also suggest a day out at the shops in Norwich tomorrow or the one after. She says yes, but we must check the weather later. All mundane stuff. Between a killer and a victim. Maybe. I have not yet decided what to do.

We are both distracted by our own thoughts. She is thinking about the boy and Elaine; mostly the boy, I suspect. And, of course, I am too. Pippa is worried where they are. I am as well, in a way — worried that they will be found.

Halfway through our omelettes, during a particularly long, quiet spell where neither of us can seem to think of anything to say, Pippa darts out of the room. She comes back with the landline phone, pressing buttons.

She sits down, pulling a piece of rocket from between her teeth on the upper left side, and puts it on the side of her plate. She waits. I hear the endless dring-dring inside the earpiece and guess she is telephoning the brother-in-law.

There are the usual pleasantries and small talk. She calls him 'James' rather than 'Jim.' This is a polite relationship rather than a close and loving one. He asks, I think, how she is, given the husband and what have you with the coroner business. She replies she is okay, considering. And then, after a minute or two, we get to it. The boy.

She asks if Dom is with him. I hear his reply, not the exact words but the tone of it: negative, no, Dom is not there. She pulls a face. With Chris, the other brother-in-law, she suggests. No, we're all here now, actually, funnily enough, is what I think he replies, shouts, and then asks her a question I can't hear clearly.

It is about the boy, I guess. She tells him about what happened — a summary, anyway. How the boy came back last night and left. She does not say why. She does not mention being pregnant. I don't know why. She stresses she does not know where Dom is. She is worried about him.

The brother-in-law's voice sounds conciliatory, not to worry, he's sure, then says, shouts again, "Perhaps Dom's got a girl!" She glances at me and shakes her head, as if to say 'Idiot.' There is more small talk; they'll let each other know if — when — they hear from the boy, and then they say goodbye.

"No luck?" I say, sipping my glass of tap water and trying to sound interested.

She shakes her head, muttering, "I don't know ... James is such a ... I don't know ... a wally." Then, "Can I borrow your mobile?"

I'd rather wait until we've finished eating — we have a cheesecake and fresh cream for dessert — but I go and fetch it from my room. The dog watches me wearily as I go by.

I hand my mobile phone to her as I return, and I watch as her fingers and thumbs dart around the keypad.

"Do you know ..." Pippa says, looking at me as she clicks away, checking the weather for tomorrow or the next day. Then she stops and thinks.

"I've always wanted to live in America ... Florida, did I say? The winter. Maybe for ever."

I shake my head, as if to say, 'No, I don't recall.' Her mind flutters over so many things all the time that she may have mentioned it some time or other. I cannot remember every single thing.

She stops what she is doing, and looks at me. "This would be a great time to go, wouldn't it? Or soon anyway. We could get a place on the coast. Sarasota's meant to be nice ... all that sunshine. Later, if we lived there, we could take Florence to the beach after school."

I look at her, not sure how to reply. It's a pipe dream, surely. Just wishful thinking. I'm not sure, though. Pippa has such a butterfly personality.

"Are you serious?" I say, a little more sharply than I mean to. Almost angrily, thinking that if I'd known this, that we might go abroad, I did not need to have done what I did with Elaine and the boy. We could have just gone!

She does not notice the tone of my voice. Just smiles to herself and then adds, "Why not? One day soon ... we could open an ice-cream parlour ... or a nail bar ... Sharon and Pippa's." And I feel my anger rise.

I want to shout at her, Do you know what I've done for you? Your stupid husband ... Elaine ... your dirty boy! All of them ... so we could be together.

I bite my tongue as she reaches across and gathers up the plates, knives and forks and glasses. She tips the last of the water from the jug into our two glasses and puts my phone on the table next to me. I turn and watch as she goes into the kitchen, clattering all the items into the dishwasher. Everything is as it ever was, her mind full of brainless nonsense: Norwich shopping tomorrow and Florida beaches next year. Lah! De! Lah! De! Lah!

She has not said anything further about the boy. I had assumed, after her phone call with the brother-in-law, she would become ever more hysterical, and I would have to talk her down — "Give it a few days yet" — from telephoning the police straightaway, 999, reporting the boy missing. But she is surprisingly calm. I could not face having a local community police officer here, snooping about and asking intrusive questions.

And, a blessed relief, she has not mentioned stupid Elaine again. There is no mention of going round there where, inevitably, Pippa would push open the back gate, notice the kitchen door was open, and hurry across before recoiling at the smell. Elaine had a rather distinctive odour at the best of times. Her rotting corpse would be much worse, possibly.

"Big piece or little piece of cheesecake?" Pippa shouts from the kitchen, distracting me from my thoughts. I call back, saying I'm not sure, how big is it? She says she'll bring a knife through; I can decide. "Do you want cream?" she shouts again, and I reply yes, please. "I'll put it in that little jug Elaine bought me," she replies. I curse to myself, realising Elaine is about to become a topic of discussion. But, as with the boy, the moment may pass.

I idly move the phone towards me, turn it over, and go to check the weather that Pippa has been looking at, for Norwich for the next couple of days. We like to sit in a park there, and as long as it's not raining, I think we will be good to go. What a treat.

The page Pippa has been looking at is still there on my phone. It is not the BBC weather, but the local police website. 'Missing people. To report a missing person, submit our online form or call 101.' This jolts me into shock.

Pippa comes back in, puts the cheesecake and plates on the table, and takes spoons from her pockets, and places them next to the cheesecake and plates. She shakes her head and makes a comment about being ditsy, and that she is going back to the kitchen to fetch the jug of cream and the knife to cut the cheesecake. I call after her, in a cheery voice, "You've been on the police website about missing people?"

"Yes," she replies, coming back through with the jug of cream in one hand and the kitchen knife in the other. She puts the jug down. "I've filled out a form to report both

Dom and Elaine missing. And once we've had our desserts, we'll put our coats on and go round to Elaine's. And we'll drive by the Grove on the way. There's something just been put on one of the Facebook pages ... the police have put cordons up there ... I wonder if they've found a herd of muntjac deer?"

I explode with rage, all the fury in me bubbling over, horrified the game is up, tonight, if not now.

"All I've ever wanted is for the two of us to be together as soulmates! That's all I've ever wanted!" I shout so loudly, spilling into madness. Pippa's face is frozen in shock as I go on. I cannot help myself. "Everything I've done, to all of them, is so that we can be together forever!"

I stop, realising, in essence, what I have said, or at least implied. The implication turning to certainty soon enough.

Pippa's face still looks shocked, and bewildered too, as though she cannot comprehend what I am saying. About the husband. Elaine. And the boy. She does not take it in — she is just stunned that I am screaming at her in an insane fury.

"You're so fucking stupid!" I yell, grabbing her hand and snatching the knife from it. I have no choice now but to kill her, take as much money and as many cards as I can, and run for my life. What else can I do?

I GO to move round the table to stab her with the knife.

She reacts instinctively, her body doing what her mind cannot, pushing the table hard against me.

I stumble backwards and fall over, the knife clattering away across the hard wooden floor.

As I struggle to get up, Pippa comes round the table with

the heavy fruit bowl, the centrepiece of the table, in her hands.

She looks terrified as she raises it above her head. I roll to one side as it crashes down towards my head, missing me by centimetres.

"Sharon," she says, in a whimper. "Sharon." As if she can't believe what is happening. Is almost begging me to stop.

She stands there shaking. But I have no choice. I have to kill her. I will do it as quickly and as painlessly as I can.

I move across the room to the bottom of the stairs, retrieving the knife. As I pick it up, it slips from my fingers and spins further away.

Now I have it, turning towards Pippa. But she has gone, running into the kitchen, and I hear her on the landline phone.

I am close to her as she presses 999 and starts shouting, "Police! Help! Help me!" I knock the phone out of her hand, over the floor to the fridge.

And then I stand there, panting, as Pippa looks at me with such an expression: disbelief and fear and God knows what.

I have to finish this and jab her with the knife, but it goes into her arm as she brings them both across her stomach, protecting the baby.

"No, Sharon, no!" she pleads. "Not my baby, not my baby."

I pull the knife back and jab again, harder this time, into the other protective arm. She screams in pain. Her arms drop to the sides as I pull the knife out.

I move in for the kill. I know where the heart is. I have seen enough programmes, read so many crime books.

It will take two or three stabs, at most. I don't want to hurt her more than I have to.

Pippa turns towards the block of knives on the side close by her.

It all happens so fast. She is younger than me and quicker.

I stagger back, looking down to see a kitchen knife in my stomach. I double forwards in pain as I realise, then somehow pull it out, screaming.

It slips from my grip and lands on the floor. Pippa looks at me. I stare back at her. I am wounded now. There are two knives that Pippa can go for to finish me off.

I hear the operator on the phone, speaking, calling, seeking an answer. She will have heard all of this, of course.

I turn, back towards the living room, to head for the front door and away.

But Pippa is behind me now, chasing. She won't let me escape.

Somehow, she trips me, and I go sprawling across the wooden floor.

And then she is above, that heavy fruit bowl in her hands again.

I rise as best I can onto my elbows. "No, Pippa, no."

She hesitates for an instant, a look of uncertainty on her face. Horror at what she is about to do.

"I love you, Pips. You're my soulmate."

That seems to enrage her for some reason. I don't know why.

She hits me with the heavy bowl on the head, a glancing blow, as I twist to the side and fall flat on my back.

I am stunned, but not fatally wounded. I think I have the

strength to get back up on my feet, to somehow fight her off and get away.

But I am unable to, my head rolling to the side. I find myself staring at the wretched dog lying in its basket. It looks back at me, only half-awake.

I go to call to it, hoping somehow it might do something to help me. But it just rolls over, making a slobbering noise, back into sleep.

Finally, I turn my head, my eyes bloody, towards Pippa and watch, as if in slow motion, as she heaves the fruit bowl on to my head one last time.

EPILOGUE

I reread and slightly edit my clumsy, semi-literate poem.

You are my soulmate, my one true love.
I have searched for you all my days.
Knowing you were out there somewhere.
All I had to do was to find you.
And now I have, my darling Ruth.
We will be together forever.
Holding hands. Laughing. Loving.
Our hearts and minds as one.
Our souls entwined.

I do not really care how it reads to anyone. I adore it and so, I believe, will Ruth, the love of my life.

I have had what I thought were soulmates before. Some I think about; others I don't. They are all dead. Good riddance to all of them.

Pippa was not my soulmate. Truth is, she tried to kill me.

I survived. In court, later, as I was sentenced, I cried out, "I love you," but she just turned away without even looking in my direction.

I am in prison now and will be for the rest of my days. I confessed to everything. I could not let the landlord's son, Alan, or anyone else report me to the police first and have the last laugh.

I would have thought that being locked up would break me, but it hasn't. Not at all. If anything, I am thriving.

At the moment, I am having psychiatric assessments to determine the prison I will eventually be sent to. The bed is warm. The food is tolerable. There are activities to pass the time. It is far better than the streets.

One of the assessors is called Ruth. She is ever so nice to me. I called her 'Ruthie' for the first time this morning. She smiled warmly. Ruthie is my soulmate.

THE END

ABOUT THE AUTHOR

Did you enjoy *The Soulmate*? If you could spend a moment to write an honest review on Amazon, no matter how short, we would be extremely grateful. They really do help readers discover new authors.

Iain Maitland is the author of five previous psych thrillers, *The Perfect Husband* (2022), *The Girl Downstairs* (2021), *The Scribbler* (2020), *Mr Todd's Reckoning* (2019) and *Sweet William* (2017).

He is also the author of two memoirs, *Dear Michael, Love Dad* (Hodder, 2016), a book of letters written to his eldest son who experienced depression and anorexia, and (co-authored with Michael) *Out Of The Madhouse* (Jessica Kingsley, 2018). His most recent book is the semi-autobiographical novel *The Old Man, His Dog & Their Longest Journey* (2023).

Iain is an Ambassador for Stem4, the teenage mental health charity. He talks regularly about mental health issues in schools and colleges and workplaces.

You can find Iain on his website:
www.iainmaitland.net

ACKNOWLEDGMENTS

As always, I 'd like to thank ...

Brian and Garret and all at Inkubator Books for publishing *The Soulmate*. Another grand job!

Nebojsa Zoric – for your cover.

Barbara Nadel – for the cover quote and your ongoing support.

Jodi – for your line edit and making sure everything made sense to our US readers.

Pauline – for reading the proofs.

Alice Latchford – for seeing the MS through production.

Tracey, Michael, Georgia, Sophie, Glyn, Adam, Sophie, Jonah and Halley, Dolly and Zack – for being there.

AUTHOR'S NOTES

The Soulmate is my third psych thriller with Inkubator Books, following *The Perfect Husband* (2022) and *The Girl Downstairs* (2021) - I hope there will be many more. I just wanted to end *The Soulmate* by answering questions that I'd expect to be asked about the book at author signings and literary events.

The first question that's usually asked is 'Where did you get the idea for *The Soulmate*?' It really comes from a book I wrote back in 2019, *Mr Todd's Reckoning*, about a just-made-redundant tax inspector, Malcolm Todd, who lived with his unemployed, twenty-something son, in a cramped and run-down bungalow during one of the hottest summers on record. Mr Todd is a psychopath.

This had some success as a paperback and as an audio, narrated by the superb actor Michael Simkins. It was also picked up for television by AbbottVision and was due to be turned into a six-part series starring the hugely talented Paul

Ritter. Tragically, Paul passed away, and the TV series did not proceed.

I moved on and wrote more books, both psych thrillers and others, including *The Wickham Market Murder*, an Agatha Christie-ish type mystery, and a semi-autobiographical novel, *The Old Man, His Dog & Their Longest Journey*, which is currently doing the rounds of TV and film production companies.

But Todd's always kind of been there - I still get emails and what have you from readers. I was, when the TV series was going to happen, going to write two sequels to *Mr Todd's Reckoning* – having been told that there would be a demand for more series after the first one. So I had two stories in my mind, ready to write. But then, of course, the TV series did not progress.

This – *The Soulmate* – is, in a way, one of those stories. The main character falls in love with someone – completely and utterly inappropriate - and then does everything they can to be with them, including killing anyone who gets in their way.

The second question is usually about the main character. Sharon Meyer is based upon a now-deceased member of my wife Tracey's extended family. She was, quite simply, the sourest person I've ever met in my life, being sweet-faced to Tracey whilst bad-mouthing her relatives to her. And then, vice versa, being really nasty about Tracey, myself and our children to them. Everyone saw through her, but she never realised.

Having an anti-hero as your lead is tricky – usually, readers will be rooting for that main character whereas, with a baddie, many readers are hoping for their downfall. I've tried to make Sharon Meyer as rounded as I can – revealing something of her past, her former loves, and the sadness of her current life.

Pippa, of course, her soulmate, is the one I think readers will root for – and that she will survive and thrive by the end of the book. Pippa is lovely. I've also added in as rich a cast of characters as I can – the landlord and his son, the oddball, Mr Grunt and Mrs Groan, Peter, Dominic and Elaine. These are all characters from my imagination.

Another question will usually be about humour, which I put in every book. When *Mr Todd's Reckoning* was published, I did a lot of interviews and remember, having finished one podcast, the interviewer saying to me, 'I thought you'd be really miserable!' It had been a rather jolly interview, so I asked why she would think that. It was, she said, because *Mr Todd's Reckoning* was 'so bleak and dark.' That surprised me, as I thought the book was full of humour.

"'Iain Maitland has pulled off a masterstroke. Combining the ingenuity of an Agatha Christie, the horror of *Rillington Place* and the wit of the best of British, the story keeps you on your toes, fills you with dread and makes you laugh out loud." Martin Carr, AbbottVision.' Fact is, most people missed the humour, and it was only when the press release for the upcoming TV series came out that they started to claim they saw it.

So there is humour, pitch black and thinly spread, in *The Soulmate*. It's part of the story, much of it coming from Sharon's asides. I think it kind of offsets some of the sadness and horror of what happens through the book. If you don't notice the humour, I hope it won't affect your enjoyment of the book. If you do, I trust it adds to it.

And finally, the most oft-asked question, 'Do you have an ending in mind when you start writing?' I typically begin with my main characters and a rough story in mind. Then, as the book progresses, the characters – mad as it sounds – seem to take over and take the story where they want it to go.

With this story, I had the first part clear in my mind and most of the second – the third part, which seemed to get faster and faster, differs from my original notes. I won't write too much here in case you are reading this before the book itself. But Sharon starts to lose control of things, and that was really exciting to write.

The ending – the last scene. When readers review a book, love it or not, some will say that they knew that would be the ending, or, sometimes, that they never saw that coming. With this last scene, I did not know how it would unfold until I started writing it. So I did not know the ending, nor did I see it coming.

What's next? I'm just finishing my latest psych thriller for Inkubator Books, provisionally titled *The New Son*. That should be out soon. And I'm drafting half a dozen outlines, which will hopefully see me writing three more psychs over the next year. If you've enjoyed *The Soulmate* and can't wait to read the next, please check out *The Perfect Husband* and *The Girl Downstairs*.

Thank you – I hope to see you again soon.

Iain Maitland
15 July 2023

ALSO BY IAIN MAITLAND

Printed in Great Britain
by Amazon

29395512R00172